COWBOY,
CROSS MY
HEART

DONNA GRANT

St. Martin's Paperbacks

COWBOY, CROSS MY HEART

Copyright © 2018 by Donna Grant.

All rights reserved.

For information address St. Martin's Press, 175 Fifth Avenue, New York, NY 10010.

ISBN: 978-1-250-16900-6

Our books may be purchased in bulk for promotional, educational, or business use. Please contact your local bookseller or the Macmillan Corporate and Premium Sales Department at 1-800-221-7945, ext. 5442, or by e-mail at MacmillanSpecialMarkets@macmillan.com.

Printed in the United States of America

St. Martin's Paperbacks edition / September 2018

St. Martin's Paperbacks are published by St. Martin's Press, 175 Fifth Avenue, New York, NY 10010.

10 9 8 7 6 5 4 3 2 1

The Dark Warrior series

"The world of the Immortal Warriors is a thoroughly engaging one, blending powerful ancient gods, fiery desire, and touchingly human love, which readers will surely want to revisit." —*RT Book Reviews*

"[Grant] blends ancient gods, love, desire, and evil-doers into a world you will want to revisit over and over again." —*Night Owl Reviews*

"Sizzling love scenes and engaging characters."
—*Publishers Weekly*

"Ms. Grant mixes adventure, magic, and sweet love to create the perfect romance[s]." —*Single Title Reviews*

The Dark Sword series

"Grant creates a vivid picture of Britain centuries after the Celts and Druids tried to expel the Romans, deftly merging magic and history. The result is a wonderfully dark, delightfully well-written [series]. Readers will eagerly await the next Dark Sword book."
—*RT Book Reviews*

"Another fantastic series that melds the paranormal with the historical life of the Scottish highlander in this arousing and exciting adventure." —*Bitten By Books*

"These are some of the hottest brothers around in paranormal fiction." —*Nocturne Romance Reads*

"Will keep readers spellbound."
—*Romance Reviews Today*

Writing is a solitary business, but it takes a team of dedicated people in order to put a story out.
This book goes out to my editor extraordinaire, Monique Patterson. For the past ten years she has pushed me to grow as a writer as well as offered me opportunities to write in different genres—including cowboys.

Dragon Kings, Reapers, Warriors, Druids, cowboys, or military men—each has been a pleasure and a privilege to write for you! Can't wait to see what the next ten years bring.

Acknowledgments

A very special thanks to everyone at SMP for this book—from the art department, to marketing, to publicity, to production. I'd also like to thank Alexandra Sehulster for being such a big help for so many things. It goes without saying that a shoutout is directed at my editor, Monique Patterson.

More thanks to my agent, Natanya Wheeler, who is always there to support me in whatever direction I happen to be headed in.

A special thanks to my kiddos, Gillian and Connor, as well as my family for the never-ending support and love.

Hats off to my incredible readers who have fallen for my cowboys!

Chapter 1

March

Excitement rushed through everyone as the lights suddenly cut out in the arena. Naomi slid to the edge of the metal bench in the darkness, her heart kicking up a notch as silence fell over the crowd of several thousand. The only sound was the occasional stamp of a hoof from the animals or the jingle of a bridle.

A spotlight came on and swung to the gates. It had been years since Naomi had been to a rodeo, but it took just a few seconds for the memories of that splendid time in her life to fill her.

Seemingly as one, everyone rose to their feet and put their hands over their hearts. Her mind halted at the first strings of the national anthem that played loudly over the speakers. The first horse came walking out of the gates, with the American flag being held by none other than Naomi's best friend, Whitney Nolan.

Behind Whitney was another woman with the Texas flag. The two made their way around the edge of the arena several times, the horses moving from a walk to a trot to a gallop, and then a full-out run with the flags rippling in the wind. As Whitney neared her, Naomi flashed her a smile, the tears gathering.

Naomi blinked through them as her mind went back to high school and the third member of their group, Suellen, who had dreamed of being exactly where Whitney was. It was one reason Naomi had returned now.

Besides, it had been too long since she had done more than talk to her best friend over the phone or visit her mother.

Whitney and the other woman halted in the middle of the arena at the crescendo of music. The spotlight caught on the rhinestones of her friend's white chaps with writing claiming Whitney the Rodeo Queen of Baxter County.

Naomi grinned at the large crown fitted on the white Stetson hat atop Whitney's long, golden waves. When the anthem concluded, applause erupted as the lights came back on.

After a tribute to the military and a prayer had commenced, Naomi discreetly took pictures of everything. She resumed her seat and watched Whitney return through the gates as the event began.

Naomi laughed when the rodeo clowns rushed into the arena to get the crowd going. She snapped photos while enjoying the show. Part of her wished she had made it in time for the day rodeo when she could have seen the youngsters doing the steer racing.

It wasn't long before she was once more sucked back into a world she had so easily left behind. She lost track of time as she cheered the events from calf roping, steer wrestling, and bareback riding.

When it came time for the barrel racers, Naomi's heart

missed a beat. This had been her event. And she had loved every second of it.

With every rider that rushed through the gates and worked their horse around the barrels, she held her breath until they crossed over the finish line. When the final rider finished, the scoreboard went up, and her camera nearly slipped through her fingers.

Her time had yet to be beaten. There were some that came close, but somehow, she was still the rider to beat. Even after all these years.

She nearly forgot her camera when the event shifted to team roping. Naomi paid no attention to the announcer as he spouted off the names of the first contestants while the clowns hurried to remove the barrels.

Naomi lifted her camera and looked through the viewfinder. She took rapid shots to get everything from the moment the gate was pulled and the steer rushed from the header box, to when the lead roper—called a header—got the rope around the steer's horns. Once the header had the steer turned, the heeler would rope its back legs.

It was a timed event, so it was always fun to watch who was the quickest. Naomi loved that women competed in the teams, as well. Some duos were mixed, some not.

Naomi swung her camera to the next two up for the event and snapped a couple of pictures.

"Ladies and gentlemen," the announcer said over the speaker. "The winners of the past three years are once more in the arena. Let's give a warm welcome to the Harper brothers, Brice and Caleb."

The applause was deafening. Naomi looked down at her camera and pulled up the picture she'd just taken. She stared at the guy in a tan Stetson and a red and orange plaid button-down who looked at the arena as if it were his battlefield, while the other wore a mischievous grin that had obviously broken many hearts, along with a brown Stetson and a chambray shirt.

"These brothers are the ones to beat," the announcer finished.

Naomi had to admit, both were handsome, but there was something about the serious one that kept drawing her gaze. For the first time, she pulled her head away from her camera to the gates and watched as the cowboy maneuvered his horse into the header slot.

Somehow, she wasn't surprised that he was in that position. Was he the eldest? She imagined he might be.

She lifted her camera again and took picture after picture, shocked at how skilled—and quick—the brothers were. No one seemed surprised when they won the first round of the event.

When she lowered her camera, her gaze remained on the serious one and strayed to his ass. Because there was just something about a man in Wranglers that she couldn't resist.

As he wound his rope, his eyes lifted and looked right at her.

Naomi's heart missed a beat. She smiled nervously. Right before he grabbed the reins, he tipped his hat at her and rode off.

At least she thought he'd been looking at her, but the women behind her giggled loudly, each wondering if she had been the object of his greeting.

Naomi laughed at herself and readied for the first round of bull riding, which was the main affair at any rodeo. She'd once dated a bull rider. Briefly. She had been too young for their wild, reckless ways and how they eagerly put their lives in danger each time they climbed on a bull, hoping to hear the buzzer on that eight-second ride.

But people lived for the event. The crazier the bull, the louder the crowd cheered. Naomi took more pictures, her heart in her throat each time a cowboy was bucked off, and the bull went after them.

One of her pictures captured how close the bull's horns had been to gorging the cowboy. Yet, with each near-death experience, the crowd gasped then cheered both the rider for getting away and the rodeo clowns for coming between the bull and the contestant.

Her uncle had been a rodeo clown, and she knew their jobs were the hardest of everyone's. They were out there between each event and always at the ready for any participant or animal that got into trouble. They were also the ones with the most injuries.

In fact, her uncle had died when a bull's horn pierced his chest. But the cowboy her uncle had been helping got to safety. And that's what the clowns were for.

With the rodeo coming to a close for the night, Naomi was the first on her feet to give the clowns an ovation. As soon as the closing ceremony finished, Naomi made her way out of the stands to the back of the arena.

She paid only a passing courtesy to the many cowboys who murmured "ma'am" and tipped their hats as she walked past. When she finally reached the area where the pageant contestants were, she easily found Whitney's white hat, sparkling crown, and blond locks.

Naomi watched her friend in her element for a long minute. Then Naomi whistled loudly. Whitney turned, her blue gaze scanning the people until she spotted Naomi. Whitley let out a loud squeal and rushed her. Naomi threw open her arms and hugged her friend tightly.

"It's been so long," Whitney murmured.

Naomi knew she was thinking of Suellen. "Too long."

Whitney leaned back and beamed at her. "I worried you might change your mind."

"Never. Weather delayed my plane, but I told you I'd be here."

"And you always keep your word." Whitney moved to her side and linked arms with her as they started walking slowly. "Well?"

Naomi shook her head, chuckling, as she glanced at Whitney. "Fine. I'll admit that I miss being involved in the rodeo."

"I knew it," her friend said with a pump of her arm.

"Don't get any ideas. I've got a nice life in DC, and that's where I'll be returning in a couple of days."

Whitney rolled her eyes. "You say that now, but I think if I can find the right cowboy for you, you'll change your mind."

"You forget I know all I want to know about cowboys."

"True," Whitney said with a twist of her lips. They both stopped and watched a couple of men walk past, their gazes on their fine asses. "Then again. . . ."

Naomi swung her head to Whitney, and they both laughed. "If I do any riding, it will only be on a horse."

"Yeah, we'll see about that," Whitney declared with a grin.

"I mean it, Whit. I'm here to spend time with you and Mom. That's all."

Whitney nodded. "Yep. I hear you loud and clear."

Then why was it that Naomi suspected her friend had other ideas?

"Are you ready?" Whitney asked.

Naomi looked at all the women in rhinestones and

hairspray ahead of them. Each beautiful and impeccably dressed in denim and boots. But anyone who believed rodeo pageants were like other talent and beauty contests was sorely mistaken.

The women were expert riders. While competing, they were given a horse they had never ridden before and had ninety seconds to flawlessly complete an intricate routine.

But it went further than that. The girls weren't allowed to be married or have children. Each contestant also had a chaperone. Hell, even the judges had escorts. And the girls who competed were discouraged from even having boyfriends.

At her silence, Whitney raised a brow. "Is it too much?"

Naomi took a deep breath. "Yes. And no."

"Even after all these years, I still see Suellen everywhere," Whitney murmured.

Naomi tightened her hand on her friend's arm. Whitney, Suellen, and Naomi had been inseparable. They'd traded wins in barrel racing, and were always there to cheer each other on.

Suellen was the one who'd decided to do a rodeo pageant. Her dream was to win Miss Rodeo America and claim the thirty grand that came along with it. While neither Naomi nor Whitney had any interest in the pageant, they'd supported Suellen fully.

And when Suellen won her first title in a local rodeo, the three went out to celebrate. Suellen put the top down on her convertible on that balmy night. And they had the music blaring, singing loudly as they drove down the dark, winding roads.

They had the entire world before them. And they planned to conquer it together.

Until a car hit them head-on.

Naomi could still hear her scream mixed with the sounds of tires screeching. And the crunch of metal.

Whitney had suffered two broken arms and a broken collarbone. Naomi broke her femur, had several lacerations, and a concussion. Suellen . . . died.

Naomi had missed Suellen's funeral because of the surgery on her leg. She had tried to escape the hospital to go, and in the end, the doctors had to sedate her. She didn't talk to her parents for four days after that.

"Suellen would be so proud of you," Naomi said to Whitney.

They shared a look, tears gathering before Whitney sniffed and hurriedly looked away. Then Whitney pulled her toward the corral where her horse was. "When was the last time you rode?"

"A horse?" Naomi teased.

Whitney threw back her head and laughed. Naomi took a quick picture of her friend. The sound was loud and glorious and infectious. Everyone paused and looked at Whitney because they had no choice. Suellen had been fearless and bold, but Whitney was captivating and charming.

"Oh, you are as naughty as always," Whitney said with a wide smile. "God, I've missed your humor."

Naomi put her elbow on the railing. "I've not been on a horse since I left for college."

"And men?" Whitney asked with a twinkle in her blue eyes.

Naomi forced the smile to stay in place. "None since Rick."

"That was over a year ago."

As if she needed a reminder of how long it'd been since she called off her engagement. It had been the right thing to do. Rick was an amazing man, but she knew marrying him would be a mistake. So she'd saved them heartache—and a divorce. Though he didn't see it that way.

"Well," Whitney said with a sigh. "By the way the men here are looking at you, you should be riding soon."

Naomi rolled her eyes as she laughed. Maybe she would use this time to explore her options. What did she have to lose?

Your heart.

She laughed off her inner voice. As if that would happen.

Chapter 2

"Good boy," Brice murmured to his stallion, Jigsaw, as he rubbed the horse down after removing the saddle and bridle.

"It's almost too easy winning," Caleb grumbled as he led his gray gelding into the trailer and shut the gate.

Brice looked up at his younger brother. "You're the one who wanted to enter this year."

With one hand, Caleb grabbed his saddle beneath the gullet of the horn and swung it up, resting it on his shoulder before picking up the saddle blanket and heading to the front of the horse trailer to put it all away. "So I did."

Something had been bothering Caleb for days now, and Brice suspected he knew what it was. As soon as he had announced that he'd bought his own ranch, Caleb had become withdrawn. Their sister, Abby, and her husband, Clayton East, had been thrilled.

Or at least they seemed to be.

There would be a lot of changes coming. For everyone. Even for him. Ever since Abby and Clayton had fallen in love twelve years ago, the East Ranch had been his home. He could happily remain there for the rest of his life, but he needed to push himself to see what he could accomplish on his own.

He owed everything he had learned to Clayton, who hadn't only welcomed them into the family but was also happy to show him and Caleb the ins and outs of running a large ranch.

Not that Brice wasn't terrified of failing. But that was partly why he'd decided to do this. To see what he could accomplish without the East name backing him.

He'd put his entire life savings into the three-hundred-acre ranch. And there were significant upgrades and repairs that needed to be done to the barns and corrals if he was going to have any chance of starting his horse business.

Brice led his black and white paint stallion into the trailer and secured the horse before putting away his tack. When he finished, he looked around for Caleb. It didn't take him long to find his brother with a foot on the lowest rung of a fence as he leaned on it, flirting with two women.

It didn't matter where they were or what they were doing, women always found his brother. Brice grinned and motioned to Caleb that he was going to check on things for tomorrow.

Caleb was right. The first round of team roping was easy. Brice was ready for a challenge, which happened in the finals. It was getting to that last stage that sometimes made him irritable.

He walked through the back of the arena where the women who were part of the pageant were located. Brice didn't bother to even look their way since the chaperones stared him down, daring him to make eye contact with the women.

Halfway through, he heard a laugh that was sweet and seductive at once. Unable to help himself, his head swung toward the sound, and he found his gaze on the same woman he'd seen in the stands.

Wheat-colored hair hung straight and thick to her shoulders. His footsteps slowed as he stared at her oval face alight with mirth. Her smile was wide, her eyes crinkled at the corners. He wished he knew their color.

She wore a body-hugging denim jacket over a white V-neck tee shirt that was tucked into dark jeans. She had a well-worn, olive green bag slung over one shoulder. His gaze lingered on her curves before he heard someone clear their throat.

Brice tipped his hat at the line of chaperones, not bothering to discern who had made the sound, and continued on his way. The woman wasn't dolled up like the other contestants, and he wondered what she was doing there.

It was the first time since his breakup with his girlfriend that he found himself thinking about a woman. Not that he would do anything about it. He had to keep his eye on his goals. There was no time for a dalliance of any sort in his plans.

"I saw that."

He jerked his head around at the sound of Caleb's voice. "Saw what?"

"You looking at that woman."

Brice shrugged, hoping his brother would let it go. "You realize that females make up half the population, right? I do look at them from time to time."

Caleb rolled his dark eyes as he came even with Brice. "I'm laughing on the inside."

"What's the big deal about me looking anyway?"

One brown brow shot up in Caleb's forehead as they walked together. "Did you seriously just ask me that? I've been trying to set you up for months now. You keep telling me you aren't interested."

"Because I'm not," Brice interjected.

Caleb halted. "Yeah. All this time, I thought you were torn up about the breakup with Jill. When, really, you were getting on with your life."

Brice stopped and turned to look at his brother. "I'm not leaving. The ranch is less than thirty minutes away."

"You're leaving our ranch," Caleb said. "What was it? What wasn't enough? We were a team."

Brice blew out a breath. "We're still a team. You'll always be my brother. Always. Besides, we can't run the East ranch. It's Clayton's, and it'll pass to his and Abby's children."

"Clayton said we'd always have a place there."

Brice walked back to his brother and put a hand on his shoulder. "I know that. But I want more. I need something that's mine. We always talked about having a ranch together."

"Yeah." Caleb looked away. "Together."

"I was going to do this later when we were at home, but I don't think I should wait," he began.

Caleb's brown eyes swung back to him, a worried frown on his brow. "You want to stop competing, don't you?"

"No," Brice said, taken aback as he dropped his arm to his side. "Not at all."

"Oh." Caleb hooked his thumb through his belt loop. "What, then?"

Brice waited until his brother looked at him. "You said yourself, we're a team. A damn good one."

"Unbeatable," Caleb stated.

"That's right. The East Ranch is all about cattle. I want to focus on horses. And no one breaks horses better than you."

This time, Caleb's frown was full of confusion. "What are you asking?"

"For you to join me. We go into business together. It's what I wanted from the beginning, but every time I brought up leaving, you changed the subject. When I found the ranch, I knew I couldn't wait. It was too good of a deal to let it pass by."

Caleb stared at him in silence for a long time.

Finally, Brice shifted his feet nervously. "Say something, damn it."

"Tell me this isn't a handout."

Anger shot through him. "It isn't. Why would you think that?"

"You could've told me about this at any time. Even after you put the initial payment down to buy the ranch. You didn't. You waited until now. After you closed on it two weeks ago."

"Caleb," Brice began. "I held off specifically because I knew you would think it was charity."

Caleb took off his hat and scratched his head before replacing it. "We did use to talk about starting our own ranch. As partners. But this is in your name. I'd be working for you. *Partners* implies that I would be involved in all the decision making. You've proven that you want to do things on your own."

Brice watched his brother return to the truck. He put his hands on his hips and looked up as he blew out a breath. Fuck. That hadn't gone as he'd hoped. Actually, it had gone so much worse than he'd initially feared.

He yanked off his hat and slapped it against his leg before he continued on to find Darnell Pruitt, who ran the rodeo. After a brief conversation about the next day, Brice headed back to his brother and the silent ride home he knew was coming. That was if Caleb had waited for him. It'd be just like his brother to leave.

It wouldn't be the first time.

He paused and drew out his cell phone. With the punch of a button, he dialed a number and brought the phone to his ear. After two rings, the call was answered. "Abby."

"What happened?" she asked, immediately concerned. "Did either of you get hurt?"

That made him smile. From the first rodeo Clayton had entered them in, it was always his sister's initial question whether she was with them or not.

"Naw, sis. We're good."

She let out a loud sigh. "Thank God." After a hesitation, she asked, "You told Caleb, didn't you?"

"I did. Well, part of it."

Abby might be his sister, but she'd raised him and Caleb after their mother ran off when he was only ten and Abby just eighteen.

Brice hadn't seen or heard from his mother since. And he hoped he never did. Abby was the one he considered his mother. She was the one who'd looked after them, raised them, fed them, and cared for them as if they were her own. She could've handed them over to the state. But that wasn't his sister.

Abby made a sound on the other end of the line. "That good, huh?"

"He thinks it's a handout."

"Clayton and I warned you that would happen when you didn't take him with you to buy the ranch. Does he know the rest?"

Brice looked down at his boots. "He walked off before I could tell him."

"You better let him cool down. You know Caleb needs to think on things for a bit before he's ready to talk again."

"Yeah."

"Shit. Did he drive off and leave you again? Do I need to send Clayton to pick you up?"

Brice grinned. "I've not checked. I'll find a way home if Caleb left me."

"If he did, I'm going to give him an earful when he gets back."

"Leave it. He's hurting, and it's my fault. I should've told him everything to begin with instead of doing it on my own."

Abby blew out a breath. "Tell him the rest soon."

"I will."

"Brice, I mean it," she stated in a stern voice.

"I heard you. And you do realize I'm not a kid anymore, right?"

She hesitated a moment. "I know. I just hate when the two of you fight."

"We're brothers. It happens all the time," he said, hoping to lighten the mood. "By the way, we won the first round."

"Of course you did," she said, a smile in her voice. "Hurry home. But be careful."

"Yes, ma'am," he said and ended the call.

Brice put the phone back into his pocket and looked toward the parking lot where, hopefully, a ride home waited for him. Abby was right. He needed to tell Caleb the rest of it. But not tonight when his brother was so angry.

Brice started walking to the truck. He did a quick look around for the blonde that he'd spotted earlier when he reached the group of women, but she wasn't there.

It bothered him that he was searching for her. More than likely, he'd never see her again. He recognized the women who made the circuit with the cowboys in the rodeo, and she wasn't one of them. Which meant that she was probably just visiting.

That was too bad. He would've liked to know the color of her eyes and get her name. And maybe buy her a cup of coffee.

He was walking through the fenced area where the cattle and horses were kept. The crowds had gone, as had most everyone in the rodeo. So when he heard the shout of distress, it stopped him in his tracks.

Brice listened, trying to determine which direction it had come from. About the time he thought he might have mistaken the sound, there was another yell.

He didn't hesitate as he took off running toward it.

Chapter 3

Something was wrong. Naomi knew it within the space of a few minutes after she'd gotten her friend away from the others. The way Whitney kept looking around as if expecting someone to jump out at any second was impossible to miss.

Naomi had taken photos all over the world in various situations, and she'd learned to pick up on the subtle nuances of people and their surroundings. To discover such tension and anxiety at the rodeo was a surprise.

"What is it?" Naomi asked in a soft voice.

Whitney flashed her a bright smile, showing off her even, white teeth. "What do you mean?"

"I see how you're glancing around."

"The chaperones are always near," Whitney said with a laugh. But it was forced. "It's nice to get away from them for a bit."

Naomi nodded, accepting her answer for now. She pulled out her camera and began snapping pictures of the horses and cattle as they munched lazily on hay or stood with eyes closed, trying to sleep.

"The part of a rodeo few see," Whitney murmured.

Naomi lifted her head from the camera to look at her a quiet moment. Then Naomi focused on one of the bulls that was known for his wildness. Yet now, he stood half asleep, barely paying them any mind.

"The spectators want a show. And they get it."

Naomi frowned at Whitney's words. "You know you can tell me whatever is bothering you?"

Whitney smiled again and shook her head. "I'm just tired. It's been an exhausting day, and there are many more coming before the next pageant. I'll be going up for Miss Rodeo Texas."

"You sure you still want to do it?"

"Absolutely. The contacts I'm making are well worth the constant chaperones and all of this," she said, gesturing to her heavy makeup, styled hair, and clothes.

Naomi took several more photos of the bull before moving to the next pen. Whitney was silent for a long time. Naomi became so engrossed in her work that she forgot about her friend for a moment. When she looked out of the corner of her eye, Whitney was staring off to the side into a darkened area away from Naomi. The way her friend's chest rose and fell rapidly told her all Naomi needed to know.

She turned gradually, taking pictures until she faced the direction Whitney was looking. Suddenly, a blur of movement came out of the shadows.

The person slammed into Whitney, knocking her against a pen, startling a bull. Whitney gave a shout of surprise. Naomi raised her elbow, connecting with the attacker's face. To her shock, strong hands grabbed for her camera.

"Hey!" Naomi shouted and protected her equipment with both hands. She kicked her foot at the man's knee and smiled in satisfaction when he let out a curse as she connected with his leg.

But the man persisted. His hat and the shadows hid his face, but she could feel his angry eyes, hear his heavy breathing and grunts as he attempted to get the camera. She was yanked this way and that, and she could feel her fingers slipping as his stronger hold won out.

The next thing she knew, someone else was there. The newcomer pulled her attacker off her, but his hands were still around the camera. She no longer had the strength to hold on. It went flying from her grasp and fell to the ground with a crunch that made her cringe.

Naomi forgot her equipment and rushed to help Whitney. By the time her friend had her feet under her again, the attacker was gone, and their rescuer climbed to his feet with his back turned.

But she recognized the red and orange plaid. Her eyes fastened on his thick, deep brown locks. She held Whitney as Brice Harper bent and retrieved his hat. He dusted it off before setting it back on his head. Then he turned to them.

She found herself staring into pale blue eyes. They entranced her, ensnared her. If she had thought him handsome while working his horse in the event, he was breathtaking standing before her now.

Tall and broad-shouldered with a quiet intensity that made her heart skip a beat. Her gaze raked along the hard line of his jaw and his wide lips. Her fingers itched for her camera to capture the moment.

His clothes were dusty from the scuffle, the corner of his lip bleeding, but he gazed at her with surprise, worry, and . . . interest.

She could only watch as he walked to her camera and retrieved it. Then he slowly made his way to them, his gaze darting to Whitney before returning to her.

"Are either of you hurt?"

Naomi shook her head before turning to Whitney. "What about you?"

Whitney lowered her eyes to the ground and quickly said, "I'm fine."

"Who was that?" Naomi asked.

Brice shrugged, his lips twisting. "I didn't get a look at his face."

Naomi twisted to make Whitney look at her. "Do you know who it was?"

"No."

It was a lie. But why would Whitney lie to her? Naomi wiped the frown from her face when she turned back to Brice. "Thank you for helping us."

"My pleasure."

"I'm Naomi, by the way. Naomi Pierce."

"Brice Harper. I'm afraid this might be broken," he said and held out her camera.

She winced as she saw the cracked lens. There was no telling what else was broken, and she wouldn't know until she was able to open it up and look.

Naomi turned the camera over in her hand. "He wanted this." She looked from Whitney to Brice. "I think because I got him on film."

"He didn't do anything," Whitney said as she lifted her head.

Naomi looked at the darkened area where the guy had

been. She recalled Whitney's earlier anxiety and swung her gaze to her friend, who wouldn't meet her eyes.

What the hell was going on?

Naomi turned her attention to Brice. He wore a frown as he looked Whitney over. Did he notice that something was off, as well? Surely, it wasn't all in her head.

"You took a picture of him?" Brice asked her.

Naomi eyed her friend to see her reaction as she said, "I noticed that Whitney was staring into those shadows, and she seemed nervous."

"It's nothing," Whitney said. "I let my imagination get the better of me."

"Then why did he go after the camera?" Brice asked.

Whitney looked at Naomi for a long, silent minute. Just as she was opening her mouth to speak, someone called out Whitney's name.

A few seconds later, a woman in her late fifties with short, bleached hair and caked-on makeup appeared. Her pink shirt was embroidered with flowers at the collar and tucked into too-tight jeans that made her stomach bulge over the waist.

"Oh, there you are," the woman said when she saw Whitney. But the welcoming smile vanished when she spied Brice. Then she noticed the dirt on Whitney's shirt. "What happened?"

Naomi didn't wait for her friend to speak. "A man pushed Whitney down and tried to take my camera. Luckily, Mr. Harper was near and helped us."

Brice tipped his hat to the woman. "I'm glad I arrived in time."

"Thank you," the woman said and ushered Whitney away.

Naomi didn't follow. She was still shaken by the attack,

but also her certainty that her friend was hiding something. When she pulled her gaze from Whitney's retreating back, it was to find Brice squatting near the shadows where the man had been.

"Did you find something?" Naomi asked as she walked to him.

Brice straightened before he turned his head to her. "Which way did y'all come?"

"Um," Naomi said as she spun around. "There, there, and then there," she said pointing to the way they'd weaved through the pens.

Brice didn't say anything else as he walked to the spots that she had indicated. Each time, he squatted and inspected the ground.

"Someone was following the two of you," he finally said.

A shiver went down her back. "I didn't notice. I was too intent on the animals. But I knew something was wrong with Whitney."

"How so?" he pressed.

Naomi shrugged, trying to find the words to express her feelings. "Just a general sense. Whitney kept looking around like she expected to see someone."

"And then the man appeared?"

"Not until I took his picture," Naomi said. "He might have remained in the shadows, but Whitney's anxiety was palpable. I wanted to know what would do that to her. I've known her since grade school, and we talk several times a week."

Brice pushed the hat on his head back. "Whitney and the other pageant girls have chaperones so they should be safe."

Naomi laughed. "You think this guy was after me? No.

It's not me. It has to be Whitney. I just arrived today from DC."

"Whitney's a local girl."

Naomi had to give Brice props for his subtle way of learning information. "I grew up here. I moved to go to college."

"And stayed."

She chuckled. "Something like that."

"Are you sure you're okay? Nothing hurt?"

"Just this," she said and lifted the camera, thinking about the expense of getting it fixed. "I have others, but this was a favorite."

Brice adjusted his hat. "Can I walk you back to Whitney and the others?"

"Assuming you aren't with the man who attacked us?" she asked, brow raised, and a grin on her lips.

Brice smiled, showing even, white teeth. His eyes crinkled at the corners as he wiped at his bloody lip. "Assuming."

"Thanks. I'd rather not be alone at the moment."

They fell into step together as they headed back to Whitney. After a few moments, Naomi asked, "If the chaperones are always around, why did Whitney get to walk away with me? No one stopped us? And why did it seem as if Whitney knew who was there and wanted to protect them?"

"Maybe she's protecting herself," Brice suggested.

Naomi didn't like that thought. "I can't imagine that. Once, in high school, a guy cornered one of our friends. Whitney walked up and punched him, breaking his nose. She's that type of person."

"Could something have happened that you don't know about?"

She slowed until she came to a stop. "Anything is possible. We stayed in touch, even after I left for college. Sometimes, Whitney came to see me, and sometimes, I'd return home. But the last two years have been busy for both of us. She with the rodeo circuit and pageant, and me with my business. But we don't keep secrets from each other."

"Everyone keeps secrets," he said.

She looked into his blue eyes and realized he was right. "Have you heard anything about Whitney? Anything that would suggest something happened?"

"Not a word, but that doesn't mean something didn't happen. Whitney could just be tired and on edge."

Naomi looked down at her camera. Whoever had come at her wanted to make sure she couldn't find out who he was. And in her mind, that meant the creep had done more than follow Whitney around.

Because Naomi knew this involved her friend. After losing Suellen, Naomi wasn't going to sit around and do nothing. No matter what, she would get to the bottom of things and help Whitney out in whatever fashion she needed.

"I'm almost afraid to ask what you're thinking," Brice stated.

She blinked and found him grinning at her. Naomi couldn't help but return his smile. "You don't want to know."

His gaze briefly moved away as the smile disappeared. "Look, I have a sister and a niece. If there is something going on, you shouldn't be investigating on your own. Find someone to help. Even if it's nothing more than watching your back. Because if anyone is stalking Whitney, they'll be examining you now, as well."

"Thanks for the tip. And the help earlier," she said and lifted the camera.

"I'm sorry I couldn't save it."

She swallowed, trying to think of something to say that would keep him talking more. Then someone honked a horn, loud and long.

Brice shook his head as he chuckled. "That's my brother. Are you sure you're all right?"

"Yeah. Thanks again."

He tipped his hat and walked away. Naomi watched him go. Brice Harper reminded her of all the things she loved about Texas and cowboys. It was the first time since she had left for college that she wondered why she hadn't returned for good.

Chapter 4

The drive back to the ranch was as silent as Brice thought it would be. The radio was paired with his phone and played Dwight Yoakam's "A Thousand Miles from Nowhere."

He glanced at Caleb, but his brother was slouched in the passenger seat with his hat pulled over his eyes—his way of removing himself from any conversation. Brice turned up the volume and drummed his fingers on the wheel as he stared at the white lines on the blacktop road.

His mind returned to Naomi Pierce. He smiled when he thought about finally discovering the color of her eyes. Chestnut. Warm brown with hints of orange. Stunning, expressive eyes that seized him.

That grin faded when he recalled seeing the man wrestling with her to get her camera. All Brice had wanted was to get the attacker away. He hadn't thought of the animals or how any one of them could have fallen into the enclosures with the bulls and thus been trampled.

He'd ended up with a busted lip thanks to a lucky hit from the guy's elbow, but Brice had landed several punches himself. The fact that he hadn't gotten a look at the man irritated him.

If only Brice would've turned him around. But he'd been so intent on yanking the bastard away from Naomi that he had thought of little else. Now, Brice could walk right past this guy and never know it. And that didn't sit well with him.

Brice pulled into the long drive that led to the ranch. Lights were still on in the house despite the late hour. Apparently, Caleb saw them too because he sat up and adjusted his hat.

As Brice drove past the house to the barn, he and Caleb looked into the windows of the dwelling to see if they could spot who was up, but he didn't see anything.

He parked near the barns. Caleb was out before Brice turned off the ignition. He blew out a breath and opened the truck door. He was slow to rage, but Caleb was the opposite. He had always been quick to anger. Normally, Caleb cooled down just as quickly, though.

Not so with Brice. It took him a while to reach the point of furiousness. And when he got there, it took a long time for him to let it go.

So he knew the best course was to let Caleb sleep on things and then try to talk to him again in the morning. His brother could never stay mad at him longer than a few hours.

Brice made his way to the back of the trailer. Caleb had already led Jigsaw to the barn, so he got Sullivan and brought him to his stall.

When Brice went into the feed room and tried to get the buckets of food for their horses, Caleb yanked both of them out of Brice's hand and stalked out. Brice drew in a breath and went to Jigsaw to rub his horse down and settle him for the night.

Caleb was still tending to Sullivan when Brice murmured a goodnight and headed to the house. He was quiet when he walked in through the back door and spotted Clayton putting a blanket over Abby and their two kids who were curled up together on the sofa.

Clayton motioned him to his office. Once there, Brice closed the door to keep their voices from reaching Abby and the kids and waking them.

"There was a thunderstorm," Clayton said as he poured two glasses of bourbon.

Brice accepted the drink and thought about Wynter, who had feared the storms from the moment she was born seven years earlier. And whenever she got up, her brother, Brody, three years her junior, was always with her.

"How's Abby feeling?" Brice asked.

It had come as a surprise to everyone, including Abby and Clayton, when she announced that she was pregnant eight months ago. This pregnancy hadn't been an easy one. There were some medical issues that had Abby staying off her feet as much as possible.

Her first two pregnancies had been easy and uneventful, so when she began having issues and feeling poorly with this one, everyone grew concerned.

"She had a pretty good day," Clayton said. "She's ready for the baby to come."

Brice took a sip of the alcohol and walked to the sofa, where he sat on the edge of the cushion. He looked at the glass he held between his hands.

"Caleb will calm down," Clayton said as he sank into the chair behind his desk.

Brice lifted his gaze to meet his brother-in-law's green eyes. "I hope so."

"You shouldn't have waited to tell him."

"I know. I was trying to find a way where he wouldn't get pissed off."

Clayton chuckled as he finished his drink and set the empty tumbler on his desk. "This is Caleb we're talking about."

Brice smiled briefly. He leaned back on the sofa. "Are you upset?"

"About you going your own way?" Clayton shook his head of dark blond hair. "To be honest, I expected both you and Caleb to leave once you joined the military. This will always be your home, and y'all can stay as long as you want—which would make your sister and my kids deliriously happy. But I know that feeling of wanting to do something on your own. Abby and the kids are sad, but they understand they'll still get to see you."

"Sunday dinners. Always," Brice said with a nod.

Clayton leaned back in his chair, his hands linked behind his head. "Is that all that's wrong? I'm hoping that split lip is Caleb's doing, but you would've said if you two got into a scuffle."

Brice reached up and touched the corner of his lip. "I came upon a guy attacking a woman."

"Attacking?" Clayton said in shocked anger as he sat up and dropped his arms.

"He was trying to get a camera from her. It seems she took a picture of him."

Clayton frowned and shook his head. "I don't understand."

"The creep had been following the woman, Naomi, and her friend Whitney."

"Whitney Nolan?"

"Yep."

Brice wasn't surprised that Clayton knew Whitney. Everyone knew the rodeo queen in their small town. She was one of their local celebrities.

Clayton drew in a deep breath. "Where was Whitney's chaperone?"

"Nowhere near them. The guy pushed Whitney down and went after Naomi. I got him off her."

"I gather you got in your share of hits?"

"Of course," Brice said with a flat look. "The bastard got the one elbow against my lip. But I never saw his face."

Clayton drummed his fingers on the arm of the chair. "Did you notice anything? Clothes, smell, anything?"

"He was in Wranglers and a black shirt."

Clayton grunted. "That could be anyone."

"He had dark hair. I did see that when I knocked his hat off, but that only narrows things down a little."

"Did either of the girls see his face?"

Brice shook his head. "The lights were dimmed so the animals could sleep, but Naomi thinks Whitney knows who it was. She said Whitney had been acting apprehensive."

"Maybe Naomi got a picture of him."

"The camera broke."

"Damn," Clayton said. "With as closely guarded as the pageant girls are, I don't understand how no one saw anything."

Brice swirled his glass and looked at the liquid that made him think of Naomi's eyes. "Yeah."

"Need help looking into things?"

He lifted his eyes to Clayton and grinned. "You know I'd welcome it, but you need to be with Abby."

"Let me know if you change your mind." Clayton rose and gave him a nod on the way out of the office.

Brice remained for another thirty minutes as he finished his bourbon while watching his brother through the windows. Caleb left the barn and turned out the lights, but he didn't come to the house. Instead, he rode the ATV out to the bunkhouse.

Which meant that Caleb was well and truly livid.

Brice stood and grabbed his and Clayton's empty glass and brought them to the kitchen. The lights were off throughout the house, with the only illumination coming from under the cabinets in the kitchen.

Brice glanced into the living room, but the sofa was empty. After checking the door locks, he made his way upstairs to his room and showered before getting into bed.

However, he didn't rest easy. His mind kept going from Caleb to Naomi with little sleep in between. He was grateful when dawn finally came and he could start a new day.

He dressed and went downstairs to make a mug of coffee when he heard the truck start. Brice turned and looked out the window to see Caleb pulling out with the horses already loaded into the trailer.

"At least he got Jigsaw for you," Abby said as she waddled into the kitchen.

"I suppose. You look like shit."

She flashed a sarcastic smile at him. "How about I put a watermelon in your stomach that presses on your bladder so you get up every thirty minutes to pee? Then I can make your boobs swell to three times their size and become so sore that just looking at them makes them hurt. Then there is the constant hunger. Oh, and let's not forget that moving is normally impossible for the most part."

"I can attest to that," Clayton said as he walked down

the stairs. "She hasn't been able to put on her underwear by herself for four months."

Abby rolled her eyes and climbed onto a barstool. "I have to toss them on the ground and work my feet into the holes."

Brice shook his head as he dumped three teaspoons of sugar into his mug. "I don't need to hear this."

"Then," Abby continued, ignoring him, "I have to scoot my feet on the floor, careful not to let the panties come off until I can get to the bed. That's when I lay back and lift my legs up so that my underwear can fall down enough so I can grab them and pull them on."

Clayton grinned at Brice. "That was the routine for a while. Now that she can't bend at all, I dress her."

Brice brought his mug to his lips to hide his smile.

"I hate you both," Abby grumbled and slid from the stool to walk to the fridge.

"Sit, baby," Clayton said. "I'll make breakfast."

Abby busted out crying as she stood in the open fridge. Brice frowned as Clayton comforted her. After a moment, Abby lifted her face and sniffed loudly. "You mean, I can eat all by myself? Without sharing food with the kids?"

"That's right," Clayton said, rubbing her back.

Which only made Abby cry harder.

Brice couldn't remember his sister acting like this when she carried Wynter or Brody, but maybe he'd just missed those episodes.

While Clayton got Abby comfortable, Brice cooked the eggs and bacon. He managed to snag one slice of salty goodness before Abby devoured the rest.

Once she'd scraped her third serving from her plate, she pushed it away and looked at Brice. "Clayton told me about Naomi and Whitney. I want to help."

"Abby," Brice began the same time Clayton said, "Honey."

She held up a hand to silence them both. "From the house. I'm not an idiot. I have enough trouble getting up and down the stairs. When I was awake last night, I started thinking. The organizers of the rodeo pageant are very strict, but that doesn't mean things don't happen."

"Nothing has been in the papers or news," Clayton said.

Brice raised his brows. "And there has been no talk amongst those in the rodeo, which you know there would have been."

"That doesn't mean it's not out there." Abby grinned. "It's all about asking the right people."

Brice traded a look with Clayton. "If you can find anything, I'd like to know, but I don't think you will. All I have to go on is that Whitney wanted me and Naomi to drop it, and Naomi said her friend was anxious."

Clayton pushed a glass of orange juice to Abby. "I'll do some checking on my own. Discreetly, of course."

"Thanks," Brice said, suddenly eager to get back to the rodeo so he could find Naomi.

He hadn't asked if she was staying, but hopefully, she would be around for a little while.

Chapter 5

Brice Harper was certainly on her mind. Naomi flipped the switch and waited for the red light of the darkroom to flicker on.

She looked around the space, which was significantly larger than the one she had. Then again, this one was for a community college. She had fought all night against opening her camera to see how much was broken, but if there were even a chance that she'd gotten the guy on film, she wanted to take all the precautions.

So she'd driven her rental car to the college early that morning and spoke to the professor, who'd gladly allowed her into the darkroom.

Naomi set the camera on the table and gently opened the compartment with the film. She cringed when she heard the various broken parts falling. She would see to the camera later. Right now, her focus was on the film.

She took her time removing the roll. With methodical purpose, she set about making a contact print of the negatives as a reference to see which images to save.

Bent over the table, Naomi searched the squares until she came to the last set before the camera had been torn from her hands. There were four images she decided to print.

Naomi put the negative on the enlarger and controlled the focus. Then she decided to give additional exposure to the areas of the pictures that were shadowed to, hopefully, better see the attacker. The burning process added another layer to the time it took to print the photos.

Next, she exposed a sheet of photographic paper to the enlarged image before moving the sheet into a tray of chemicals. As she waited for that image to process, Naomi moved on to the next one.

Once all four were sitting in the chemicals, she pulled out the other rolls of film from the day before and made contract prints of each of them, as well. When she found the roll that had the pictures she'd taken of Brice and his brother, Naomi opted to print three more photos.

It wasn't long before she had the seven photos hanging up to dry. She checked her phone then and saw that she had missed a call from Whitney and another from a local number.

Naomi sent Whitney a quick text to let her know where she was, then tried a reverse search on the unknown number to no avail. The caller hadn't left a message. Normally, Naomi wouldn't think twice about it, but after the previous night, she was on edge about many things.

She remained in the darkroom until all the prints were dry, looking over the photos. Despite the steps she'd taken, she still couldn't make out the assailant's face. But Whitney might recognize something about him.

Naomi put the pictures into an envelope and flicked the

switch that shut off the red light before she turned on the regular lights. Naomi made sure to stop by the professor's office to impart her thanks once more.

On the drive to meet up with Whitney, she thought back over the night before. After Whitney's chaperone, Ms. Biermann, had arrived, Whitney refused to even discuss what had occurred. Even when she and Whitney were alone.

Naomi checked her watch. She had an hour before lunch with Whitney, so she stopped and dropped off her camera for repairs before buying flowers and heading to the cemetery.

She went to her family's plots first, placing flowers on her uncle's, father's, and grandparents' headstones. Naomi then made her way to Suellen's grave.

"It's been a while," Naomi said as she squatted next to the tombstone and set the flowers down. "I wish you were here. Maybe then, Whitney would listen. Or, at the very least, we could gang up on her. She never did stand a chance when you and I stood together."

Naomi let out a loud sigh. "I know something is going on with her, but I can't figure it out. I'm used to being behind the camera, Suellen. I see things differently from that angle. Others look at the world as a whole. I see parts of it at a time. And I'm afraid I'm going to miss something that will help Whit."

She straightened and put her hands into the pockets of her olive green jacket. "I'll stop by and see your parents while I'm here. My mom is still a firecracker. The woman doesn't stop. She takes oil painting classes. And she has a personal trainer. Her schedule is busier than mine will ever be. I swear, I don't have a clue where she gets the energy."

Naomi lifted her gaze and looked out across the cemetery. She should've come as soon as she arrived in town, but it was always such a difficult stop to make.

"I miss you," she said and kissed her fingers before putting them against the granite of the gravestone.

She walked back to her car and drove straight to a coffee shop and ordered the largest they had. Naomi sat in her vehicle with her hands around the cup and watched the people driving and walking past.

She finished her coffee before heading to meet up with Whitney. Unfortunately, her friend wasn't alone. Ms. Biermann was with her.

The restaurant was one that Naomi, Whitney, and Suellen had visited often. And she was irrationally irritated that Ms. Biermann was there.

"Goodness, I'm already tired," Whitney said once they took their seats in the booth.

Ms. Biermann smiled and raised her menu to cover her face. Naomi used that chance to hold out her hands, raise her eyebrows, and shake her head. Whitney's gaze darted to the side where her chaperone sat before she issued a little half shrug.

"Mom wants to know if you want to come by for dinner while I'm in town," Naomi said.

Whitney smiled. "I've been salivating for your mom's chicken and dumplings."

"She said she'd make whatever you want."

Whitney laughed and moved aside the menu. "She should be cooking for you."

"Oh, she is, believe me," Naomi said with a roll of her eyes. "An army wouldn't be able to eat everything she's made. And I'm not sure when she has time between volunteering at the nursing home, the library, *and* the theatre. Then there are her painting classes, and the regimen her personal trainer has her on."

Whitney laughed loudly. "Your mom was always like that, though."

"No. It's worse. Soooooo much worse."

They shared a smile, and for a moment, Naomi forgot that they weren't alone. Then the waitress arrived, and the three placed their orders.

Before Naomi could get back to their conversation, Ms. Biermann turned to her. "Whitney told me you used to be part of the rodeo circuit with her."

"That's right," Naomi replied stiffly. She didn't know what it was about the older woman that she didn't like, and try as she might not to let it show, it was a losing battle.

"Were you any good?"

Whitney gawked at the woman. "Surely you've seen the unbeatable score for barrel racing for the entire county. Naomi holds that record."

When Ms. Biermann's gray gaze slid back to Naomi, there was respect there. "Interesting."

Naomi stopped short of rolling her eyes. Instead, she focused on Whitney. "I've had some requests for country-side pictures, so I'm going to take an extra day or two and drive around to get those. Want to come?"

"She can't," Ms. Biermann stated before Whitney could reply. "She has engagements to attend."

Whitney smiled ruefully. "Sorry."

"No worries. I'll take Mom."

As soon as the words were out of her mouth, Naomi knew that wouldn't happen. She loved her mother dearly, but Diana Pierce couldn't even sit still long enough to watch a movie. Driving around and looking for the perfect setting for pictures would be agonizing for her.

And Naomi.

So, she would save herself and her mother the headache and go on her own. Perhaps she might run into Brice in the process.

What should have been a fun lunch catching up seemed stilted and strained. Naomi was grateful when it was finally over—and more than a happy to place the blame on Ms. Biermann. She picked up the tab when the chaperone hurried Whitney to finish eating so they could leave.

Naomi remained and finished her burger and fries after the two had left to get ready for the rodeo. Then she headed to the arena. She parked and got out, her eyes immediately scanning for any sign of Brice.

It was silly, really. She barely knew him, but he was the only one she could talk to about the attack. It was why Naomi hadn't brought it up at lunch with Ms. Biermann there. Had it just been her and Whitney, she'd planned to show her friend the pictures.

Naomi held the envelope close to her chest as she adjusted her bag. She rose up on her tiptoes and looked toward the area where the contestants were gathered. Two burly cowboys blocked the entrance, eyeing her as if she might attempt to dart past them.

No doubt some women tried to get to the men.

"Looking for someone?"

At the sound of the deep voice, Naomi whirled around and looked into dark brown eyes. She recognized him immediately from his charming smile and the pictures she'd taken the day before. "Actually, I am."

He touched the brim of his hat. "I'm Caleb Harper. Please say I'm the one you're searching for."

She laughed. She couldn't help it. There was something so easy-going and likable about him that she was immediately drawn in. She held out her hand. "Naomi Pierce."

"Naomi," he repeated and looked deep into her eyes, giving her hand a firm squeeze before releasing her. "A beautiful name."

She shook her head, the smile still in place. "How many hearts have you broken?"

He twisted his lips, shrugging. "I've no idea what you mean."

"Oh, sure you do." She laughed again. "No doubt the number is in the triple digits."

He put his hand over his heart and gave her a surprised look that was ruined by a wink. "I'm innocent, ma'am."

"Naomi?"

Her head swung to the side at the sound of Brice's voice. Her heart sped up as he strode over to her.

"Ah. I see," Caleb murmured.

Naomi looked at him, but the smile was gone. He nodded his head at her and walked off before his brother reached them. She turned to Brice before glancing over her shoulder at Caleb.

"Is everything all right between you two?" she asked Brice.

He looked at his brother's retreating back. "I messed up. Normally, he's over his anger by now." Blue eyes slid to her. "How are you?"

"Fine," she assured him. "I developed the pictures this morning. I tried to lighten the area to see the attacker's face, but it was just too dark. I was hoping you might look at them and find something I might have missed when I looked."

One side of his lips lifted in a grin. "I'd love to. I've been thinking about the incident all night. Come with me."

Now that she was with Brice, the two men at the gate smiled and waved her through. The sounds of the rodeo in progress were loud and overwhelming. From the crowd cheering to the bulls stamping their hooves and blowing out air to cowboys laughing in groups while others drifted off by themselves, readying for their events.

Brice put a hand on her lower back and guided her into an area where the sounds were dimmed enough that they could talk normally.

He checked the vicinity to make sure they were alone before he turned to her. "I don't think you should be walking around alone. Especially here."

"You think he'd try something in the middle of a crowd?"

"I'd rather not find out."

She bit her bottom lip. "My mom is busy today, so I'm alone until Whitney is finished. I'm here to take some more pictures and be with Whitney."

"Stick close to the pageant officials as much as you can."

"And if I can't?"

His chest expanded as he took a breath. "Then stick with me."

She looked into his eyes and smiled. Spending the day with him sounded nice.

Chapter 6

Danger. It hung in the air like an invisible menace. Brice couldn't put his finger on it, but it was there. Somewhere in the vast area of the arena.

And it involved someone associated with the rodeo.

Again, he had no definitive person to blame. All he had was the feeling inside him.

He looked into Naomi's brown eyes and felt an overwhelming need to protect her. She had become involved, simply by her association with Whitney. It made him wonder what would have happened that night had Naomi not been with Whitney.

But he knew that Naomi shouldn't be alone. It was why he made the offer.

"You compete today," Naomi said.

Brice shrugged. "We can work around that."

She rocked back on her heels and turned the envelope in her hands. "If anyone was coming after me, they had all night and this morning to do it. I was by myself until I met Whitney for lunch."

"I gather you developed the film earlier today?"

She nodded her head, tucking a strand of wheat-colored hair behind her ear.

He glimpsed a pair of black and white stud earrings that looked like a dog's face. "Did you notice if anyone was following you?"

Her lips parted as she frowned. "Uh . . . I can't say that I did."

"It may be nothing. The guy might have given up, but I'd rather be safe than sorry."

She wrinkled her nose and bit her bottom lip. "I would, as well."

"Want to show me those?" he said and jerked his chin to the envelope.

"Oh." She issued a small laugh and handed him the packet.

Brice glanced at her before he opened the envelope and pulled out several 8×10 pictures. He spent a while studying each one, noting where Whitney was, as well as how her head was turned toward the shadows.

Naomi caught the attacker coming out of the dark and shoving Whitney aside before he reached for the camera. Unfortunately, there wasn't much to see of the man.

"I gave the exposure as much extra light as I could, hoping to catch something of the guy," Naomi explained as she stood in front of him and adjusted the strap of her bag.

"The angle of his hat makes seeing his face nearly impossible."

"Yeah, I tried to see him," Naomi said.

He met her gaze and said, "It's not your fault."

Brice moved that photo behind the others and looked

over the next. He noted Whitney staring right at the guy as he pushed her down. Why had she been so adamant that it was nothing?

Odds were that Whitney knew the man. And for some reason, she didn't want his identity confirmed.

Perhaps Brice should talk to her privately. If she wouldn't tell her friend the truth, she probably wouldn't tell him either, but he was going to try.

He studied the next couple of photos, but when he flipped one more, he stilled. It was one of him and Caleb from yesterday's team roping. His eyes were on the steer, his arm up, and the lasso overhead right before he threw it. Caleb's rope was also out, but while his brother had a grin on his face, Brice didn't.

"I didn't know if you ever had anyone take such pictures of you two. I'm sure you have," she hurried to say. "It's my gift to you. But you don't have to take it if you don't want it."

"You captured the moment perfectly," he said.

She rocked back on her heels again and beamed. "I've always found life easier behind the camera. I see things others don't."

"And you bring it out in them. It's a great picture." He lifted his gaze to her. "Thank you."

Her smile widened as she lifted her shoulders in a shrug. "There's a few more."

Brice moved to the following photo. This one was a close-up of Caleb in the chute. He was leaned over his horse, whispering something to Sullivan.

The next one was of Brice. His face took up nearly the entire photo. His gaze was straight ahead, intense and thoroughly focused. Brice knew exactly when this had been taken. It was right before the steer had been loose. He always envisioned how he would rope the cattle, going through the motions in his head over and over.

"I can't remember the last time someone took my picture," he said. "Not like this. The pics my sister takes at family functions don't count."

"The camera loves you," Naomi said.

That wasn't something he'd heard before. It was an odd feeling to see yourself through someone else's eyes. Naomi had captured a specific moment in time during an event that he not only loved but also excelled at with his brother.

"Thank you for these. I can't wait to show Caleb."

Naomi pulled her hands from her pockets. "If he doesn't like those, I've got others. And I plan on taking more pictures over the next few days while the rodeo is ongoing. That is if neither of you mind."

He tucked the pictures back into the envelope. "Not at all. So, this is what you do?"

"Not often. Mostly, I take pictures of things and sell them to companies or individuals to use for advertising."

"Really?" he asked, surprised.

She laughed softly. "I promise you won't see your face up on my site for sale. I have to get permission from people before that can happen. The pictures I'm taking now are for a scrapbook for Whitney."

"You're very talented."

She briefly looked at the ground. "It's nice to be good at what you love. And to be able to make a living doing it."

"I agree."

Naomi then pointed at his belt buckle, which was from the Houston Livestock Show and Rodeo. "You're obviously good at what you do."

He glanced down at the silver and gold buckle that pronounced him and Caleb winners. "My brother and I are blessed."

They stared at each other in silence for a moment. Brice searched his mind for something to say to continue the conversation. He wasn't ready for Naomi to leave.

"Um," she said, motioning to the envelope. "Keep the pictures of the attacker. I can make more."

"I have a couple of friends I'd like to show them to. Maybe they'll recognize something I missed."

She nodded eagerly. "Sure. I want to know who this guy is and why he was following Whitney. And why he was so upset about me finding out who he is."

Brice heard his name called behind him. He looked over his shoulder and waved to Jace and Cooper.

"I guess you need to go," Naomi said.

He looked back at her. "You can stay."

"I'm not sure that's a good idea. You have things you need to do. I don't want to be in the way."

Brice turned to the side next to Naomi and motioned his friends over. "If you won't stay with me, then promise you'll go find Whitney. I'm going to introduce you to two of my closest friends. They'll keep an eye on you, as well."

"I wish I could say I don't need them, but I appreciate it."

He didn't have a chance to say more as his friends arrived, both grinning knowingly. Brice wanted to punch them, but it would have to wait until later.

"Hey," Jace said to Brice and tipped his black Stetson at Naomi. "Everything all right?"

Brice looked from Jace to Cooper and pulled out the photos of the attacker. "Not really. We need your help. Jace Wilder and Cooper Owens let me introduce Naomi

Pierce. Naomi, this is Jace and Cooper. They may be able to charm the scales off a snake, but I trust them."

"Then so shall I," she replied with a smile.

Cooper narrowed his dark green eyes. "The same Naomi Pierce who holds the barrel racing record?"

Brice's head jerked to Naomi to find her smiling proudly. How had he not made the connection?

"It was a long time ago," she said. "And I had an amazing horse."

Brice definitely wanted to know more about Naomi because there was much to discover. He'd never figured her as someone part of the rodeo circuit. Apparently, he'd been dead wrong.

He cleared his throat and quickly filled in his friends on what had happened the night before. They looked at the pictures, but neither recognized anything about the man.

"You shouldn't be alone," Jace told Naomi.

She cut her gaze to Brice. "He's already mentioned that, and I agree with him. I hope we're all overreacting—"

"It's better to be careful," Cooper stated.

Jace tipped his hat to her again. "Let us know if you need anything. We'll keep an eye out for you."

"We'll be here the rest of the day," Cooper said. "Don't hesitate to find us."

Naomi smiled at them. "Thank you both. I appreciate it."

When she turned to him, Brice knew she was leaving. He wanted her to remain, but he couldn't force her.

"I'm going to go look for Whitney," Naomi said. "I'll be with her or someone else. Or," she spoke over him when he parted his lips, "I'll come find you."

Brice shot her a grin. "And don't leave by yourself."

"Yes, sir," she replied with a smile.

After one more look, she waved to Cooper and Jace and walked away. Brice watched her, an uneasy feeling falling over him.

"You should've made her stay with us," Cooper said.

Brice swung his head to his friends. "I plan on ensuring she isn't alone."

"You can't be with her everywhere," Jace pointed out.

"That's why I have you two," Brice said with a grin.

Jace raised a blond brow. "And Caleb, right?"

"Yeah." Brice needed to fill his brother in. If Caleb would even listen to him.

Cooper held out his hand. "Can I see the photos again?"

"Did you recognize something?" Brice asked as he handed them over.

"No, but I heard a rumor a few years back about someone stalking the girls in the pageant."

Jace frowned as he crossed his arms over his chest. "It was just the once." He looked at Brice. "It came from the momma of a girl who didn't win."

"So everyone chalked it up to her being sore about losing," Brice said.

Cooper tilted his head to the side in a shrug. "Especially since the woman didn't repeat anything about it, and there hasn't been that kind of rumor since."

"Until last night," Brice said.

Jace elbowed Cooper. "Hey, what happened to that girl? What was her name?"

"Jamie Adcock," Cooper said. "And I have no idea. She and her mother moved away."

Brice put the name to memory. He was going to do some digging. "Let me know if either of you remember any more about Jamie. Let's keep this to ourselves for now."

"Agreed," Jace said. "I don't like the idea of anyone stalking, but it chaps my ass when someone attacks a woman."

"Even if it was just for her camera," Cooper added.

Brice slapped Jace on the back as the two walked away. Now, he needed to find Caleb.

Chapter 7

She was smiling. A true, couldn't-wipe-it-away-if-she-tried smile. And Naomi knew it was because of Brice.

The grin had begun when he complimented her work. She'd initially been afraid that he didn't like the pictures of him and his brother. The way he'd stood so still staring at them had made her want to snatch them away and take better ones.

She waved to Whitney when her friend shouted her name. Naomi adjusted her bag and walked through the line of chaperones guarding the girls.

At least no one could get to Whitney here. Which meant that Naomi was safe, as well.

When she passed Ms. Biermann, she met the woman's cold gaze. Then again, if the man following Whitney were part of the pageant, her friend was right in the crosshairs. That shook Naomi enough that it wiped the smile from her lips.

"Hey," Whitney said as she met her halfway. "You okay?"

Naomi shook off her reservations. "Fine."

"I'm sorry about lunch. Sharon won't let me out of her sight after what happened last night."

"That's good, I suppose."

Whitney hooked her arm with Naomi's. "So, tonight, after the rodeo, I want you to come with me and the other girls. We're going out. The chaperones will be there, of course, but they tend to give us room when we're all together."

"Yeah, sure. Sounds good." Naomi stopped walking and faced Whitney. "Will you please talk to me about last night?"

Just like that, Whitney's attitude changed. Her gaze darted to the chaperones while her face became tight with agitation. "Drop it, Naomi."

"Why? I don't understand."

Whitney's hand wrapped painfully around Naomi's upper arm as her friend literally dragged her into a corner where there was only a horse that could hear them.

"Why can't you drop it?" Whitney demanded, arms crossed over her chest.

Naomi looked at the crown atop Whitney's hat. "Because the girl I grew up with wouldn't step aside when something bad happened."

"You have no concept of what my life is."

"Then help me understand," Naomi pleaded. She took a deep breath when Whitney remained silent. "I remember life in the rodeo. It's all about being Christians, having family values, and showing patriotism. And it passes to the pageants. The chaperones are here to make sure nothing improper happens to any of you. Same with the judges. I understand rodeo values just as you do, so don't tell me I don't get it."

Whitney's blue eyes cut to her. "I'm begging you to let it go. Please don't say anything else. If you're my friend, you won't ask any more questions."

"You know who the guy is, don't you?"

Whitney dropped her arms and turned to walk away. Naomi followed her to the back fence where Whitney grabbed her chaps and buckled them on.

Naomi saw her friend's name stitched on the band of the chaps near her waist at the back. Whatever it was that Whitney wanted to keep hidden, it was serious. And she was going to extremes to keep Naomi from finding out what it was.

"I'll leave it," Naomi said after a long, silent minute. "But only if you promise me that you haven't been hurt."

"I haven't," Whitney replied without looking at her.

"That's no—"

Whitney whirled around. "Who are you to come into the world that you left years ago—*my* world—and tell me how to do things? You know nothing about this life anymore. Nothing. You should never have come."

Naomi watched Whitney walk away. She was stunned by Whitney's words, and it made her rethink everything. Maybe her friend was right. She had left the rodeo life and never looked back.

It didn't mean that she'd deserted Whitney but, apparently, her friend thought differently. Naomi drew in a deep breath and turned to see if anyone had witnessed the exchange. Thankfully, it appeared that no one had.

She was walking out of the pageant area when a group of girls who were friends of the other contestants asked if she wanted to sit with them.

Brice's words of warning came back to her. Naomi accepted the invitation and followed them into the stands.

There was a section roped off just for the group, who were obviously considered VIPs of some sort. The seats were the best in the arena and next to the railing to get an up-close view of everything.

They had just taken their places when the rodeo began. Naomi was used to being on her own, but she liked the group of young women. They were chatty and easy to talk to. Soon, she was laughing along with them as they clapped and cheered.

Brice slapped the envelope against his leg as he looked for Caleb. He checked on their horses to make sure they were fine.

After giving Jigsaw and Sullivan each a carrot, Brice turned and continued his search. He paused and watched Jace compete in the steer wrestling event. His friend came in second and easily moved on to the next round.

Jace nodded to Brice as he rode past on his horse. "She's in the arena."

Brice didn't need to ask who Jace meant. Even during his event, Jace had managed to locate Naomi in the stands. Brice was glad he'd brought his friends in on things. Especially now, when he couldn't find his brother.

"Where are you, Caleb?" he murmured to himself.

Brice decided to check the truck. His brother might be there just to avoid him. Brice moved away from the crowds of cowboys and cowgirls waiting for their events and walked amid the animal pens when a sudden pain exploded in his head.

He hit the ground, his face smashing into the dirt as he fought to stay conscious. The envelope was yanked from his hand. He instinctively knew that this had something to do with Naomi. He needed to warn her.

As the blackness claimed him, he felt the heel of a boot step onto his right hand.

"Brice? Brice!"

He woke to the sound of his name being called again and again.

"Brice? Shit, man," Cooper said with a sigh as he grabbed an arm. "There you are."

Jace grasped Brice's other arm. "We got you. Easy does it now."

"What the fuck?" Caleb shouted as he rushed to them.

Brice tried to push up, but his right hand erupted in agony as his brother came running over. His head felt as if it were being kicked between two horses over and over again. He was seeing double and was nauseous.

"Naomi," he muttered when his friends pulled him to his feet. He met Caleb's gaze then.

His brother gave a nod. "I saw her in the stands. I'll get her."

Thank God Caleb hadn't asked for an explanation. Brice tried to follow him, but the world began to spin. The nausea combined with the throbbing in his head and hand made it impossible for Brice to stand without leaning.

"Did you not hear me tell you to take it easy?" Jace demanded and held him tighter.

Cooper grunted. "Stubborn as a damn mule."

"We should get Karl and Marina," Jace said. "Your head is bleeding bad."

Brice felt something warm and thick slide down the side of his face. He reached up to feel it with his injured hand and gasped at the pain.

"Son of a bitch," Cooper exclaimed.

Brice blinked and finally looked at his hand, which was

turning a sick shade of yellow and green even as he looked at it. His hand hadn't been stepped on. It had been stomped.

"Your roping hand," Jace said.

Naomi jumped up and clapped loudly as she shouted her praise for the chuck wagon racing. It was a wild, crazy event that drove the crowd insane.

She leaned forward to get a better look at the wagons as they drove away from her when she felt something shove into her back. Her hands propelled wildly as she pitched forward.

Naomi saw the old woman and tried to twist to miss her, which caused Naomi to slam awkwardly into the railing. There was nothing to grab onto, so she fell forward. Right over the barrier and into the arena.

She landed hard on her back, right on her bag that she rarely took off. The unmistakable sound of equipment cracking filled her ears, but it was drowned out by the gasp of the crowd.

And the approaching wagons.

Naomi knew she had to get up and move. She tried to roll onto her side toward the fence, but something stopped her. The ground shook as the horses and wagons thundered toward her. The screams of the crowd told her that if she didn't get out of the way, she was going to be trampled.

She pushed up onto her hands and saw the horses. Her gaze briefly met the guy driving the wagon closest to her. The other two wagons prevented him from moving away from the barrier. It was all up to her.

Gritting her teeth, she rolled toward the fence and felt the whoosh of wind as the wagons rushed past her. She clutched the bars of the barrier, her heart slamming against her ribs as she shook.

Something hit the ground next to her, and then there was a body protecting her.

"It's gonna be okay," he said. "The wagons have stopped, and the medics are on their way. Nod that you understand me, Naomi. Brice will kick my ass if you don't."

Caleb. She knew he was joking, but she couldn't form a smile. Instead, she did as he asked and nodded.

"Good. You're doing fine. The ambulance is pulling into the arena now. It's over."

"It's just beginning," she whispered.

He pulled her hair away from her face. "I gather you didn't fall?"

She swallowed and looked to where the ambulance approached. "Pushed."

"You and Brice attacked at nearly the same time? What the hell is going on?"

That got her attention. She tried to turn to see him, but she couldn't release the fence. "Is he hurt?"

"He sent me to you. Naomi, the medics are here. They're my friends. I need you to let go of the wall so they can help you."

His voice was relaxed and comforting as he attempted to calm her, but she had almost died. She heard the medics talking, mumbling something about being in shock.

Caleb put an arm around her while his other hand lightly gripped her wrist. "If you want to see how Brice is, you're going to have to let go."

He was right, of course. But someone had pushed her. Someone had wanted her to die.

"No one is going to hurt you now," Caleb said. "Trust me."

Naomi swallowed and loosened her fingers. Next thing she knew, she was on a stretcher and hastily put into the ambulance. Caleb climbed in with her and gave her a reassuring smile as the doors closed and they drove out of the arena.

The ambulance didn't go far, though. They stopped while the paramedic examined her for any injuries. She began to shake, and she was hastily wrapped in a blanket as they raised the bed so she could sit up.

Caleb was talking, but she couldn't hear him. She still felt the hand on her back. It was imprinted there, like a burn. Evil had touched her, and it terrified her.

Then the ambulance doors were suddenly thrown open, and Brice stood there. She immediately spotted the blood running down the side of his face from his dark hair. He climbed into the truck without taking his eyes from her.

"She's unscathed other than a few bruises," the paramedic said.

Brice sighed and glanced at his brother. That's when Naomi saw Brice's hand, which was swollen and turning violent shades of green and purple.

"Let me look at you," the paramedic said to Brice.

Immediately, the elder Harper shook his head. "You treat me, you have to report it."

"Brice, dammit," the guy said. "I'll keep this between us."

Naomi turned her head and read his nametag: *Karl Vega*.

"Let Karl tend you, or I'll do it," said a woman who turned in the driver's seat.

Naomi then remembered that Caleb had said he knew

the medics. And Brice needed to be looked at. "Let them see your injuries," she urged.

Brice's lips flattened, but he nodded in agreement.

Caleb slid over on the seat as his brother sat beside him. "Someone is going to tell me why the hell the two of you were attacked. And by someone, I mean you," he informed Brice. "Now."

Naomi met Brice's gaze for a long, silent minute, a look passing between them before he pulled in a breath and began the story.

Chapter 8

When Brice finished speaking, the silence in the ambulance was loud. He remained still while Karl cleaned the blood from his face.

"Shit," Caleb muttered as he took off his hat and ran a hand through his light brown hair.

Brice jerked his head away from Karl when he pushed against sensitive flesh. "That hurts."

"This will go quicker if you stay still," Karl said with a flat look.

Brice stayed motionless and fought not to reach for Naomi's hand. She was white as a sheet as she huddled beneath the foil blanket. Her brown eyes held fear for all to see.

"Your hat may have saved you from stitches," Karl said as he sat back. "But you're going to have one whopper of a headache."

"Obviously," Brice replied tersely.

He didn't know where his hat was, and frankly, he didn't care. Even something as minor as breathing made his head pound to the point where he had a hard time focusing.

Caleb blew out a breath. "Karl, check my brother's hand. And Brice, if you tell me it doesn't hurt, I may punch you. In the face. Think how that will feel with that headache of yours."

"Asshole," Brice muttered while he held out his hand to Karl.

Marina chuckled softly and fussed over Naomi. When Brice had heard the gasp from the arena and then the screams, he'd been terrified that Naomi was seriously injured.

While Marina spoke with Naomi, Brice raised his brows in a silent question to his brother.

Caleb glanced at Naomi and mouthed, *"It was close."*

"How is Naomi?" Brice asked.

Karl glanced at him but remained focused on Brice's hand. "She's going to be bruised, but nothing is broken."

"My bag," Naomi suddenly said and sat upright.

Marina reached over and lifted it. "It's right here."

Naomi held out her hand for the bag. "My equipment."

Brice pressed his lips together. She'd already had one camera ruined. He hoped the rest fared better, but he was doubtful.

"Dammit," he growled and glared when Karl prodded a knuckle.

Karl raised a black brow. "You're a terrible patient."

"You don't know the half of it," Caleb said with a grin.

Brice turned his gaze back to Naomi to see her carefully pulling out each piece of equipment from her bag. The way her face furrowed with deep lines told him that there was damage. Hopefully, the pieces could be fixed.

It felt like forever before Karl finished examining his

hand. Caleb had joked with Marina, trying to keep the atmosphere light until Naomi put the cameras and lenses back into the bag and sighed.

"How bad is it?" Brice asked.

Her chestnut gaze swung to him. "Some cracked lenses, and a few hairline fissures in my cameras. I'll take them to be looked at."

"Whoever hit me took the printed pictures."

No sooner had the last word left his mouth than Jace and Cooper walked up. Brice didn't like the frowns his friends wore.

"A vehicle was broken into," Cooper said.

Everyone looked at Naomi.

She swallowed loudly. "A red Jeep Wrangler?"

Jace nodded. "I take that to mean it's yours?"

"Yeah," Naomi replied. "A rental."

Cooper put one hand on the ambulance door and leaned on it. "They tore the Jeep up."

"The pictures weren't enough," Caleb said. "They're looking for the film."

Son of a bitch. This was getting out of control. Brice had to get Naomi away from the rodeo.

Naomi laughed then. He looked at her, worried that everything may have sent her over the edge.

But her eyes were clear as she met his gaze. "I hid the film. It wasn't in my Jeep."

"Which means you can reprint those pictures," Jace said with a grin.

Caleb took off his hat and hung it on his knee. "I'd sure like to see what was so important for someone to go to such trouble."

"Count me in," Marina said.

Karl finally released Brice's hand. "Add me to the list.

But based on what happened today, I think everyone needs to tread carefully. Brice, you won't be able to use your hand for a day or two. After that, it's going to be very sore."

"Your event," Naomi exclaimed.

Brice traded looks with his brother and grinned. "Don't worry about that. I agree with Karl. If this guy was after the film, he's going to keep looking until he finds it."

"The only way to stop him is for the guy to believe he's gotten the roll," Naomi said. A slow smile pulled at her lips. "That should be easy enough."

Caleb's eyes looked from Brice to Naomi. "I suppose you have an idea?"

Naomi reached into her bag and pulled out a roll of film. "I sure do." She then tossed it to Caleb. "You need to be seen with that. It should draw the creep out."

"Gladly," he replied.

Jace nodded as he hooked his thumbs through his belt loops. "Cooper and I will be waiting for him."

"It's about time we corner this jerk," Brice added.

Caleb replaced his hat and tucked the film into his pocket. "What about Whitney? Should we bring her in on this?"

"No," Naomi hurried to answer. "She made it clear earlier that she doesn't want to talk about it."

Cooper turned his head and looked at something on the other side of the ambulance. "Speaking of. She's on her way."

Everyone went silent when Whitney came running around the ambulance and stood between Jace and Cooper. She stared at Naomi with wide eyes, her chest heaving from the exertion. "I just heard. Are you okay? Shouldn't you be at the hospital?" Whitney turned her gaze to Marina. "Why isn't she at the hospital?"

"Because, miraculously, she's unhurt," Marina replied.

Whitney shook her head of long, blond hair, curled and sprayed. "Naomi, how did you fall over?"

"I was pushed."

Brice watched Whitney's face after Naomi's statement. The rodeo queen blinked and shook her head, but there was no denying the flicker of dread that she hadn't been able to hide.

"Pushed?" Whitney repeated. "How? Why?"

"You know why," Brice said.

Whitney's blue eyes swung to him. She opened her mouth to say something before her gaze lowered to his injured hand. "Did you save her?"

"I did," Caleb replied. "After Brice was found lying on the ground because someone knocked him on the head and stomped on his hand."

Whitney swallowed and looked at Cooper and Jace before sliding her gaze to Naomi. "I was the one who found your Jeep. I was coming to look for you when I heard about the accident in the arena."

Caleb got to his feet and shimmied past Brice and Karl as he climbed out of the ambulance. He stood before Whitney, staring at her a long minute. "You have no idea how close Naomi came to being trampled by the horses and wagons. Whatever you're hiding, it's time you tell us."

"I can't," Whitney said in a hoarse whisper. Then buried her face in her hands.

Brice cut his eyes to Naomi and found her dropping the blanket and rising from the gurney. Caleb moved out of the way while Cooper helped Naomi out of the ambulance. Naomi wrapped her arms around Whitney as her friend's shoulders shook with her tears.

"Y'all, anyone could be watching this," Jace said as he looked around.

Brice braced his elbow on his knee and slowly lowered his forehead to his good hand. He could barely think straight with the pounding in his head.

And he still had his event to do.

He'd ridden with a headache before, but nothing had ever hurt as badly as this one. His scalp was sore and throbbing from being bashed and split open.

Not to mention the agony of his hand. Thankfully, he could rope with both hands. It was a skill learned from Clayton, who'd warned both Brice and Caleb that anything could happen on a ranch and that a man needed to be able to do every job with either hand.

Brice had never roped with his left arm at a rodeo, so no one other than Caleb, Jace, and Cooper knew he had the ability. If the man who'd hit him wanted to take him out of the event, the bastard would be in for a surprise.

"Do you need something for the pain?" Karl leaned close and whispered.

Brice lifted his head and shot him a quick grin. "Aspirin only."

"I can do that."

Brice gladly accepted the two pills and water and downed them. They would hopefully take the edge off the throbbing. While he was thinking about what to do with Naomi and Whitney, Marina handed Karl an elastic bandage that he wrapped around Brice's hand. Brice didn't even complain because it actually felt good, like the bandage was snuggly holding everything together.

"What do you want to do?" Cooper asked Naomi.

Brice watched as she lifted her tear-streaked face and sniffed. "That depends on Whitney."

The rodeo queen accepted a tissue from Marina and dabbed at her face. "I swear, I never thought it would come to this."

"Just tell us who it is," Caleb urged.

Whitney looked at Naomi. "I can't."

Naomi rubbed her hands up and down Whitney's upper arms. "Then tell us what you can."

"If I do, he'll know."

Brice shrugged. "Chances are, he thinks you've already told us."

Whitney shook her head and snorted. "I doubt that."

"How can you be sure?" Cooper asked.

Whitney looked down at her hands and turned the tissue around in her fingers. "Because you'll start asking other questions."

"This is about the pageant, isn't it?" Naomi asked.

Whitney briefly met Naomi's gaze. "Yeah."

Naomi turned and looked at Brice. He rubbed his eyes with the thumb and forefinger of his left hand. "We can't help you if you don't tell us."

"That's just it," Whitney said as she lifted her face. "If I tell you, these accidents will increase."

Caleb's forehead furrowed in a frown. "What will happen to you?"

Whitney shrugged, but the fear on her face said it all.

Brice climbed out of the ambulance to stand beside Naomi. "If you want to keep living like this, Whitney, none of us can stop you. But this has gone beyond you. This now involves me and Naomi."

"I know," she replied irritably.

"You have people here willing to protect you," Brice continued. "We'll put ourselves out there for this bastard to come at us. That is if you're keen on telling us whatever it is you're hiding."

Whitney sniffed and shook her head. "I would've kept my mouth shut. I would've continued to ignore all of it." She then wrapped an arm around Naomi. "But my best friend was hurt. I can't lose another."

Naomi gave her a watery smile and hugged Whitney.

"This is nice and all," Caleb said, "but I'm not comfortable standing out here where anyone can see us."

Cooper glanced at the arena. "It won't be long before my calf roping event. Team roping is right after."

"I'm finished for the day," Jacc said.

Brice nodded to Jace. "Take my truck and bring the girls to the ranch."

"I can't leave," Whitney said. "Besides, if I leave now, whoever it is will think I've told you."

Naomi lifted her chin. "If she isn't going, neither am I."

"No," Whitney said. "I'll feel better if you're safe."

Brice was glad that Whitney agreed with him. "As soon as our event finishes, we'll be on our way."

"You can trust me, Naomi," Jace said with a grin.

From inside the ambulance, Marina said, "We'll keep watch for anything unusual."

Karl nodded. "You bet."

"Jace will keep you safe until you get to the ranch and the rest of us arrive," Cooper said. "I'll bring Whitney."

Naomi turned her head to Brice. "Looks like I'm leaving."

"I'll be along shortly. Promise."

She moved to him and gently held his injured hand between hers. Then she looked into his eyes. "Be careful."

"Always."

Chapter 9

Clayton East paused in mounting his horse and pulled out his cell phone when it buzzed. The short text from Brice saying that the ranch was about to have special company had him frowning.

He dropped the reins and gave the horse a pat before he pivoted and walked from the barn to the house. He stepped inside and almost expected to hear his mother's shout from the kitchen.

When his dad died two years ago of a stroke, his mother soon lost the will to live. She joined her beloved Ben eight months later. Clayton missed them terribly, and he always would. But his parents had been deliriously happy with the addition of Abby and her brothers into the family.

And then came their grandchildren. Clayton didn't think there were grandkids more spoiled than his two. He just wished his parents were there to see the arrival of his next child.

He closed the door behind him and listened, trying to discern where Abby was in the house. After she'd come downstairs in the mornings, she rarely went back up until it was time for bed. Before the pregnancy, she would go into the office and keep up with the books and taxes after the kids had headed off to school.

Clayton walked through the kitchen, noting that Abby had gotten into the cookies as well as eaten an orange. He grinned. His wife was an amazing woman. He'd realized it from their first meeting at the police station when Brice was arrested for cattle rustling.

Abby had drive, and it hadn't taken her long to get her degree and pass the state exam to be a CPA. Clayton urged her to open her own business, but she wanted to focus on the ranch. Still, she insisted that they hire a large accounting firm in Fort Worth to oversee her.

He found his wife asleep on the couch, her laptop open as pictures of their kids scrolled on the screensaver. He quietly walked to her and moved her hands before lifting the computer.

The screensaver vanished, showing a browser screen with news on their area's rodeo pageants. Except Abby had searched for any scandals or negative news. Of course, there were always adverse articles about everything, so he wasn't surprised about those. But he did frown at a story headline toward the bottom of the page.

He knelt next to the sofa and set the laptop on the coffee table. Just as he clicked the link, Abby touched his shoulder.

He turned his head to her and smiled. "I didn't mean to wake you."

"You didn't. The baby did," she replied with a yawn before pushing herself up farther on the couch. "Feel."

He put his hand on her stomach and laughed at the tiny feet that pummeled his palm. "Goodness."

"Just wait." She then moved his hand to another part of her stomach.

Clayton laughed when he felt the little hands shoving against Abby's stomach.

"It's a boy. I know it," she muttered.

Each time she had been pregnant, they'd decided not to find out the sex of the baby until the birth. They made bets with each other. So far, they had both won.

He rubbed her belly softly before planting a kiss on it then another on her lips.

"I'm appalled at how much I sleep during the day, and yet I'm wide-awake at night. Neither of the other two pregnancies seemed to drain me like this one."

"Sleep as long as you need."

She leaned her head back and sighed. "Believe me, I am." Her gaze then landed on the computer screen. "Have you read that?"

"I just pulled it up."

Her lips flattened in distaste. "You need to read it."

"I will. I came in to tell you that Brice texted to say we're going to have a special guest."

Abby frowned as she shifted to sit up straight. "Is that all he said?"

"Yep."

"Did you reply to him?"

Clayton moved to sit next to her when she tucked her legs against her. "Not yet."

She stared at him with raised brows.

He shook his head and pulled out his phone from his pocket. "There," he said after he'd texted to see if everything was all right.

No sooner had the message gone through than Abby's phone rang. She reached for it where it lay on the back of the couch. "It's Caleb," she told Clayton before answering it.

There was a pause before Abby's blue eyes met his and she said, "Oh. Okay. Hang on."

Clayton watched as she lowered the phone between them and put it on speaker.

"He's here," Abby said.

The sounds of the rodeo could be heard in the background before Caleb said, "Jace is headed to the ranch with Naomi Pierce."

"The woman Brice helped last night?" Clayton asked.

"The very one," Caleb replied. He blew out a breath and lowered his voice to make sure no one else could hear him. "The shit has hit the fan here. Brice wants to wait until he gets home to tell you, but you'll see Naomi, and Jace will probably tell you anyway."

Abby's face tightened. "Caleb, you're worrying me. Just tell us."

"There was an accident. Two actually. Well, you could say three."

"Caleb," Clayton said when he saw Abby's face go white. "Is everyone all right?"

The sounds of the rodeo faded, then Caleb said, "Barely. Someone pushed Naomi into the arena during the wagon races."

"Dear God," Abby murmured.

Caleb grunted. "Moments before that, someone hit Brice on the head with something, stomped on his hand, and took the pictures Naomi developed of the guy following her and Whitney."

Clayton blew out a breath and ran his hand down his face. "Do I need to come there?"

"No," Caleb hurried to reply. "Karl and Marina were

here and checked both Brice and Naomi out. I always said Brice had a hard head, and now this proves it because he didn't even have a concussion. He bled a lot, but the wound didn't need stitches."

"And his hand?" Abby asked, her gaze meeting Clayton's.

"Not broken, but it's swollen. Karl said Brice won't be able to use it for a few days."

Clayton put his hand atop Abby's. "Sounds like whoever this guy is, he wanted to make sure Brice couldn't compete."

"Won't the bastard be in for a surprise?" Caleb said, a smile in his voice. "We all agreed that Naomi needed to get away from the rodeo. Whitney is also coming later."

Abby glanced at the computer screen and the article. "So, she does know something?"

"It looks that way. She didn't want to tell us now since she said we'd all react, but she plans on giving us the details later tonight," Caleb explained.

Clayton checked his watch. "Jace and Naomi should arrive in about twenty minutes. I'll send both you and Brice a text when she gets here, and I expect both of you to keep us updated. Otherwise, your sister might decide to make her way there."

Caleb barked in laughter. "I promise to stay in touch. And Abby, keep your ass on the sofa. I'm anxious to meet my new niece or nephew, but not before it's time. And if you leave, then Clayton will kick my ass."

"You got that right," Clayton said with a wink to Abby.

But she didn't respond with a smile. Worry filled her gaze. "How much longer until your event? I want you and Brice home."

"We'll be there as quick as we can, sis. Promise."

"Caleb," she said before he could hang up. "You and Brice need to stick together."

Caleb grunted loudly. "Yeah, I know. If anyone gets to hit my brother, it should be me. Whoever this guy is, he's messed with the wrong family."

"Damn straight," Clayton said. "Just be smart about it."

"That won't be a problem. By the way, I think there might be something developing between Brice and Naomi. I've never seen him so protective," Caleb said.

Abby looked thoughtful for a moment. "Not even with Jill?"

"Not even close," Caleb answered.

Clayton nodded. "Jace will get Naomi here, and we'll take care of her. I'll alert Shane so he and the other hands can be on the lookout. The security system will take care of the rest."

"Thanks. I've got to go," Caleb said.

The call ended, and Abby drew in a deep breath. "What did Brice get mixed up in?"

"He was coming to the defense of someone else. I don't think either he or Naomi realized what this might become." Clayton's gaze looked out the window to the driveway.

"Caleb only told us the highlights of what happened. And I hate that. He knows I need every detail."

Clayton swung his head to her and brought her hand to his lips to kiss it. "We'll get all the nitty-gritty details when Naomi and Jace arrive."

"Brice could have been seriously injured. And Naomi could have died," Abby said as she started to get agitated.

"But they didn't," he reminded her. "They're okay."

Blue eyes met his as she gazed at him in exasperation. "This time."

Clayton grinned as he shook his head. "And that is the mistake this person made. They had one chance to get Brice out of the way, and they didn't take it. Not only did they then go after Naomi, but they also brought our family into the mix."

"Either they don't know us, or they think they can get away with it."

Neither made Clayton feel any better. He had a sick feeling that it was the latter, that whoever this assailant was thought they could do whatever they wanted, though he kept that information to himself.

It was already bad enough that Abby's anxiety was up about her brothers' involvement. Clayton wasn't going to make things worse and risk upsetting Abby—and possibly causing harm to her or the baby.

He leaned over and gave her a kiss. "I'm going to find Shane."

"Don't leave me out of this," she said, giving his hand a yank when he tried to get to his feet.

"Sweetheart, these are your brothers. I wouldn't dream of it."

She shot him a flat look. "I call bullshit. I know you, Clayton East. You'll do whatever it takes to keep our children and me from harm. And that means keeping me out of this situation. But I'll tell you right now that if you do that, you'll be sleeping by yourself for the next year."

He smiled as he got to his feet. "Yes, ma'am. I hear you loud and clear."

"Good. Now, get moving," she ordered sternly.

Then ruined it with a wink.

His grin lasted until he left the house and spotted Shane in one of the pastures. The ranch manager had been around since Clayton was a small boy. Now that Shane was advancing in years, Clayton worried his old friend would want to retire. Not that he could blame Shane. The man had given his life to the East Ranch.

Clayton rested his arms on the fence and waited for Shane to ride up on his horse. "We have a situation."

"How bad?"

"Get the boys ready. Everyone needs to be on high alert. Anything, and I do mean anything, that trips the sensors around the ranch needs to be checked out by at least two men. With guns."

Shane rested both hands on the pommel of his saddle. "Well, hell."

The sound of an engine caused Clayton to turn his head. He spotted the black pickup driving toward him. "You better join me so you can hear everything."

"I'll put everyone on alert before joining you in the house," Shane said and turned his horse around before setting into a run.

Clayton pushed away from the fence as the truck came to a stop.

Chapter 10

The closest Naomi had ever gotten to the East Ranch growing up was driving on the road and gazing in wonder at the massive wood and iron entrance.

Now, she was actually on the ranch.

Jace laughed as he glanced at her. "They're really good people."

"How do Brice and Caleb know the Easts?" she asked while taking in the pastures and the cattle grazing on either side of the drive.

"I forget that not everyone knows," Jace said as he rested his wrist on top of the steering wheel and grinned. "Brice and Caleb's older sister, Abby, married Clayton East. From the time Brice was sixteen and Caleb was fourteen, they grew up here."

Naomi raised her brows in shock. "Wow."

"You'll like Abby and Clayton. They're good people. So were Ben and Justine, Clayton's parents. They passed within months of each other about a year or so ago."

Naomi licked her lips and then turned her head to stare in shock at the impressive residence. There was something about the red clay tile roof and the overall Spanish feel of it that seemed to fit the ranch. She looked in awe at the sweeping arches and windows everywhere.

Jace chuckled loudly. "It certainly is a gorgeous house."

"That isn't a house. That's a mansion," Naomi pointed out.

"Yes, ma'am, it is."

As they pulled around to the back of the home, Naomi saw a man in a straw cowboy hat at the fence talking to another man on horseback. Moments later, the cowboy on the horse rode away.

Jace parked the truck and turned off the engine. Naomi swallowed nervously as Jace opened the door and looked back at her. He hesitated, waiting until she put her hand on the handle and opened it. Only then did he exit the vehicle.

Naomi slid from the truck, wincing when her sore muscles pulled from where she'd fallen on her bag. She shut the door and found herself looking up at a tall man with pale green eyes and blond hair partially hidden by his hat.

He was exceptionally handsome with broad shoulders and an easy smile. He extended his hand as she approached. They shook, and he held her hand for a moment as he said, "You must be Naomi. I'm Clayton East. Welcome. My Abby will tell you later, but I'll say it now. Make yourself at home here. Whatever you need, don't hesitate to ask any one of us."

"That is very kind of you," she said and adjusted her bag strap.

"She's had a rough day," Jace said.

Clayton nodded, a frown furrowing his brow. "Brice texted to let me know you two were coming, but Caleb called. Abby is inside, waiting to get all the details."

"I can do that," Naomi said. "I, uh, I need to let my mom know where I am. But I seem to have lost my phone somewhere."

Clayton held out his arm toward the house. "There's a phone inside. Should I bring your mom here?"

"Oh, God, no," Naomi said hurriedly. She rolled her eyes as she realized how she sounded. "I love my mother dearly, and I don't want anything to happen to her. It's just that she's like a tornado."

Jace laughed. "Sounds like my mom. We'll keep an eye on her. If things get bad, we'll bring her."

"You can't expect to take in everyone," Naomi said to Clayton.

He raised a brow. "Have you seen the size of my home? We have plenty of room. Now, come. Let's get you inside before Abby comes looking for us."

Naomi followed Clayton toward the back of the house, where she glimpsed large, arched windows everywhere, lending to the Spanish style of the house.

They walked into the kitchen, and Naomi was immediately taken with the home. She had expected something extravagant and over-the-top, which the kitchen was, but it was also homey and welcoming.

There were bar stools along the island, and a basket of fruit as well as a covered cake stand with an assortment of cookies on the counter.

Jace immediately went to the cookies and stuffed one into his mouth before grabbing another. He lifted his brows to Naomi in a silent offering, but she shook her head in refusal.

"Eat," Clayton urged her. To Jace, he said, "Grab a couple for Abby."

Naomi walked to the island and peered at the cookies. She opted for a gingersnap and took a small bite before closing her eyes in delight. It was delicious.

"I know," Jace said. "Abby and Ms. Justine combined their recipes. I mean, Caleb and Brice are amazing friends and all, but I really come for the food."

"I heard that," came a woman's voice from another room. "And look in the fridge, Jace. I made you something."

Jace rushed by Naomi and yanked open the refrigerator doors. He groaned loudly and stuffed the cookie into his mouth to use both hands to withdraw a large covered dish.

Naomi laughed as Jace kicked the door closed with his foot and carried the bowl to a drawer, where he pulled out a spoon. Jace then yanked the foil off and tossed it on the counter before he began eating the banana pudding.

"Want a bite?" he asked Naomi.

She smiled and held up her cookie. "I'm good, thanks."

"Abby, this is better than last time," Jace said as he walked past Clayton and Naomi.

Naomi looked at Clayton. "I gather Jace spends a lot of time here."

"It wasn't long after Abby and I married that Brice and Caleb met Jace and Cooper. The four have been together ever since."

Naomi took a bite of her cookie and followed Clayton around the kitchen into the family room. It was huge. The six arched, double-door windows helped, but it was the eye-catching height of the dark-beamed cathedral ceilings that truly captured a person's attention.

The off-white marble floors were beautiful and enhanced by the various rugs. A huge fireplace on the far wall was the focal point of the room, made obvious by the three cream couches—two regular-sized and one massive, curved one—flanking it.

Naomi found Abby reclining on one of the sofas, looking as if she were going to give birth any second. Abby's long, brunette hair was pulled up into a messy bun with wisps falling around her face. Her smile reminded Naomi of Brice.

"Hi," Abby said. "I'd stand, but it takes me forever to get to my feet."

Jace glanced at Abby's feet, frowning. "Your ankles will return, right?" he asked around a mouthful of pudding.

Abby swung her head to him and narrowed her gaze. "I may not be able to move quickly right now, but Clayton can. And he'd be happy to take that pudding away from you."

Jace turned so the pudding was out of reach. He glanced at Clayton before looking back at Abby. "I think swollen ankles are beautiful."

Abby nodded, a brow raised. "That's what I thought," she said before she ruined it with a smile.

All the nervousness Naomi had initially felt quickly fell away. It was obvious that the Easts were much admired and loved.

Abby motioned to the furniture as she turned her attention to Naomi. "Please, sit and make yourself at home."

"I have food," Naomi said.

Abby then laughed and exchanged a look with Clayton. "The first time I was inside this house, Justine brought me in here and served me coffee. I was terrified I'd spill. She informed me that it was just furniture and that it could be cleaned. I've held to her thoughts on the matter. And trust me when I say this furniture gets cleaned regularly with my brothers, their friends, and my kids always spilling something."

"Told ya," Jace said to Naomi and shoveled a heaping spoonful of pudding into his mouth.

Naomi sat and listened as Clayton and Abby made small talk with Jace for a few minutes, allowing her time to settle and calm down. It was Jace who turned the conversation to why she was there.

"It wasn't until today that Brice told Cooper and me about what occurred last night with Whitney and Naomi," Jace said.

Clayton removed his hat and set it on the table. "He told me when he came home yesterday. We're more concerned about today."

Naomi cleared her throat. "I think this is my fault. I took the film and developed it at the college this morning."

"Developed it?" Abby asked. "You're a photographer?"

"I am. I take photos and sell them to individuals and companies. I use digital for that, but I've always kept a darkroom to develop my own film."

Jace smacked his lips. "Impressive."

Naomi glanced at the unfinished cookie in her hand. "I wanted to see if I had caught the attacker. I did. But no matter what filters or lighting I used, I couldn't see his face. But I thought maybe Brice or Whitney might recognize something about the guy. Brice didn't, unfortunately. Then he asked if he could keep the photos to show Jace and Cooper."

"Which he did," Jace interjected. "We didn't recognize anything either."

Clayton blew out a breath. "It was a good try, though."

"Brice urged me to remain with someone at all times, and I did," Naomi continued. "I was with a group of women. I tried to see if Whitney would tell me anything about the attacker, but she told me to leave it alone. So I went to the arena to watch the rodeo."

Jace set aside the half-eaten bowl and licked his lips. "During that time, Brice was looking for Caleb. I don't know exactly when it happened, but Cooper and I found Brice lying on the ground between the cattle pens. I saw the blood, and we tried to wake him. About the time he regained consciousness, Caleb ran up. The first thing Brice said when he came to was Naomi's name. I'd seen her in the stands and told Caleb, who rushed to find her."

Abby reached over and took Clayton's hand. "How bad is the wound on his head?"

"He got his bell rung pretty good," Jace admitted, his lips twisted. "I was more concerned about his hand that had been stomped on, but he wasn't worried about either one."

"Sounds like him," Abby said and looked at Clayton. She blinked several times and nodded. "Then what happened?"

Jace turned to Naomi. She'd been reliving what happened, but she wasn't keen to actually put it into words.

"You don't have to tell us," Clayton said.

Jace's face fell into contrite lines. "Yeah, sorry, Naomi. I can tell them."

"It's okay," she said and forced a smile. "I stood up to cheer on the wagons as the race began. The next thing I knew, I felt someone shove hard into my back. I fell toward this little old woman next to the railing, so I twisted to miss her and toppled over the fence."

"I believe the point was for her to go over regardless," Jace said.

Clayton drew in a deep breath. "I'm inclined to agree."

Naomi glanced out the window. "I hit the ground hard and landed on my bag, making it difficult to move. I knew the wagons were on their way back around when I felt the ground shake. I looked up and saw the horses bearing down on me. Somehow, I managed to roll out of the way. And then Caleb was there, putting himself between me and the horses."

"Dear God," Abby said and put her hand to her throat. "It's a miracle neither of you was killed."

"The asshole stole the photos from Brice," Jace said.

Naomi finally had a reason to smile. "I don't know why, but something told me to hide the film this morning. I can make more of the photos."

"There has to be something in them that this guy fears," Clayton said.

Abby dropped her hand to her lap and shrugged. "Like someone recognizing him."

"He broke into my Jeep to look for the film," Naomi added. "But I don't leave any in my vehicle. It's always on me."

Abby blew out a breath. "I could really use a drink right now."

"I'll have yours, darlin', because at this point, I need one, too," Clayton said.

Jace leaned his elbows on his thighs. "Whitney will be here tonight to tell us everything."

"Including the guy's name?" Abby asked.

Naomi shrugged. "That's what I'm hoping. She's very . . . reluctant."

Abby then pointed to the computer. "I think y'all need to read the article I found."

"About?" Jace prodded.

Abby's lips twisted. "It's a story that was buried about someone who stalked and sexually assaulted a contestant from a local rodeo pageant."

Jace dropped his head and took off his hat. "The girl's name is Jamie Adcock, isn't it?"

"How do you know that?" Naomi asked.

Jace lifted his head and looked at each of them. "Because her mother told everyone exactly what the article says, but no one believed them."

Chapter 11

Impatience chafed him. Like rubbing against a raw, exposed nerve. Brice looked over at the speedometer as Caleb drove down the road.

"I'm about to kick you out. While we're moving," his brother grumbled over the music playing.

"We need to hurry."

Caleb glanced at him. "I'm going as fast as I can pulling the horses. And at night, if I need to remind you."

"I know." Damn. He did know. What the hell was wrong with him?

But he knew the answer to that, as well—Naomi Pierce.

He scrubbed his good hand down his face and blew out a harsh breath.

"Naomi is safe at the ranch," Caleb said.

Brice looked out the window and nodded. "I know."

"Clayton, Jace, Shane, and the others won't let anything happen."

Brice removed his hat and scratched his head. "I should

never have sent Naomi to the ranch. Abby is there with the kids."

Caleb chuckled and shook his head as he slowed and put on his blinker. "Anyone stupid enough to try and come onto the ranch to do anyone harm deserves the double-barreled shotgun that will be aimed at them."

"Yeah."

Brice wished he could think clearly. His head had yet to stop pounding, but it was more than the hit. He was worried. Really worried. Someone had attempted to kill Naomi.

"You're thinking of that video, aren't you?" Caleb said.

A spectator had managed to capture Naomi going over the railing and falling into the arena and they'd posted it on social media. Brice saw firsthand just how close she'd come to dying.

"Seeing it was harder than you telling me," Brice admitted.

Caleb drew in a breath. "I didn't see all of it. By the time I got to the stands, Naomi had already fallen. But I'll admit, watching the video made me more than a little sick to my stomach. A member of the rodeo did that. It could be someone we know."

"I've thought of that. I'm looking at everyone differently now."

"Me, too."

Brice reached around and felt the spot on his head. Karl wanted him to go to the ER for stitches, but the bleeding had finally stopped. That didn't mean the area around the wound wasn't painful.

"How's the hand?"

Brice looked at his bandaged appendage. "I'll be fine."

"The jerkwad stomping on your hand acted infantile."

"As if he couldn't control his temper and hitting me over the head wasn't enough."

Caleb turned down the music. "I think, in his mind, you interfered. Had you not been there, he would've either taken Naomi's camera or destroyed it and the film. Your arrival halted that. And brought all of this."

"So why not try and kill me? Why only Naomi?" Brice asked as he looked at his brother.

"Hurting Naomi could be a warning to Whitney to keep her mouth shut."

Brice pinched the bridge of his nose with his thumb and forefinger. "And we interfered again."

Caleb's head jerked to him, concern evident even in the dim light of the cab. "Call Cooper now. If this guy will go after you and Naomi in the middle of a rodeo—"

"Then he won't hesitate to attack Whitney," Brice finished as he fished out his phone, fumbling with it because of his bandaged hand.

He let out a loud curse when his injured fingers wouldn't work properly and caused the phone to fall on his bad hand. Finally, he dialed Cooper's number. The longer it rang without an answer, the more anxious Brice became. When it went to voicemail, he tried again with the same results.

Brice then called Jace. No sooner had his friend answered than Brice said, "Have you heard from Copper?"

"Not since he texted to say he and Whitney were leaving the rodeo. And they aren't alone."

Brice frowned. "What do you mean?"

"Ms. Biermann is with them."

"Shit. I just tried to call Cooper, twice, with no answer."

Jace said, "They left about ten minutes after y'all did."

"Thanks," Brice said and ended the call. He looked at Caleb and said, "Whitney's chaperone is with her."

Caleb made a face. "I don't know if I'm relieved or irritated."

"Do you actually think Whitney will talk candidly with that woman around?"

His brother suddenly smiled. "You forget where we'll be. There are plenty of others around who can keep that woman occupied while we talk to Whitney."

"I want to get to the bottom of this. Otherwise, we'll be looking over our shoulders constantly."

"I agree," Caleb pointed out.

Brice felt some measure of relief when he spotted the East Ranch entrance that had spotlights lighting it for all to see. He knew Naomi was all right, but he hadn't gotten a chance to speak to her himself.

Or touch her.

He squeezed his eyes closed and fought against the sudden tide of fear he felt for Naomi. When Caleb finally turned the truck and trailer onto the drive, Brice knew every dip and bump. He kept his eyes closed until Caleb turned in front of the barn.

Brice put on his hat and turned his head to the house to see Jace and Clayton headed their way. But his gaze moved to the windows as he exited the truck. The tightness in his chest loosened when he saw Naomi with Wynter sitting beside her as she talked to Abby.

"She's safe," Clayton said as he stopped before him.

Brice pushed the vehicle door closed and nodded first to Jace then Clayton. "Thank you both."

"We've been friends too long for you to need to thank

me for helping you," Jace said with a smile. He slapped Brice on the shoulder and went to lend Caleb assistance unloading the horses.

Clayton raised a brow. "I hear someone tried to knock some sense into you."

Brice couldn't help but smile. "Very funny."

His brother-in-law's smile died. "How are you really?"

"Annoyed, angry. And uneasy."

"What of the pain?"

Brice shrugged one shoulder. "Nothing some aspirin and bourbon won't help."

"Abby already had Brody get the medicine for you. There's plenty of food waiting."

"You mean Jace didn't eat it all?" Caleb called from the barn as he put away the horses.

Jace let out a loud snort. "Not for lack of trying."

Clayton grinned and slid his gaze back to Brice. "Abby was delighted to have so many to cook for, and Naomi helped her. I think it gave everyone something to focus on other than the events of today."

"Yeah," Brice said and blew out a breath.

"Do I even need to ask how your event went?"

Jace closed the trailer doors and walked to them with Caleb beside him. It was Caleb who let out a soft laugh as he came to stand beside his brother.

Brice rolled his eyes. "It would have gone better had Caleb kept his eyes on the steer."

"I wanted to see if anyone was surprised by your appearance," his brother replied.

Jace asked, "Well? What did you see?"

Caleb's lips twisted ruefully. "Everyone was shocked that his hand was hurt and surprised that he could rope with his other arm."

"We came in second, so we move on to the next round," Brice said.

"And the hand?" Jace asked.

Brice lifted it to show the large bandage. "We'll see. Karl suggested I not use it for at least twenty-four hours. He wanted longer, but he said if I could give it at least twenty-four hours, then that would help."

"Umm, guys. We'd better get inside," Caleb said.

They all turned their heads to the house to find Abby glaring at them through the window.

Without a word, the four headed into the house. Brice was surprised to find Naomi in the kitchen. She walked to him and gave him a once over, her brow puckered in a frown.

"You're still hurting, aren't you?" she asked. "I can see it in your eyes."

"A little," he answered, not thinking clearly when she removed his hat and lightly ran her fingers through his hair, keeping far away from his injury. A shiver went through him at her casual—yet sensual—contact. And he liked it. A lot.

Too damn much, actually.

When she stopped, he wanted to reach for her and bring her hand back to his scalp.

Caleb took the hat from her and hung it up next to the back door. Naomi then smiled up at Brice. "Your sister has requested that you and Caleb take showers."

Clayton laughed as he walked into the family room. Jace headed to the fridge and got out what remained of the banana pudding while Caleb took the stairs three at a time, leaving Brice alone with her.

"How are you?" he asked softly.

She wrinkled her nose as she shrugged. "A little sore. You?"

"I've had worse cuts on my head before, I'll be fine," he said.

"You better." She then turned and grabbed a bottle of aspirin. "Take these before you shower. It'll make a world of difference."

It had been hours since he'd gotten anything from Karl, so Brice eagerly opened the bottle and dumped two pills into his hand before he walked to the sink and turned on the water. He popped the pills into his mouth and cupped the water in his hand to swallow them.

He wiped his lips on the towel and looked at Naomi. Something sharp and exciting went through him at seeing her there. He didn't want to leave her, and it had nothing to do with what happened today and everything to do with the feelings running rampant through him.

"I won't be long."

"I'm not going anywhere," she told him.

Their gazes met. There was something in her words that sounded . . . right. He was more than happy to have her with him. Not only did those he trusted surround her but it also allowed him more time with her.

Brice watched her join the others. The conversation from the family room was loud, but it didn't bother his head. Just being back at the ranch relieved much of his pain.

He headed to the stairs and made his way up to his room. Beneath the spray of the shower, he winced as the hot water hit his wound. He scrubbed the dirt, sweat, and blood of the day away before he dried off and put on clean clothes.

By the time he made it downstairs with the wrap in his hand to be reapplied, Caleb was already scooping food onto his plate. The number of dishes and variety to choose from reminded Brice of his first meal at the ranch when he met Ben and Justine.

It was weird that the memory would return out of the blue. Then again, the last time anything violent had happened to the Harpers and Easts, it had been when he was involved with stealing cattle and the men had shot at Abby.

Brice put his hands on the island counter and closed his eyes. He would never forget the sight of blood on Abby's arm or the ambulance loading her up and rushing her to the ER. Seeing her lying so still and unconscious on the hospital bed had been the worst.

It hadn't helped when he opened the ambulance doors today and saw Naomi on the gurney. If she hadn't rolled out of the way, if he hadn't sent Caleb after her, Naomi might not be with them right now.

He'd almost lost his sister because of his stupidity. He wasn't going to have Naomi, his family, or his friends hurt simply because he hadn't come to her rescue.

Someone laid a hand on his shoulder. Brice opened his eyes and turned his head to find Caleb.

"This isn't the past," Abby said as she walked up on his other side.

"It's all over your face," Caleb said when Brice frowned. "It doesn't take a genius to figure out your head is in the past and that nasty business that just happened to bring us all together."

Brice swallowed and straightened. "She could have died."

"You could have, too," Abby pointed out.

A muscle jumped in Caleb's jaw. "I'm ready to get to the bottom of all of this. No matter what it takes."

"No matter what it takes," Clayton said as he joined them.

Brice smiled at his family. Anxiety faded as anger took root. Someone would pay for what happened today, and he wasn't going to rest until he found out who was responsible.

Chapter 12

Naomi checked her watch again. Whitney and Cooper—along with Ms. Biermann—should have been there by now. For a short while, Naomi had become engrossed in the East household. It had been relatively easy to do.

Not only were Clayton and Abby pleasant and welcoming but they also made her feel right at home. As if they weren't living in a mansion.

And their two children were sweet, respectful, and so damn cute. Wynter had taken an immediate liking to her, and Naomi had to admit, the feeling was mutual.

It was Wynter who had dragged her to one of the barns to show Naomi her horse. Clayton had tagged along, showing Naomi around. Everyone within six counties knew of the East Ranch, but no amount of rumors lived up to what Naomi saw firsthand. And to think, Brice had grown up here.

After mooning over the horses—and developing a real desire to ride again—the three of them returned, and

Clayton fussed when he found Abby in the kitchen preparing dinner.

That's when Naomi learned that the pregnancy hadn't just been a surprise, it had also been fraught with complications. Clayton's worry was real. As was Abby's discomfort. So, Naomi had eagerly joined her in food prep. Eventually, Clayton and Jace got Abby to sit down and let Naomi finish.

Even the meal was lovely. Wynter and Brody talked about their day at school, and everyone went to great lengths not to reveal Naomi's reason for being at the ranch to the kids.

Despite the great company and food, Naomi had wished Brice were there. Not only because she was worried about another attack befalling him, but also because this was his family.

She inwardly groaned at herself.

Not even in her own thoughts could she admit that she wanted Brice at the ranch to be with him. She barely knew him, but she liked him. A lot.

A whole lot.

It helped that he had come to her rescue and wanted to protect her. Perhaps Naomi had spent too long in the city with men who would, without thought, run a woman over to catch a cab. Maybe that's why Brice shielding her and worrying about her made her feel . . . treasured. And very much a woman.

She'd thought she wanted the hustle of the city. The times she'd returned to Texas to visit her mom had not made her second guess her decision to move.

But all that had changed sometime over the last couple of days. It could have been the rodeo. Perhaps it was meeting Brice. Maybe it was being at the East Ranch. Whatever it was, Naomi missed the simple life she'd had growing up.

That life hadn't been easy. She'd been up at dawn mucking stalls and letting the horses out to the pasture. Then there was the training, not to mention taking care of the horses for those who rented out stalls at the Pierce barn.

She'd had very little time to sit in front of the TV or chat on the phone with anyone. But her memories were vivid and filled with love and laughter.

The country life was calling to her once more, and she wasn't sure she wanted to ignore it. Returning to Texas would certainly lower her rent. She could bring a new addition to her business as far as the pictures went.

Her thoughts came to a halt when Brice rounded the corner as he entered the family room, his gaze skating to her. His deep brown locks were damp, his denim shirt untucked and the sleeves rolled to his elbows.

"Damn," Clayton said as he looked at Brice's injured hand.

Naomi grimaced when she saw how swollen it was. The bruising was now a mix of green this side of sickly, putrid yellow, and purple quickly turning black.

"I got it," Caleb said as he took the elastic bandage from Brice and began wrapping his brother's hand.

Abby flattened her lips as she made her way around the sofa and sat. "I've seen both of you get all kinds of scrapes in your lives, but this one takes the cake."

Caleb smiled as he looked up at Brice. "And I wasn't even responsible for it this time."

"There's a first time for everything," Brice teased.

It was good to see Brice smiling again. Naomi felt a rush of warmth when his light blue eyes landed on her.

His lips curved into a sexy grin, and for just a moment, she forgot that they weren't alone.

Naomi hastily looked away and tried not to read too much into the look. But she could feel his eyes linger on her. Unable to help herself, she looked at him again. The smile was gone, replaced by an intense look that made her shift on the couch.

Once more, she tugged her gaze away. And within seconds, he pulled her back. Naomi became all too aware of how quiet everyone got.

"Someone's coming," Brody shouted and jumped off the sofa.

Jace rose and headed to the back door. "It's Cooper."

As soon as Caleb finished with the bandage, Brice walked around him and straight to Naomi. Her heart kicked up a notch when he lowered himself next to her. Everyone talked amongst themselves, waiting for Cooper, Whitney, and Ms. Biermann to arrive.

"I'm sorry about your hand," Naomi said, doing everything in her power not to touch him.

One side of his mouth lifted in a grin. "You didn't do it."

"I'm still sorry. I take it your event went well?"

He gave a single nod, his gaze briefly going toward the kitchen. "We're in the next round. It's going take a lot more before I'm unable to compete."

"Don't say that too loud," Naomi warned. An image of him with blood running down his face as he entered the ambulance flashed in her head. "I'm afraid whoever this guy is, he will make sure he prevents you."

"That's where they messed up," Abby said. "They have totally screwed with the wrong family. We Harpers are a tough lot."

Clayton leaned in from the kitchen. "Easts, sweetheart. You're an East now."

Abby tilted her head back to smile at him before looking at Naomi. "East, Harper. We're one and the same. The fact is, we will stand against anyone."

"The East money and position in society helps," Jace said with a wink as he walked into the room.

Abby picked up a pillow and threw it at him.

Jace dodged it and held up his hands. "Whoa. I'm just stating a fact. I love your cooking too much to ever do anything to jeopardize being able to eat here."

Abby laughed and threw another pillow him.

Naomi was smiling again, and she realized everyone was doing what they could to relieve the tension that had begun to build with Whitney's arrival. Her friend had the answers, and they were all clamoring for them.

It wasn't long before Naomi heard Whitney and Ms. Biermann exclaiming over the inside of the house. Clayton then walked into the family room and held out his arms. The kids rushed to him. He tossed Wynter over his shoulder as Brody climbed up his other side. Clayton brought the kids to Abby, who gave them each a kiss and whispered something to them.

"Tell everyone goodnight," Clayton urged the kids.

There was a chorus of sendoffs for the children before Clayton headed upstairs. Caleb and Cooper showed Whitney and Ms. Biermann around before offering them food.

"We're going to get the chaperone away so Whitney can talk freely," Brice leaned in close to whisper.

Naomi nodded, her gaze on Whitney. Her hat and crown were gone, as were her chaps. Whitney was in jeans, boots, and a red tee tucked into jeans to show off her belt buckle. A leather jacket completed the look. "I wondered about that."

She caught Brice staring at Whitney, which caused Naomi to grin. "Whitney has always been like that. Vivacious and outgoing. With an innate fashion sense I could never grasp."

His dark head turned to her, blue eyes meeting hers. "I like what you're wearing."

Naomi chuckled as she looked down at her jeans, booties, black Def Leppard t-shirt, and olive green jacket. "You can't really go wrong with jeans and a tee."

"You'd be surprised."

They shared a smile.

Brice leaned back on the sofa. "What were you like in school?"

"I can answer that," Whitney said as she walked into the room.

The conversation paused as Whitney was introduced to Abby. Afterward, Whitney gave Naomi a once over.

"I'm good," Naomi assured her.

Whitney sat beside Abby and gave Naomi her sternest look. "You better be. Otherwise, I'm going to kick your ass after I take you to a doctor."

"You never change," Naomi said with a shake of her head, smiling despite herself.

Whitney swung her blue eyes to Brice. "Naomi was the smart one, the quiet one. She pestered the head of the school newspaper by submitting dozens of photos every day until he finally relented and allowed her to join. There were officially no more spots, but they made one for her. As a freshman."

Naomi crossed one leg over the other, embarrassed to

her core. "You make it sound like I was some prodigy or something."

"You were," Whitney said with a laugh as Caleb, Cooper, Clayton, and Ms. Biermann walked into the room. "At least one of your photos was printed in every edition, and not even the seniors could claim that."

Naomi popped her knuckles in nervousness as everyone's gaze turned to her.

"That quiet Naomi disappeared once she was on her horse, however," Whitney said with a smile.

Naomi held her friend's gaze as dozens of memories returned.

"Is that so?" Caleb asked. "Did she become rowdy?"

Whitney shook her head of blond waves. "Determined. Focused."

"Just as you were," Naomi said. "That's how we met. At a rodeo when we were just, what, seven?"

"Eight," Whitney corrected her. "I'm still not sure why you became friends with me and Suellen."

Jace frowned and looked between Naomi and Whitney. "Who is Suellen?"

"The best horsewoman between us," Naomi said.

Whitney looked down at her hands in her lap. "The most beautiful person."

"What happened?" Clayton asked as he returned to the room.

Naomi swallowed and waited for Whitney to answer, but when it became apparent that her friend wouldn't, Naomi licked her lips to stop the tightness in her throat. "She died our senior year. We were going to celebrate her winning her first crown in the rodeo pageant when we were involved in a head-on collision. She was killed on impact."

"That's horrible," Abby said and reached over to pat Whitney's hands. "I can't imagine going through anything like that. I'm so sorry."

Naomi forced a smile. "The drunk guy who hit us is in prison. It's justice, but it won't bring Suellen back." Naomi knew if she didn't turn the conversation, she'd start crying. "Suellen was always pulling pranks on us."

"Oh, God, yes," Whitney said with a chuckle as she looked up. "And defiant against anyone who dared to wrong either of us."

Naomi laughed, nodding. "How many of your boyfriends did she threaten to shame for hurting you?"

"Three," Whitney said.

Everyone laughed, which was exactly what was needed. Abby gazed at her brothers, Cooper, and Jace. "Sounds like the four of you."

"Yeah, but I didn't punch any girls," Jace said.

Cooper shoved him while giving him a flat look. "You aren't the best horseman."

"Sure I am."

"Not even close," Cooper said.

Jace threw up his arms. "Then who is?"

Brice then replied, "Caleb."

Naomi looked between the two brothers to see some silent exchange pass between them.

"I think I'm offended," Clayton murmured.

Caleb grinned. "I thought it was just between us four, but I'm all about including you in that."

Cooper was shaking his head before Caleb finished. "No. No way, man. Clayton beats all of us."

"Yes, he certainly does," Abby stated proudly.

Clayton walked to the back of the sofa and bent over as Abby leaned her head back so they could kiss.

Naomi moved her gaze to Whitney to find her friend turning a ring round and round on her finger, her eyes on the floor, seemingly deep in thought.

This interlude had been fun, but Naomi was ready to sort out the truth of her attack.

And issue some payback of her own—Suellen style.

Chapter 13

There was something heartening about walking into the house and having Naomi there. Brice wasn't sure if it was because he'd shied away from any relationships over the past year, but suddenly, all he thought about was Naomi.

While he would have liked to remain on the sofa beside her and hear more stories about the past, they had gathered for something else entirely.

Brice swung his gaze to Abby and gave her a small nod. She frowned, unable to discern what he meant until Brice cut his eyes to Ms. Biermann. Abby's mouth formed an *O* before she winked at him.

"Ms. Biermann, my daughter has shown interest in the rodeo pageant," Abby said.

Clayton's brows snapped together in confusion. Before he could say anything, Caleb elbowed him. Clayton looked between Abby and Brice and Caleb before he realized what was going on.

"Is Wynter a good rider?" the woman asked.

Clayton let out a loud snort. "She lives here. What do you think?"

"Good," Ms. Biermann said. "That's what I wanted to hear."

When the woman started to walk around the sofa to sit, Abby held out her hand as Brice stood and helped her to her feet. His sister smiled at the chaperone. "I want to write down everything you tell me. Let's go into the office."

"But . . ." Ms. Biermann said, hesitating as she glanced at Whitney.

Clayton grinned. "No one will leave this room. You have my word."

"Okay," the woman finally relented and followed Abby out of the room.

Once they were out of earshot, Clayton looked pointedly at Brice. "You owe Abby for this. She's going to want a play-by-play of this conversation from the moment she walked away until everyone leaves."

"Maybe we should record it," Caleb teased.

Whitney's head snapped in his direction as she sat upright. "No."

"It was a joke," Naomi told her.

"Sorry," Whitney said and slowly rested back against the cushion. "It's just . . . y'all don't understand."

Clayton took Abby's place while Jace and Cooper occupied the hearth, and Caleb sat on Brice's other side. All eyes were on Whitney.

"I don't know how long we have before Ms. Biermann returns," Cooper reminded her.

Whitney nodded, swallowing loudly as she looked at the coffee table. "I don't know where to begin."

"The beginning," Naomi suggested.

Whitney's eyes lifted and landed on Naomi. "The beginning? I don't even know when that was. It just all sort of . . . happened."

"What did?" Jace asked softly.

Whitney's smile was forced as she looked around the room. It faded quickly as she shrugged. "I don't think anyone knows how hard the pageants are. I mean, we don't have to just look perfect all the time, we also have to act a certain way and ride without messing up. All the contestants want is to win. But winning comes at a steep price."

Naomi rose and went to sit beside Whitney. She took her friend's hand in her own. "You never said anything. Why didn't you tell me?"

"I got exactly what I wanted," Whitney said and turned her head to Naomi. "Why would I complain about it?"

"Because things aren't always as they seem. And you had a friend to turn to," Clayton said.

Whitney rubbed her lips together. "At the beginning, I thought it was just me being paranoid. That first win was everything I thought it would be and more. The attention, the attentiveness of everyone was unbelievable. But then things began happening."

"Like what?" Brice asked.

"Any event I was required to attend, someone always messed with my things."

Naomi's face creased in confusion. "What do you mean *messed with*?"

"My horse's bridle was either too tight or too loose where someone had moved the buckle. One of my stirrups was also either too long or too short. I thought it was some type of hazing thing from the other girls. After the third incident, I confronted them. Not a single contestant was surprised by my claims. Then, one of the girls looked at me and said it was my turn now."

Caleb scrunched up his face. "What the hell did that mean?"

"I asked," Whitney said. "No one would tell me. They all vehemently denied touching my stuff. Oddly, after that, everything went back to normal. Or so I thought." She glanced at Naomi. "I started feeling like I was being watched. I never saw anyone or had proof, but the hairs on the back of my neck would stand on end."

Naomi shifted to face Whitney. "Are you telling me this has been happening from the very beginning?"

Whitney nodded.

"For four years?" Naomi asked, her voice rising.

Whitney briefly closed her eyes. "I thought it was nothing. It stayed like that for months."

"Then what happened?" Cooper asked.

There was a long stretch of silence as Whitney stared at her hands. "Right after I won the next pageant, there was a big commotion within the ranks about a girl who'd claimed she was sexually assaulted. But as soon as it blew up, suddenly, everything about it turned to silence."

"Jamie Adcock," Jace said.

Whitney looked at him and nodded. "I didn't know her well. In fact, I'd only talked to her once or twice. She seemed nice enough. At first, the other girls were sympathetic about Jaime's assertions. Seemingly overnight, those same girls acted as if they didn't know her. She came to us right before she and her mother moved away. Jamie was crying, demanding that we stand up and admit what was going on."

"Obviously, no one did," Clayton said.

Whitney shoved a lock of blond hair over her shoulder

and shook her head. "Jamie was dragged out of the arena by the chaperones. That was the last I saw or heard from her."

"Did you believe her?" Brice asked.

After another pause, Whitney shook her head. "Jaime had been first runner-up, and she and her mother were known to cause problems when she didn't win. When they left town, I assumed it had all been a lie."

Brice met his brother's gaze. Things were moving much too slowly. At this rate, they wouldn't learn much of anything before Abby and Ms. Biermann returned.

Caleb took off his hat and tossed it onto the coffee table. "Then what?"

"I won a third pageant," Whitney replied. "Someone started touching my things again. More disturbing was the yellow rose that was always there. Everywhere I went for my title, I'd find that rose. I didn't think anything of it at first, but it didn't take long for me to get creeped out. I said something to Ms. Biermann, who said I must have an admirer, and that all rodeo queens did."

Naomi rolled her eyes and made a sound at the back of her throat. "Please tell me you didn't believe her."

"Of course not," Whitney said, making a face. "Those roses, along with the feeling of being watched, only made me hyper aware of everything. But nothing happened. Not until I found a letter attached to a rose in my car."

Naomi jumped up and stared in shock at her friend. "You told your parents, at least, right? Or Ms. Biermann?"

"What did the letter say?" Jace pressed.

Whitney linked her fingers together. "It simply said that I was beautiful and that he enjoyed watching me. That he would continue to watch me. And, yes, Naomi, I told Ms. Biermann."

"And?" Brice asked.

Whitney shrugged when she met his gaze. "She said she'd take care of it."

Naomi resumed her seat. "Did things stop?"

"For a couple of days. The next note said he could make sure I won the next pageant. I gave it to Ms. Biermann and thought nothing of it. Until I lost."

Brice rested his ankle on his knee. "Lost?"

"First runner-up," Whitney said. "I went home defeated, until a week later when Ms. Biermann showed up at my house and said the winner had given up the crown. It was mine. I asked why the winner had left, but I never got an explanation. And I never saw the girl again."

Cooper blew out a breath and rubbed his hands on his thighs. "There is so much that doesn't add up, but there is no proof."

Brice kept his gaze on Whitney. He could tell that there was still much she hadn't revealed, and he wasn't sure she was comfortable telling a roomful of men.

He got Clayton's attention. "Do you think you could get Ms. Biermann to stay here tonight?"

"I think so," Clayton replied. Then he looked at Whitney. "Is that all right with you?"

She gave her first genuine smile since the story had begun. "I would like that very much."

"Then I'll see it done," Clayton said.

The conversation stopped when Abby's voice reached them. Brice motioned for Naomi and Whitney to get up and follow them. He took the girls around to the other side of the kitchen. When Abby and Ms. Biermann got to the family area, he took the girls upstairs and showed Whitney to a bedroom.

"Ms. Biermann will want to be next to me," Whitney said.

Brice grinned. "I expected as much. I'll be sure to put her farthest away from the stairs."

Whitney shot them a smile before closing the door.

He then moved across the hall and opened another bedroom door. Naomi walked inside and turned in a circle, taking it in. "There are others if you'd prefer. I thought you might want to be close to Whitney."

"This is beautiful." She ran her fingers over the dark wood of the four-poster bed.

Brice left the door open as he made his way into the room and came to stand before her. He lowered his voice to a whisper and said, "I got the feeling Whitney may find it easier finishing the story with just the two of you."

"Very perceptive," Naomi replied with a grin. "Thank you."

"You two can sneak out to the barn later. I'll make sure the house alarm isn't set."

Naomi frowned, her head cocking to the side. "Why wouldn't we stay in the house?"

"Because I'm not convinced Ms. Biermann isn't in on whatever is happening, and I think you feel the same."

Naomi crossed her arms over her chest as her lips flattened. "You're right. I do feel that way. There's just something about that woman I don't like. I can't put my finger on it. She's nice, but. . . ."

"Odd?" Brice supplied.

"Yes. Odd works. I'm glad I'm not the only one who sees it."

Brice shifted so he could see the doorway. "The woman didn't ask how you were doing, and everyone at the rodeo knew about the accident."

Naomi's brow furrowed. "You're right. She didn't. That's just plain rude."

He wanted to stay in the room with her, but he had to get back downstairs. "If we don't get answers from Whitney, you could be attacked again."

"So could you."

"I'm more worried about you. See if you can talk to Whitney later. This may be our only chance to discover whatever it is she's hiding."

Naomi grabbed his arm when he started to turn away. "Are you sorry you helped me the other night?"

"There are a number of things I regret and wish I could change, but that isn't one of them. Not by a long shot."

Her smile was slow as she gazed up at him with her chestnut eyes.

Brice wanted to lean down and kiss her. He was sure she would accept him. Then he heard Caleb hiss his name from the hallway.

"Goodnight," he said.

She sat on the bed. "Goodnight."

Chapter 14

The minutes ticked by slowly. Naomi didn't know what Clayton said to Ms. Biermann, but everything went smoothly. She put her ear to the door as Clayton walked the chaperone up to her room, putting the older woman exactly where Brice said she would sleep for the night.

Ms. Biermann laughed and spoke amicably with Clayton before her door closed and the only sound Naomi heard was Clayton's footsteps as he walked down the hall.

She didn't know how long to give Ms. Biermann before she went knocking on Whitney's door. Obviously, she needed to give the woman time to get ready for bed.

So, Naomi walked around the room, looking at the pictures. There was an old, faded wedding picture that looked as if it were taken in the early 1800s. There were pictures of children in various eras, but all either on a horse, with a lasso in their hands, or standing next to cattle.

She studied each one, trying to determine the ages and their connection to Clayton. It was easy to determine which ones were of Clayton, yet there were some from when Clayton was younger that had another boy with him. The fact that they looked so similar meant they had to be related, but she had heard nothing of Clayton having a brother or cousin.

When Naomi came to a couple of pictures of Brice and Caleb, she smiled. The boys were young and covered in dust as they each sat atop a horse, but their wide smiles told everyone how happy they were.

Finally, she set down the pictures and walked to the window as she yawned. She very much wanted to crawl beneath the thick covers. Naomi didn't think too hard about the fact that she didn't have a change of clothes and would be right back in her clothes the next day.

She looked out the window facing the front of the house. Far in the distance, she could just make out the headlights of a passing car. She wrapped her arms around herself and thought over the things Whitney had said downstairs.

How had her friend gone through something like that— and she feared even worse things that had yet to be revealed—and not come to her? Had Whitney felt as if Naomi didn't have time for her? Was it something Naomi had said? Something she did? She really wanted to know so that she never did it again.

It made her stomach hurt to know that Whitney had gone through this alone. What would have happened had Naomi cancelled her trip?

She cut off that train of thought. It would take her to a place she wasn't comfortable with. As it was, she had a difficult time watching any kind of true crime shows because the thought of someone being that depraved and walking the street next to her made her want to never leave the house.

Her head jerked to the door when she heard a soft knock. She checked her watch to see that it had been over forty-five minutes since Ms. Biermann had come upstairs. Naomi hurried to the door and opened it to find Whitney.

"Want to take a walk outside?" Naomi asked in a whisper.

Whitney nodded, and they quietly walked down the hall to the stairs. When they reached the bottom, the lights were still on. Naomi slowly made her way into the kitchen to find Cooper, Jace, and Caleb each stuffing their faces.

Jace barely looked up from the roll he was slathering with butter. Cooper gave them a wave as he bit into two cookies at once.

Caleb set down his fork after taking a bite of his apple pie and walked to them. "Hey," he said. "Brice mentioned that y'all might want to take a walk. It's a chilly night, so grab any of the jackets hanging by the door."

"Thanks," Whitney said and moved past them.

Naomi asked, "Where's Brice?"

"Abby made him take some more aspirin and sent him to bed. He must still be hurting for him to listen to her," Caleb replied.

"I'm sorry y'all got involved."

Caleb shrugged and shot her a grin. "We aren't, so stop worrying about that."

"Giving orders now, huh?" she teased.

"You bet."

She chuckled and walked to where Whitney waited. Naomi reached for a jacket and slid into it, wondering if it were Brice's. Then she and Whitney slipped outside.

Whitney blew out a breath and put her hands into her pockets. She stepped off the porch and started toward the barn. Naomi followed, waiting for her friend to speak.

Whitney didn't even hesitate before opening the barn doors and turning on the light.

Naomi closed the doors behind them and then stopped at the first stall to rub the horse that stuck its head over the door. She'd already spent time that afternoon with the horses, but in truth, she loved the animals so much that she never really got enough of them.

"How did you leave town so easily?"

Naomi turned her head toward Whitney, surprised by the question. It was one that had been answered long ago. "I got a scholarship. You know that."

"Bullshit. You could've gone to any college," Whitney stated and leaned against the stall, her hands in her pockets.

Naomi walked to the center of the aisle and looked at her friend. "That's true. I could have. I wanted to see some of the world."

"You mean get away from here."

That's when she realized what the questions really revolved around. "This has nothing to do with Suellen's death."

"Sure it does." Whitney kicked at the dirt with the toe of her boot. "You wanted to stay in town and eat at our regular diner. I'm the one who pushed Suellen to go somewhere different."

"Suellen's death wasn't our fault. It took me a long time to realize I wasn't to blame. It's time you did the same."

Whitney shrugged and looked at the ground. "Even after all your time away, you fit right back in as if you never left. Your love of horses is just as strong. I don't know how you stay away."

"I don't either, really. I think I knew what a draw this

life was, which is why I rarely visit Mom. I was never interested in marrying a cowboy."

"And yet that's exactly who your eyes are on now," Whitney said as she looked pointedly at her.

Naomi wrinkled her nose. "I can't deny that."

"Brice is a good catch. Not because of the Easts but because he's a decent guy. I've never heard anyone in the rodeo have anything bad to say about Brice or Caleb."

"That's good to know."

Whitney pushed away from the stall and walked forward a few steps before she stopped and faced her. "If Suellen had lived, I wonder if she would have handled all of this better than I have. She never hesitated to stand up for herself."

"Neither did you."

Whitney looked away as her eyes filled with tears. She shook her head, her shoulders beginning to shake. Naomi hurried to her, but Whitney wouldn't look at her.

"Nothing you tell me will change my respect, admiration, and love for you," Naomi told her.

Whitney faced her and raised her brows. "Are you sure about that?"

"Positive," Naomi said, unease settling in her stomach.

"It's my fault. I let it happen. I didn't tell anyone. I didn't stop him. I di-didn't do anything!"

Naomi wrapped her arms around her friend as Whitney started sobbing. Naomi fought back her own tears at learning that her friend had been assaulted. She rubbed her hands up and down Whitney's back, letting her friend cry it out.

"It's okay," Naomi said, over and over.

And she prayed it would be. She didn't know what to do—or say. Her heart was broken for Whitney.

It was sometime later before Whitney leaned back and wiped at the tears. She sniffed and looked anywhere but at Naomi.

"I don't know what's going through your head, but this isn't your fault," Naomi said.

Whitney gave a bark of laughter. "Isn't it? He told me it was."

"Who? Give me his name. I have some choice words I'd like to say to him." The rage within Naomi was like a tsunami. It kept building and building until she was shaking with it.

The longer Whitney remained silent, the more concerned Naomi became. She shifted until she stood before her friend and made Whitney look at her. "What have you left out?"

"Giving you a name will do no good."

The dejection in Whitney's voice about sent Naomi over the proverbial edge. "Why? Is he that powerful? Have you taken a look at who is helping us? I don't know anyone more powerful than the Easts."

Whitney's look was doubtful. "These men are—"

"Men?" Naomi said, feeling as if she'd just been kicked in the stomach. "How many men?"

"I don't know exactly."

Naomi shoved her hair back from her face. "How many times did they . . . force you?"

Whitney shrugged.

Naomi swallowed a cry of outrage. Her beautiful, strong friend had been crushed beneath the boots of men who thought they had the right to touch her as they wanted.

"Whatever you're thinking of doing, it will do no good," Whitney said. "Jamie Adcock tried to out them. They ran her out of town and buried the story."

Naomi wasn't going to accept that. "No. You have chaperones to guard against things like this. Are all the contestants being subjected to such assaults?"

"They hand-pick a few of us at a time."

Naomi didn't understand why Whitney wasn't ready to fight. It was as if she'd accepted what had happened—what was *still* happening—as a part of life. "So there is only a handful who know what's going on."

Whitney nodded and walked to one of the horses. She pressed her forehead against the animal's and closed her eyes. "If I say anything to anyone, they will fabricate lies and strip me of my title."

"It's just a crown." Naomi knew it was the wrong thing to say as soon as it left her mouth.

Whitney lifted her head and glared at her. "Just a crown, huh? Funny, you didn't say that to Suellen. Why is it that for me? Do you know what it would mean for me if I win the state title? It's not just the money but the exposure to corporations and the chance to compete in the USA pageant. And if I win that, my God, Naomi, the possibilities are endless."

"Then do it. But first, stand against this group of men."

Whitney snorted and shook her head. "You just don't get it, do you?"

She brushed past Naomi and shoved open the doors as she strode to the house. Naomi watched her go, unsure of how things had gotten so turned around.

As tired as she was, she knew she couldn't sleep knowing that her friend had been raped. She walked to the bench and sat down, angry and dejected and confused. Naomi leaned forward and dropped her head into her hands.

She wasn't put off by the fact that it wasn't just one man

she was after. In some ways, it would be easier to find this group because someone, somewhere had to have seen or heard something. It was just a matter of finding them.

And if Whitney wouldn't—or couldn't—fight for herself, then Naomi would do it for her. She'd failed Whitney by not realizing something so bad had happened to her friend. By doing this, she might make up for it.

She lifted her head when she heard the barn doors close again, thinking Whitney had come back. Her heart did a little leap when she saw that it was Brice.

"It went that good, huh?" he asked.

She slumped against the stall. "I messed everything up."

"I doubt that," he said as he walked to her.

"I said all the wrong things. I don't know who was standing out here with me, but it wasn't Whitney."

Brice stood across from Naomi and braced his foot behind him on the stall. He rubbed the underside of a horse's chin when the animal put its head on Brice's shoulder. "People change."

Naomi glanced toward the barn doors. "She was raped, Brice. Repeatedly."

Chapter 15

It was as bad as Brice had feared. He walked to Naomi and squatted down in front of her. He put his hand over hers and found himself staring into beautiful brown eyes with lashes spiked from her tears.

"Did she give you a name?" he asked.

"That's just it. It's not just one man."

Brice hadn't expected that. He kept his face from showing his shock. "Do we have anyone to confront?"

Naomi shook her head of wheat blond hair. "Nothing. She's scared of them."

"As she has every right to be."

"No one, man or woman, should have that kind of control over someone."

Brice moved to sit beside her. "I agree, but it happens all the time."

"I never thought Whitney wouldn't stand up for herself. I mean, I know these kinds of things happen slowly and all that, but how did it even begin?"

"With men in positions of power," Brice said.

Naomi inhaled a quick breath of air. "In this day and age, I can't believe that still happens."

"But it gives us somewhere to start looking."

Her head swung to him, hope in her eyes. "Really?"

Brice gave a single nod. "There are several people in charge of the rodeo, a Board of Directors."

"You know them?"

"I do. More importantly, Clayton does, as well."

Naomi suddenly frowned. "I feel bad enough that you and Caleb are embroiled in this. Clayton and Abby have children. Not to mention, Abby is pregnant. If they can push me into the arena in the hopes that I die, I don't want to think what they might try with your family."

Brice put his hands on his knees as he considered her words. "I'd like to believe that with the security on the ranch, Abby and the kids will be safe but I don't want to test it. Now that she and Clayton know what's going on, they're going to be hard-pressed to stay out of it."

"Well, Abby can't do much in her present condition."

"Good point. Clayton will also remain near her."

Naomi tucked her hair behind her ear. "I'm sorry she's having such a difficult pregnancy."

"There have been a few problems. She's supposed to stay off her feet, but that's difficult to do. The doctor is being cautious, as we all are," he explained.

"I should never have come here."

Brice watched as she rose and made her way to one of the horses. "You think by visiting that you've put everyone in danger."

She looked over her shoulder at him and gave him a flat look. "Exactly."

"My family became mixed up in this the moment I stepped in to help you the other night."

"Yes, but I'm at your house."

"So are Whitney and Ms. Biermann. It's going to be all right," he assured her. And he prayed he was right. At this point, he really didn't know.

She turned to the side to look at him. "I feel safe with you."

"Good." It was exactly what he wanted—and needed—to hear. He rose and walked to stand beside her. "I'm going to help you no matter what direction this turns."

Her eyes focused on the buckskin mare she was petting. "My best friend suffered something horrible and didn't tell me."

"Probably because she was ashamed."

"I have so much hate inside me for those responsible. And I mean everyone. There have to be others who know what's going on. No one said anything."

He leaned against the stall. "Someone did."

"Jaime Adcock," Naomi said, her head swiveling to him. "We need to talk to her."

Brice looked toward the doors that led out in the direction of the house. "I know just the person to task with that. My sister. It'll make Abby feel like she's involved but keep her off her feet at the same time."

His gaze moved back to Naomi. He'd been pleasantly surprised to find that she had chosen his coat. It swallowed her. She had to keep pushing the sleeves up just so her hands could pet the mare.

"I miss being around horses," she said suddenly.

"We have plenty for you to use."

She smiled as her eyes met his. "Don't tempt me."

That's exactly what he wanted to do. "When was the last time you rode?"

"It's been about six years."

"Pick a horse," he urged.

She stroked the velvety nose of the buckskin and grinned. "I like her."

He scratched the horse behind the ear. "This is London. Abby was on a kick about traveling and named several horses after famous cities."

"The name suits her."

"She's fast. And the queen mare around here."

Naomi laughed and stroked the horse's neck. "If it wasn't so late, I'd saddle you up."

"There's always tomorrow."

His heart skipped a beat when her gaze briefly met his, a small smile playing on her full lips. God, he really hoped she stayed. He liked Naomi more than expected. Her beauty might have caught his attention, but it was her strength, steadfastness, heart, and authenticity that kept pulling him back to her.

Not that he'd tried to get away. The woman was ideal for him in every way. After his disastrous relationship with Jill, he'd thought it would be several years before he would be ready to even contemplate another relationship. Then he'd spotted Naomi, and he hadn't been able to stop thinking about her.

After meeting her, she filled his thoughts constantly. Partly because of their current situation but also because of the attraction.

"It's tecȲically tomorrow," she said and met his gaze again.

He grinned and moved closer. "Shall I saddle London?"

"You want to ride in the dark?"

"Don't tell me you've never done that?"

She laughed and dropped her hands when the mare

pulled her head back to munch on some hay. "I think I did as a kid."

"To have nothing but the moonlight and the stars . . . it's amazing."

"Obviously, I've been missing out."

His balls tightened when she leaned against the stall, putting her body within inches of his. "We should remedy that."

The barn door suddenly swung open, and Caleb strolled in. "We've been waiting for y'all. Whitney came in a while ago, crying."

"Sorry," Brice said and put his hand on Naomi's back as she turned and they walked toward his brother.

"Well?" Caleb asked when they reached him.

Brice looked at Naomi, who glanced at the house. "It's not one man we need to look for."

"Oh, for fuck's sake," Caleb grumbled and put his hands on his hips. "How many?"

"I don't know," Naomi answered. "I barely got that much out of Whitney."

Caleb ran a hand over his jaw. "Is that all she told you?"

Brice shook his head. "She was sexually assaulted. Several times."

"Damn," Caleb said and lowered his gaze to the ground as his lips twisted. "I thought it might be something like that."

Naomi drew in a deep breath. "The others need to know, but I think it'd be better if no one said anything to Whitney."

"Of course," Brice said.

Caleb nodded. "She's been hurt enough. There's no need to add more to it."

"We should get some rest while we can," Brice said.

Naomi nodded and huddled in the jacket. "I really thought we'd have all the answers and could approach the asshole tomorrow. I feel like we've taken two steps back."

"Not true," Brice told her. "We have more information now. It might not be a lot, but as I told you, these are men in power."

Caleb raised a brow. "You're thinking the Board of Directors, aren't you?"

"Yeah. I also think we should talk to Jamie Adcock."

"Abby could look into that."

Brice grinned. "I'd already planned to turn her in that direction."

Caleb twisted his lips. "But the Board of Directors? We can't just approach them and demand they confess."

"Not to mention, they may not be mixed up in this," Naomi pointed out. "In which case, we've tipped our hand."

Brice looked at the house. "What about Ms. Biermann?"

"What about her?" Caleb asked.

Naomi huddled beneath his jacket. "You think she might be involved?"

"She's Whitney's chaperone. Can either of you honestly stand there and tell me that she doesn't know anything?" he asked.

Naomi's eyes widened. "She'd have to have seen or heard something."

"That's true. Things happened to Whitney outside of her home," Caleb added.

Brice looked from his brother to Naomi. "We can't really plan until Whitney and Ms. Biermann are gone."

"Wait," Caleb said, his brows drawn together. "I thought Whitney was helping us."

Naomi's lips turned down as she shook her head. "I think Whitney has been as involved as she's comfortable being. She's terrified, and frankly, I'm scared for her. If we're going to succeed in this, then we need to keep her as far from this as we can."

"I don't think that's possible," Caleb said. "You and Whitney have been seen together multiple times. Not to mention the attack. The only way to distance yourself is to return home."

Naomi gawked at him. "I'm not leaving my friend."

Brice held up his hands before him. "That's not what Caleb is saying. What he attempted to recommend— badly, I might add—is that you pretend to leave."

"Oh," she said and considered it. "That might work."

Caleb winked. "Of course, it will. Now, let's get inside before Abby comes downstairs."

Once they left the barn, Caleb closed the door and followed them. Brice and Naomi didn't speak as they made their way to the house.

At the porch, Caleb said, "I'll fill Jace and Cooper in. They're crashing here tonight, as well."

"Just make sure Jace calls his mom. She's still pissed at us from last month," Brice said.

Caleb made a face. "Good point. 'Night," he said and entered the house.

Brice held the door open for Naomi. As she took off his coat and hung it up, she asked, "What happened last month?"

"Jace and Cooper rode the fence line with us, which they often do, but Jace purposefully left his cell phone at the house so the girl he broke up with couldn't reach him," he explained.

Naomi nodded, smiling. "But that also meant his mother couldn't."

"And Jace was so focused on the ex that he forgot to tell his mom where he was. She was fit to be tied. Needless to say, she came here and spoke to Abby, who then called Caleb."

"I can't imagine the things the four of you have gotten into."

Brice walked her to the stairs. "Trust me, you really don't want to know. But Cooper and Jace are like brothers to us. We'd do anything for them. And they, anything for us."

"Like me, Whitney, and Suellen," Naomi said and looked up the stairs.

He put his hand on her lower back, his hand warming at the contact. They shared a look before slowly ascending the steps. Brice walked her to her room. He whispered goodnight and waited until her door shut before he turned away.

Chapter 16

"Do you think they know?"

Raymond inhaled on his cigar and looked at the men sitting around his poker table. Smoke hovered above them, though each had yet to remove their hats. They hadn't converged to play this night. No, they were there because Naomi Pierce had gotten in the way.

His gaze shifted to Ethan Ross, who had posed the question. Ethan sweated profusely, a sign of his nervousness. Ethan was also mayor of their fine town.

Raymond took another puff of his cigar before tossing back the last bit of bourbon in his glass. He leaned forward and grabbed the bottle and refilled his glass. "No one knows anything," he stated.

"We went too far today," Curtis Moore stated, his bloodshot, brown eyes darting around the room at everyone. "Taking the pictures from Brice Harper, yes, but did you have to stomp on his hand?"

Raymond raised a brow and stared down at Curtis until

the man lowered his gaze. "Let me get this straight. You feel bad about Harper's hand getting hurt, but not the girl nearly dying? Or the pleasure you've taken from the other girls all these years?"

Just as he expected, Curtis shifted uncomfortably in his seat but didn't utter a word.

Raymond leaned back. "I offered each of you a chair for poker and our side entertainment because I thought you could keep your mouths shut and do whatever needed to be done. Grow some balls."

Billy Gonzalez leaned his forearms on the burgundy felt table and turned his black eyes to Raymond. "Curtis might be fine sitting back and saying nothing, but I'm not. You had one of your men push the photographer into the arena. Have you seen the video? Do you have any idea how close she came to getting killed?"

"I know exactly," Raymond stated. "I was there. And had she died, we wouldn't be having this conversation."

Curtis reached for the bottle of bourbon and topped off his glass. He drank it down before he set the glass on the table and released a breath while sitting back in his chair. "We have the pictures, and while it appears Naomi did get me on film, you can't see my face. Once we have the film, we wait things out until she returns home and all this dies down."

"Yes," Ethan said, nodding his head. "I like that plan."

Larry Anderson had yet to say anything. Raymond's gaze settled on his oldest friend and waited. After a minute, Larry's hazel eyes met his, and a pale brow rose briefly as he shrugged. That was his friend's silent agreement for whatever Raymond decided.

Raymond held his cigar between his fingers as he rested his hand on the table. On the other side of his house, his wife was watching a movie with his daughters and son. They knew better than to disturb him when he had his friends over.

"The fact is, there is a real possibility that attention is on us," he told the men. "Sharon Biermann phoned before each of you arrived and said that nothing about either Naomi's or Brice's accident was mentioned at the Easts'. That's good news. It was the perfect opportunity for them to speak privately, but they didn't."

Billy wrapped his fingers around his glass. "But you still believe the Harpers will look into things?"

Raymond nodded slowly. "Had Curtis not tried to take Naomi's camera, Brice Harper would never have gotten involved, but he is. And that means we need to take precautions. We need to let him and his family know just what we're capable of."

"We need to be careful," Larry said. "I know what kind of power the Easts have, and Brice and Caleb Harper are essentially Easts. We've given them a reason to dig into us. We can all get through it unscathed if we handle things correctly."

Ethan smiled. "I can do that."

Curtis snorted loudly. "Do you think you can keep your prick in your pants long enough?"

"You're the one with the hard-on for Whitney," Ethan retorted.

"And we're the ones who have to remind you we don't coerce little girls."

Ethan's face went red with anger. "Why you—" he began and lunged from his chair.

Billy and Larry shoved Ethan back down. This wasn't the first time that particular argument had taken place, and it wouldn't be the last.

Frankly, Raymond understood Curtis's obsession with Whitney Nolan. She was a spectacular beauty with long legs and a vibrant soul. He had enjoyed making her suck his cock. In fact, he very much wanted to visit her again. More so now than before.

But if he wanted his men to hold off, that meant he would have to, as well.

"Have you calmed down?" Raymond asked Ethan as he took off his hat and rested it on the floor by his chair.

Ethan gave a brief nod, his eyes on Curtis full of hatred.

Raymond smoothed his hands over his black hair that held just a hint of gray at his temples. He started to speak when his cell phone rang.

He reached into his sports jacket and fished it out. He was careful to keep his face impassive when he saw that it was Sharon who called. It wasn't a good sign that she was phoning again.

"Hello?" he answered.

"We have a problem," she whispered frantically into the phone.

He looked up at the men who were staring at him. "Meaning?"

"Whitney and Naomi snuck out of the house and went to the barn."

Raymond shrugged. "So?"

"Whitney returned a little later. I can hear her crying through the wall. I think she told Naomi."

Fuck. This was not what he wanted. "But you aren't sure."

"I saw Whitney's face when she left the barn. She told Naomi."

"Thanks," he said and hung up. Raymond returned the

phone to his pocket and took a deep breath. "Plans have changed."

Billy raised a black brow. "How so?"

"Sharon suspects that Whitney told Naomi about us."

Ethan's face went white as he got to his feet. "Names? My God, Raymond. My political career will be over."

"Sit your stupid ass down and shut the fuck up," Curtis stated. "And your career isn't the only thing that'll be over. Everything each of us has worked for and garnered over the years will be gone."

Larry finally lifted his glass to his lips and took a sip of the bourbon. "If Naomi had our names, Clayton would have already called Danny, and our man in the sheriff's department would've informed us."

"Good point," Billy stated.

Raymond brought his cigar back to his lips and took a long drag, letting the smoke fill his lungs before blowing it out. "Obviously, the mishaps with Naomi and Brice weren't enough to remind Whitney to keep her mouth shut."

"Do you have something else in mind?" Curtis asked.

"I do, actually."

Billy raised his brows as he asked, "Care to share?"

Raymond shook his head. "I'm still putting it all together. I'll let you know. Until then, do not approach any of the girls. Don't do anything to bring any sort of attention to yourselves. And if, by chance, the Harpers or Naomi Pierce visit you, you know the drill."

"As if we'd admit to anything," Ethan replied irritably.

"Goodnight, my friends," Raymond said as he got to his feet, ending the meeting.

He motioned to Larry to hang back. At the front door, Raymond waved to Curtis as he got into his truck and drove away. After talking with Billy, Larry, and Ethan, the mayor finally made his way to his car and left.

Raymond wasn't surprised when Billy remained behind, talking for a bit longer in the light of the front door. Out of all the men, Billy was the wildcard.

Ethan liked the idea of forcing young girls, and Curtis bordered on being a stalker with one girl until she left the rodeo and he was forced to find another to obsess over.

He, like Larry, wanted to dominate women. All women. But it was a high to show women his power and how easily he could help them—or destroy them.

But while Billy had sampled many of the girls, Raymond had yet to determine just what he got off on. Billy never hesitated to follow him in all ventures, but that didn't mean Raymond didn't keep an eye on him.

Only after Billy had driven off did Raymond walk away from the house with Larry trailing after him. They strolled for several minutes before Raymond paused and looked over the subdivision he'd developed.

"What are you thinking?" Larry asked.

"Sharon has always done as we asked. We've paid her a lot of money over the years to keep her mouth shut and dissuade the girls from telling anyone about our visits."

Larry crossed his arms over his chest. "You think she's going to talk?"

"She might. Clayton East has the ability to get people to do what he wants. I'd rather not find out if she is more afraid of him or us."

Larry nodded slowly.

Raymond turned to face him. "Whitney, Sharon, and Cooper Owens will be on their way back from the East Ranch tomorrow morning."

"I know just the man to call."

"No. I want you to take care of it."

Larry shrugged. "Sure. But why?"

"We've made a point to keep our hands clean of such things. Those we've blackmailed or bribed have agreed to help us. But we've never resorted to such . . . extremes."

"True," Larry agreed. "Does it have to be in the morning?"

"It does. I want the Easts and the Harpers to be very, very concerned."

His friend rubbed his chin, a troubled look on his face. "This could push the family into digging in their heels and exposing us."

"Or they could be so devastated that they decide to leave well enough alone."

"You're taking a chance, Raymond."

He thought a moment and nodded. "My entire life, I've taken such chances. Look around. Look what we've created. I'm sought after in the community, wanted to help young businessmen and -women. I'm on the Board of Directors for the rodeo, and I have a successful construction company. And you're in the background as you've always preferred."

"I don't regret anything we've done," Larry said. "I just don't want it all to fall apart either. We've got a good thing here. There has only been one girl who tried to say anything, and we ran her out of town. The others, we paid off. We can continue like this if we back off for a while."

Raymond raised a brow. "You mean you want us to leave Whitney and the others alone? You want me to allow that photographer to print more pictures and attempt to find out who was following Whitney?"

"I do. I think it's the smart move."

It was the first time they had differing views on such

an important issue. It wasn't that Raymond didn't respect Larry's opinion, but Raymond knew to gain anything, chances had to be taken. And this was no exception.

"Do you know what might happen if we tell Ethan or Curtis that they can't have one of the girls?" Raymond asked.

Larry raised a brow. "What do you think Curtis will do when he finds out you've killed Whitney?"

"I'll shove another pretty girl into his lap and let her suck his dick. It won't take him long to become just as obsessed," Raymond stated.

"I'll do as you ask, but I wish you'd reconsider."

"You'll thank me when all of this blows over. And if by some chance the Easts and Harpers start poking around, the next time I hit Brice over the head, I'll make sure he never gets back up again. No one is going to ruin what we've built here. No one."

Chapter 17

How could she be this happy? Naomi stretched beneath the covers before she threw them off and jumped up to grab a quick shower.

She tied her hair up and stood beneath the hot spray as she grinned like a silly schoolgirl with her first crush. Ever since Brice had asked her to go riding, she'd pictured them racing horses over the land.

Her smile faltered as she thought about Whitney. Brice said nothing could be planned until Whitney and Ms. Biermann left the ranch. Naomi hadn't thought about what she would say to remain behind. Or if Brice even wanted her to.

She thought he might. He had mentioned a horseback ride, so obviously he wanted her to stay. Right?

Naomi dropped her head back to look at the ceiling and the steam swirling above her. She didn't know. And she didn't want to presume. When she assumed anything, it was always as her father used to tell her.

"Don't assume anything, Naomi. Because it'll make an ass out of you and me."

Despite his warning, she'd learned the hard way. Time and time again. She wasn't going to do that today.

Her good mood dissipated some as she finished washing and turned off the shower. She dried off then stood before the mirror. After swiping the towel over it to clear it of steam, she looked at herself.

She'd never been much for makeup. It wasn't that she didn't like it, it was that she couldn't seem to make her hands do what was needed to put it on properly. Her mascara ended up everywhere but on her lashes. And don't even get her started on eyeliner.

Yet she found herself wishing for the highlighting powder she had bought and her favorite lipstick. Since she didn't have it, she'd have to make do. She used the old-school method and pinched her cheeks before letting her hair down.

She shook it out and dressed before combing her fingers through her tresses. Next, she flipped her hair over as she bent to give it some volume.

When she straightened, she gave herself another look. She squared her shoulders before walking quietly from the room. Halfway down the stairs, she heard the conversations from the kitchen.

It was barely six o'clock, but the house was buzzing. How she'd forgotten country life. She was used to waking up at seven. Well, she set her alarm for seven but didn't get up until around eight.

She stifled a yawn and walked into the kitchen. Her eyes immediately landed on Brice, who was taking a drink of coffee. He smiled at her, the delight in his blue eyes evident even to her.

Suddenly, it felt as if there were a dozen butterflies in her stomach. Her nervousness was off the charts. Her hands were clammy, her heart was pounding, and she couldn't catch her breath. All because of Brice.

"Morning," he drawled.

She grinned and walked to an empty stool at the island. "Good morning."

Naomi made herself look around the kitchen at the others. The only one not up was Whitney. Brice placed a mug of coffee in front of her. She smiled her thanks and wrapped her cold hands around it.

Ms. Biermann passed the sugar and cream, but Naomi only reached for the sugar. She sighed in contentment at the first sip of the heavenly caffeinated beverage. If she had one vice, it was coffee.

Caleb chuckled as he came up on the opposite side of the island. "I don't function without coffee either."

"It's an addiction," Naomi replied. "And I have no desire to stop drinking it."

"Me either." Caleb winked at her before helping Brody with his backpack while Brice spoke with Wynter.

Naomi watched the interaction with interest. Clayton and Abby walked the kids to the door, where they handed them off to an older man.

"That's Shane, the ranch manager," Brice explained.

"Ah, okay," Naomi said and took another drink of coffee.

Once the kids were gone, Abby sat while Clayton began getting eggs and bacon out of the refrigerator. Jace pulled out pans while Cooper refilled his mug and shook his head at his friend.

"One day, Jace, you're actually going to get full," Cooper said.

Jace grinned at him. "Doubtful."

"We really need to get going," Ms. Biermann said.

Naomi turned her head to the woman and said, "Whitney isn't even awake yet."

"I plan to get her up."

"Why?" Naomi felt defensive and protective of her friend. "Whitney had a long day yesterday. Let her sleep."

Ms. Biermann's gray eyes met hers. "Whitney is a rodeo queen. That role requires her to be at events as well as the rodeo to represent her title. She'll be able to rest when her reign has ended."

Naomi had the overwhelming desire to knock the woman off the stool. She hadn't been raised to retaliate with violence, but after what Whitney had endured, Naomi wasn't sure she could hold back.

"You told me just a few minutes ago that Whitney didn't have to be anywhere until after lunch," Abby said.

Naomi smiled in triumph at Ms. Biermann, who pinched her lips as if she were sucking on something sour. "So Whitney can sleep as long as she needs and eat a nice breakfast," Naomi stated.

"She certainly can," Brice added.

Cooper and Abby struck up a conversation while Ms. Biermann stewed in her anger. Brice's conspiratorial wink made Naomi grin.

"Need some help?" Naomi asked Clayton.

He shook his head as he glanced her way with a grin. "No, ma'am. I've got this covered."

Naomi reached around to check her phone when she realized she'd lost it sometime yesterday. "Can I borrow a phone?"

"Sure," Brice said and handed her his.

"Thanks. Be right back," she told him as she slid off the stool and jogged up the stairs.

She opened the door to her bedroom and glanced at her bag. She didn't allow herself to look at her ruined equipment again. That was for another time, and she was having too much fun this morning to wreck it.

Naomi sat on the bed and punched in her mother's number.

"Hello?" her mother asked in a voice roughened by sleep.

"Hey, Mom."

There was a pause. "Naomi, what in God's name are you doing up at this hour and sounding so chipper?"

"We used to get up this early."

"That was a long time ago, honey. You didn't come home last night. Are you okay?"

Naomi grinned. "I am. I suppose that means you didn't check your messages after we talked yesterday, did you? I left you two."

"It was a late night, and I always forget when I put it on vibrate. And yes, I did get the messages, but it's early and my brain needs a minute to function properly. I'd love to ask if you went home with a hot cowboy, but I already know you did," her mother said in a teasing voice.

Naomi didn't bat an eye as she replied, "No, that's something you'd do."

"Damn right," Diana replied with a chuckle. Then she said in a serious tone, "I saw the video of your fall. It's much worse than what you said in the messages."

She sighed, feeling as if the weight of the world rested on her shoulders. "There is so much I have to tell you, but now isn't the time."

"Do I need to be concerned?"

"Yes, but not for me."

Her mother made a sound in the back of her throat. "I've been worrying about you since I learned I was carrying you. It hasn't stopped, and it never will. You could have died yesterday, and you didn't come home for me to fuss over. I also didn't get upset when you asked me not to come to the ranch."

"I know," Naomi said in a small voice. "I asked that for your safety, Mom. If I had thought for a minute you were in danger, I'd be right there with you."

"It's something big, isn't it?" Diana asked.

Naomi licked her lips. "Yeah."

"We always urged you to stand up for yourself and those who needed you, so I'm not going to ask you to step out of this. But, baby, you need to be careful."

"I will, Mom. I promise. Now that I know what kind of people I'm up against, I know what to look for."

Her mother snorted loudly. "You're smart, Naomi, so you know that the kind of people who could push a woman into an arena to be run over have no scruples. They will do anything to anyone to achieve their goals."

Naomi swallowed as unease churned in her stomach. "True."

"I heard a rumor that Brice Harper was also in a bit of an accident."

"He was hit over the head, and his hand stomped on. The culprit also got away with the photos I printed."

"Hm," her mother said. "I was hoping you'd caught something on film. Can you print more?"

Naomi grinned. "Of course."

"Then do it. Put them up everywhere. Make it so that if anything else happens to you or the Harpers or anyone else, everyone will know where to look."

"But you can't see anything in the picture."

"Someone will recognize something."

Naomi considered her mother's words. "Momma, have I told you what a wise woman you are?"

"Not nearly often enough."

"I'll get it on a plaque for you," she replied with a grin.

Diana laughed softly. "It's so good when you come home. I'd hoped to see more of you this trip."

"I can't keep up with you," Naomi exclaimed. "You run rings around me."

"You should take some pointers from me. I could find you a man quick enough."

Naomi shook her head, laughing. "Thanks. I'm doing fine on my own."

"Obviously, if you're at the East Ranch. Just promise you'll stay in touch daily. If not, I'll come out there myself."

"I promise."

"Good," Diana replied. "Now go have fun and live a little. You deserve it since you're always working so hard. And don't tell me you don't work too much," she said before Naomi could argue. "I'm your mother, the wise and all-knowing."

Naomi laughed again. "Yes, ma'am."

"Love you, doodlebug."

It had been forever since she'd heard her mother's pet name for her. "Love you, too, Mom."

The call ended. When she rose and looked at the door, Whitney was standing there with her arms crossed over her chest, her hair up in a messy bun, and a smile on her face.

"I don't even need to ask how that call went," Whitney said. "Diana always did have a way with words."

Naomi rose and walked to her friend. "You look better this morning."

Whitney wiped her hands over her face. "It feels really good to not be sitting down and putting on makeup. It was the smell of bacon that woke me."

"Well, I'll warn you that Ms. Biermann wanted to get you up earlier so y'all could leave."

"Why?" Whitney asked with a frown.

"I don't know. I don't like that woman."

Whitney's lips twisted. "She's not that bad."

Naomi didn't bother to argue. "I know you don't have anything until after lunch. Do you think you'll stay here until then?"

"I don't think so," she said with a shake of her head. "I've got to get home and start the long process of getting ready."

"Then let's get down for some breakfast before the guys eat it all."

Whitney laughed as she linked her arm with Naomi's. "You obviously haven't been around many pregnant women if you're concerned about the men. Abby is liable to take all of it for herself."

"Oh. Good point."

They raced from the room and down the stairs to come to a laughing stop with everyone in the kitchen looking at them.

Naomi pressed her lips together in an effort to stop laughing. "We were hungry."

"Good thing I'm cooking for an army then," Clayton said with a wink.

But Naomi's eyes were only for Brice.

Chapter 18

There were just some days that remained in a person's memory forever. Not a single event from that day. But that day itself.

Naomi's excitement built during breakfast. Whitney laughed and acted like her old self. No one mentioned the accidents or that they knew about her assault. And Naomi would be forever grateful to everyone for that.

Well, everyone except Ms. Biermann. Naomi really didn't like the woman, and the longer she was around her, the more she detested the chaperone.

For a short time, Naomi forgot that they were immersed in a conspiracy of epic proportions. She forgot that her friend had been raped. She forgot that Brice had been attacked. She forgot that she'd come close to being killed.

It was an enjoyable breakfast with an old friend and new ones. And Ms. Biermann.

When the chaperone asked Cooper to drive her back into town, Naomi was all too happy to see the woman leave. However, that meant Whitney was going with her.

"You sure you can't stay?" Naomi asked one last time. "Play hooky and all that?"

Whitney looked at the clear sky and laughed. "I wish. I did some thinking last night. I'm through with pageants. I'll finish my duties over the next month, but after that, I'm out."

Naomi halted them and stared in shock at her friend. "What about winning the USA crown? What about the money?"

"Well," Whitney said and rolled her eyes. "There is this old friend of mine who reminded me of who I was. It seems I needed a jolt back to reality."

She threw her arms around Whitney and hugged her tightly. "Are you sure it's what you want?"

"It's what I need." She leaned back and looked at Naomi. "I also plan to out the group who has : . . done those things to me and the other girls."

"That's good."

Whitney's smile was wide. "I thought you might like that."

"Tell me who they are so we can help you."

"No," Whitney said and shook her head. "I'm going to do this on my own. Once I release their names, I'll come to you and Brice and all the others affected by these monsters. Until then, leave things to me. Can you do that? I need to do this myself."

Naomi hesitated. She didn't want to walk away from this. Not because she didn't think Whitney would carry through with her plan, but because she wanted to support her friend.

"I can do this," Whitney assured her. "I have years of dirt on them. I know their names. And I have proof."

Naomi's eyes widened. "Proof."

"And I'm going to use it," she proclaimed proudly. "But I won't tarnish the last weeks of my reign with it. I get to choose the time."

"What if they come to you again?"

Whitney glanced over at the truck where Ms. Biermann waited. "I've thought of that. I plan to make sure I have cameras recording."

Naomi nodded, impressed. This was the girl she'd grown up with. "Now I want to help."

"You did," she said. "You pushed me to see that what was done to me isn't my fault. You made me realize just how far I've strayed from my path. I didn't like the person I saw in the mirror last night. I had a good cry, and I took a long look at myself. It's time for a change."

"Good for you." Naomi was so proud of her.

They continued walking to the others, and Naomi noticed that Brice was staring at her. She pretended she didn't see, but she was giddy for the day to continue.

When she was washing the dishes, Brice had come up behind her and leaned close to her ear before asking if she was still up for a ride.

"So," Whitney said. "I gather you're not coming back with us."

Naomi pulled her eyes away from Brice. "Huh? Oh, no. I'm staying for a ride."

"On a horse or that cowboy who can't keep his eyes off you?" Whitney asked with a knowing grin.

Naomi lifted one shoulder in a shrug. "I haven't decided."

Whitney let out a loud laugh. "Oh, you most certainly have."

They stopped next to the crew cab truck. Cooper and Jace were laughing with Clayton, Caleb, and Brice. Ms. Biermann was already in the front passenger seat.

Whitney turned her back to the woman and rolled her eyes before whispering, "Apparently, I'm being punished and made to sit in the back."

Naomi stifled a giggled. They embraced once more before Whitney waved to Abby, who stood on the porch, and then she thanked everyone one last time before climbing into the truck.

Naomi turned away when Cooper drove off and came face-to-face with Brice.

"What are y'all going to do?" Jace asked as he looked between Brice and Naomi.

Caleb dragged Jace away, saying, "Let's go."

"To do what?"

"Something," Caleb said.

Naomi smiled at Clayton as he followed Caleb and Jace into the house. Then her gaze slid to Brice.

"Do you know how much control it's taken me not to drag you out of the house?" he asked.

She rocked back on her heels. "How much?"

"Everything I had," he replied.

"It's just us now."

"Thank God," he said and turned her toward the barn.

They walked in silence. There was a crazy mix of excitement and nervousness inside her. She wasn't sure if she wanted to do a jig or throw up, and she was afraid she might do both.

It wasn't as if other men hadn't asked her out. She just hadn't accepted any offers. But from the instant she'd seen Brice, she'd known there was something different about him, something that kept drawing her attention.

He brought her to the tack room, where rows of saddles were laid out before her. "Pick whichever one you want."

Since her family had boarded horses, they had also kept the tack, but their room was never this impressive. She picked a well-worn saddle, blanket, and bridle, while Brice did the same. Naomi then carried them to London's stall and placed the saddle on the ground as she grabbed a brush.

She walked into the stall, talking softly to the buckskin mare before she started brushing her. Naomi may not have been around horses for years, but they had been her life from the time she could walk until she left for college. It wasn't something she would ever forget.

After checking the mare over to make sure there were no injuries, Naomi placed the saddle blanket onto the horse's back. She carefully lifted the saddle and set it on the mare. One of her pet peeves was when people just threw the saddle on a horse.

Naomi took her time cinching the saddle before she adjusted the stirrups. Then she slipped the bridle over the mare's head, happy to see that it was one without a metal bit.

By the time Naomi led London from the stall, Brice was waiting for her. She shrugged. "It's been a while."

"You were being careful. Nothing wrong with that," he said. "Ready?"

She watched as he mounted a big bay gelding. Naomi patted London on the neck before she put her foot into the stirrup and reached for the saddle horn as she swung her other leg over the saddle.

Her right foot slipped comfortably into the stirrup as if she hadn't stopped riding. She gathered the reins in her hand and took a deep breath.

"Where can we go?" she asked.

Brice shrugged and looked around. "Pick a direction."

"Take me to your favorite place."

"I can do that," he said.

He clicked to his horse to start walking. Naomi hurried to follow him. After they had passed through a couple of gates, Brice nudged his horse into a trot. Not wanting to be left behind, Naomi quickly came even with him.

She was the one who let London shift into a gallop. Naomi laughed as the wind whipped through her air and the ground moved swiftly beneath her.

How in the world could she have given this up? Who in their right mind would leave behind something so freeing? And who wouldn't quickly return home after seeing the error of their ways?

Certainly not Naomi.

Brice looked at her and grinned before he leaned low over the gelding's neck. His horse leapt into a run.

"Come on, girl," Naomi said to London.

The mare's ears swiveled back to Naomi as she spoke. Naomi bent low as the mare quickly lengthened her strides into a run. Within moments, they caught Brice. He hadn't been joking when he'd said that London was fast.

Naomi was in love with the mare. Her gait was smooth, her hooves fleet of foot, and her attention focused.

Suddenly, Brice halted his horse. Naomi sat up and tugged on the reins as she said, "Whoa, London."

Naomi turned the mare around and trotted back to Brice, who had moved to an ATV driven by Caleb. There was something about the look Brice gave her that caused a chill to race down Naomi's back. Caleb nodded before he drove off.

She reached Brice and frowned. "Everything okay?"

"We need to head back."

"What is it?"

He studied her a long, silent minute. "There's been an accident."

"Let's go."

It wasn't until they were running the horses back to the house that Naomi realized she hadn't asked what kind of accident or who was involved. Her mind raced with possibilities. Was it her mom? Abby's kids? Abby?

When they reached the barn, Brice jumped from his horse and came to her as she dismounted. "Leave the horses."

"What?" she asked. "No."

"Look," he said and nodded to a man who walked up and took the reins of both animals.

Naomi swung her head back to Brice. "Tell me what's going on."

"Let's go into the house with the others."

She shook her head. "No. Tell me. If it was Abby, you'd already be inside."

The back door of the house flew open as Jace rushed out. Caleb was right behind him. They jumped into Caleb's truck and drove off so quickly that dirt and rocks kicked up.

Naomi's eyes were drawn back to the house when Clayton came outside. He came to a stop when he spotted her and Brice. That's when she knew. Whoever had been hurt was someone close to her.

"Tell me," she urged Brice.

He held her gaze, his blue eyes full of sorrow and regret. "About a mile from the house, someone hit Cooper's truck."

"Okay," she said with a nod. Car accidents happened all the time. "How bad?"

Brice took a deep breath and slowly released it. "Ms. Biermann was killed on impact."

Naomi let that register as she struggled to pull air into her lungs. He hadn't said Whitney was dead. That was a good sign, right?

"And?" she prompted.

"Cooper and Whitney are being rushed to the hospital now."

Naomi tried to swallow. "Were either conscious?"

"No."

"Are they critical?"

The fact that he hesitated was all the answer she needed. The world began to spin, but his arms quickly came around her.

"I can drive you to the hospital."

She focused on his blue eyes and nodded. "I have to see her. And her parents. I need to call them."

"Already being done," he said as he led her to the truck.

She blinked, and they were driving down the road. She didn't remember getting in the truck or leaving the ranch, but that didn't matter.

She'd already lost one best friend to a car accident. She couldn't lose another.

"Hang on, Whitney," she whispered.

Naomi felt something tighten on her hand and looked down to find Brice's injured fingers linked with hers.

Chapter 19

Brice sped down the road on the way to the hospital. As soon as he'd seen Caleb drive up on the ATV, he'd known something had happened. He just hadn't thought it would be something so . . . awful.

He glanced over at Naomi, who stared out the windshield, her face ashen. There was no telling what was going through her head, but he could take a guess. Because they were the same thoughts going through his.

"Where did the accident happen?" she asked.

"About a mile from the ranch."

She nodded. "Right. You said that already. Sorry."

"It's okay," he assured her.

Naomi licked her lips. "What happened to them exactly?"

"I don't know specifics."

"But you know more than you're telling me." Her head turned to him. "You're taking us the opposite way."

He shot her a quick look. "I am."

"Because it's that bad."

"Because it's that bad, and the road is blocked."

She drew in a deep breath. "Knowing is better than the scenarios that keep running through my head."

Brice hesitated, but he gave in despite his reservations. "A dump truck hit them."

"How?" she pushed.

Damn. She was relentless. She'd pull it all out of him eventually, so he'd be better off just telling her. "They were t-boned. Danny said—"

"Danny?" she asked.

"He's the sheriff and a family friend."

Naomi nodded. "Go on."

"He got the call about an accident and was one of the first to arrive at the scene. Whoever had driven the dump truck was long gone, and to make matters worse, it was stolen."

She closed her eyes and shook her head. A moment later, she shifted in the seat to face him. "It's these men, isn't it?"

"We don't know that."

"Brice," she said sternly.

He blew out a breath. "I don't know. It could be." He slammed his free hand on the steering wheel. "Shit. It probably is."

"They were trying to kill Whitney."

Brice slowed to turn off the road and glanced at Naomi. "We don't know that yet."

"You mean you don't believe that." Naomi straightened and turned her head to look out her window. "I know it."

They were quiet the rest of the way to the hospital. Brice went over what little Caleb had shared. It was everything Brice had told Naomi, but he wanted more. He *needed* more.

He pulled into the hospital parking lot, and they both jumped out and ran into the building. After stopping a nurse, they got directions to the ER, but there, they were denied entry.

Brice walked into the waiting room and found Caleb sitting in a chair, bent over with his head in his hands. Jace was pacing, his gaze going to the ER doors every few seconds.

"Naomi."

They turned, and Brice saw an older couple that looked worried walk up. Naomi rushed to the duo, hugging the woman first and then the man. They shared a quiet word. That's when Brice realized they must be Whitney's parents.

Naomi gently guided them to the nurse's station, where they were taken back to see their daughter. Brice went to Naomi and put his arm around her.

She rested her head against him and wrapped her arms around herself. "They wanted me to tell them what happened. I . . . I couldn't."

"It's okay," he said and rubbed his hand up and down her back. "Someone will."

Brice's head jerked to Jace when he ran down the hall. He spotted Cooper's mother, who sobbed on Jace's shoulder for a few moments. Then Jace motioned a nurse over and gave Betty's information to the nurse.

But Betty wouldn't release Jace. "He's coming with me," she informed the nurse.

Brice gave a nod to Jace as they walked past. The waiting was the hardest, but Brice knew Jace would come out and fill them in as soon as he could.

After he and Naomi had gotten coffee for themselves and Caleb, they took seats in the waiting room. Less than thirty minutes later, Clayton and Abby arrived.

"What are y'all doing here?" Brice asked as he rose to greet them.

Clayton glared at Abby. "As if I would leave y'all to deal with this on your own. And your sister refused to stay at home."

"I'm not having this argument again," Abby stated and walked away to sit next to Naomi as Abby spoke with her and Caleb.

Brice turned his back to the group and looked at his brother-in-law. "How the fuck did this happen?" he whispered.

Clayton shook his head and crossed his arms over his chest. "I don't know. Danny said he'd be here as soon as he could with more details. He sounded odd."

"Odd?" Brice asked with a frown. "What does that mean?"

"His position is elected, remember? That also means that he is in contact with the mayor on some things. And Ethan Ross has called three times already."

Brice shrugged in confusion. "It was a bad accident. Doesn't the mayor normally want information on things like that?"

"Unless he knows someone in the accident, he usually waits for Danny to contact him."

That got Brice's attention. "I know Cooper doesn't know the mayor. That leaves Whitney or Ms. Biermann."

"Yeah. We can't ask Ms. Biermann, and Whitney is unconscious."

"You think this has something to do with the pictures Naomi took?"

Clayton blew out a breath as he looked over Brice's shoulder at the others. "I don't have any proof, so I don't want to speculate. Honestly, I'd rather wait until Danny gets here."

"Naomi thinks the group of men who assaulted Whitney tried to kill her."

Clayton's brows shot up as his head briefly tilted to the side. "Danny did say that it looked as if Cooper tried to turn the truck away, but he didn't have time."

Brice wasn't finished talking, but Clayton slapped him on the back and went to join his wife. Sitting wasn't something Brice could do with all the things running through his head. He pulled out his phone and did a quick search on local news. Sure enough, there was already a story up—including pictures.

His stomach dropped at the sight of Cooper's crew cab smashed in the middle with the front and back curved inward from the force of the hit. The crumpled metal on the front passenger door that had been forced open by the fire department had blood on it.

Brice hoped for more pictures of the truck, but that was the only one included. He finished the article and checked the other local news sites. Each had similar photos of the vehicle, and the verbiage in each was almost identical.

More frustrated than ever, he put away his phone and returned to the others. The conversation that transpired was stilted and done in low tones as each of them was lost in their own thoughts.

Hours went by before Jace finally came out. Everyone but Abby stood at his approach.

"Tell us good news," Caleb said.

Jace ran a hand down his face. "The doctors say Cooper has a concussion. He's pretty banged up."

"But he's going to be okay, right?" Brice asked.

Jace nodded as he blew out a breath. "Half of his face is all bruised from slamming against the window and the airbag, but their focus is on his concussion. He's also cut up from the windows busting, but they'll be moving him to a normal room within the hour."

"Oh, thank God," Caleb said.

Naomi moved a step closer. "Did you see Whitney?"

Jace glanced at Brice before he looked at Naomi. "For just a moment, yes."

"And?" Clayton urged.

"She's not doing so good," Jace said after a small hesitation.

Brice walked to Naomi and put his arm around her again. She was trembling, but she stood tall and straight, waiting for the rest of the news.

"Don't keep it from her or any of us," Abby told Jace. "It only makes things worse."

Caleb nodded in agreement. "She's right. We've been sitting here for hours, waiting for someone to tell us something. Anything."

"I understand," Jace said and shifted nervously. "It's just . . . I'm not any good at this kind of thing."

Clayton put his hand on Jace's shoulder for a heartbeat. "No one is."

Jace slid his hazel eyes back to Naomi. "Whitney was rushed into surgery just a bit ago. Both of her legs are broken, and her right hip is shattered."

Naomi's breath left her in a whoosh as her eyes teared up.

But Jace wasn't finished. "Her right arm is broken in three different places, and two of her broken ribs punctured her lungs. Also . . . she has a spinal injury."

"Dear God," Abby mumbled.

Brice held Naomi tighter. And the longer he stood there

listening to Jace rattle off all the injuries Whitney had suffered, the more he began to agree with Naomi that the group of men who assaulted Whitney were the ones responsible for this.

"I saw her as they were rushing her past us into the OR," Jace continued. "It was just a brief look. Once we got in to see Cooper and spoke with the doctor, I asked about Whitney. I tried to get out here to y'all sooner, but Betty needed me."

Abby shot him a kind smile. "Of course. No need to explain, Jace. Go back to her."

"Yeah," Caleb said. "Cooper is all she has."

Brice glanced at everyone around him. "That's not true. She has us."

"That's right," Clayton agreed.

Jace rubbed his eyes with his thumb and forefinger. "Abby, can I ask something of you?"

"I'll call your parents, sweetheart," she said, knowing what he would ask.

Jace's smile was forced. "Thanks. They'll want to be up here. And I want them to know I wasn't involved."

"Good thinking," Clayton said.

Caleb gave a nod. "We'll take care of everything. Get back in there to Cooper."

"I'll let y'all know what room he's in," Jace said before he disappeared through the doors again.

The entire time Naomi stood there with soft tears rolling down her face. Brice wished he could offer some other kind of comfort, but he didn't know the words to ease her. At this point, there was nothing anyone could say that would make things better.

Naomi sniffed loudly and rested her head on his shoulder. "It's a miracle she's alive."

"But she is. That's the important thing to focus on," he reminded her.

"I know," she said and lifted her eyes to him. "It's just . . ."

He squeezed her shoulder. "I know."

"Brice," Clayton said, an urgent tone in his voice.

He turned and saw Clayton striding off. When Brice looked down the hallway, he spotted Danny coming toward them in his tan sheriff's uniform.

"Not without me," Abby said as Caleb helped her to her feet.

"Wait," Naomi said as she hurried to stop a nurse with a wheelchair. A moment later, she returned and helped Abby into it.

Brice smiled at Naomi as Caleb wheeled their sister after Clayton. To Brice's surprise, Naomi held out her hand. He clasped his fingers to hers.

"I couldn't do this without you," she said.

He looked into her eyes. "Yes, you could."

"But I'm glad I don't have to."

Chapter 20

Naomi had originally wanted to spend the day racing over the land on top of London with Brice, or maybe even kissing him beneath the bright blue sky. But the day had taken a darker turn. Still, there was no one else she wanted by her side at that moment than Brice.

She was terrified of the group of men that had done such a thing to her friend. There was no doubt in her mind that they were responsible, and until someone showed her proof that it was an accident, she would continue to think so.

She'd already learned firsthand what the group was capable of. Who was to say they wouldn't come after her or Brice again. Or worse, Abby, the kids, or anyone else at the ranch.

Naomi's heart pounded as she and Brice followed the others out of the hospital. Sheriff Danny Oldman was young and good-looking. He had short, dark hair and kind, hazel eyes that were more gold than green.

"Why are we outside?" Clayton asked, concern cutting a deep frown on his face.

Danny took off his dark brown Stetson and slapped it on his leg before replacing it on his head. "Because I don't know who I can trust."

"Why would you say that?" Abby asked.

Danny looked down at her and raised a brow. "What the hell are you doing here?"

"She's damn stubborn, that's why," Clayton mumbled.

Abby sighed loudly and rolled her eyes. "Because this involves Cooper, who, like Jace, is part of our family. And because Whitney and Naomi were at the house last night."

Naomi felt the weight of the sheriff's gaze land on her. He studied her a moment before his eyes briefly lowered to her and Brice's hands.

Danny returned his attention to her face. "Clayton called me yesterday about what happened to the two of you at the rodeo. Brice, your hand looks like shit."

"Feels like it, too," Brice added.

Naomi gasped and looked down when she realized she was holding his bad hand, but he tightened his grip, refusing to release her. She turned her head to Danny as she felt his gaze on her.

"I recognize your name," he said. "It took me a moment to place from where. I was friends with your uncle, JoŸny."

Naomi cocked her head to the side as she looked at Danny. A memory returned as her lips parted. "You were one of his pallbearers."

"Yes, ma'am," he said with a nod. "JoŸny was a good man, and one hell of a rodeo clown. He helped save my brother a time or two in the arena."

Naomi, already emotional from the morning, felt a tear slide down her cheek. She hastily wiped it away. "It's what he lived for."

Danny shifted his feet, his hazel eyes full of sorrow. "I was sorry to hear about your father's passing so quickly after JoŸny's. How's your mother?"

Oh, God. Her mom. Naomi hadn't called her about the accident. "She's good."

Abby smiled at them. "Small-town life, huh? It never entered my mind that you might know Naomi, Danny, but I should have realized."

"I figured it out last night after Clayton called," Danny said. "Then I watched the video of Naomi being pushed, and it clicked how I knew the name Pierce."

Brice looked at her. Naomi swiveled her head to him. Their gazes clashed. With a simple glance, Brice told her so much. That he was sorry she'd lost her uncle and her father, and that he would continue to stand beside her, and with her, for whatever she needed him for.

But it was the desire he didn't try to hide that helped push away the weight of despair that had consumed her since learning of the wreck.

Danny cleared his throat, catching everyone's attention. "Look, I'm going to tell all of you things that I shouldn't." He paused and looked at the hospital doors a moment. "The dump truck was reported stolen late last night. There are no prints other than the owner's, and he has an alibi for when the accident took place."

"Any sign of the driver?" Caleb asked. "No one saw anything?"

"Not that we've found. I plan on putting out a call on the evening news. Hopefully then we'll hear something," Danny explained.

Brice glanced at the ground. "So you don't have any suspects?"

"No," the sheriff said with a soft shake of his head.

Abby rubbed her stomach in soft circles. "I know that look of yours, Danny. There's something you're keeping to yourself."

The sheriff looked at Abby, a brow raised. "There is something."

"Then tell us," Clayton urged.

Danny shrugged and rested his hand on the butt of his gun. "It's just a feeling."

"What kind of feeling?" Brice pressed.

"The kind that says there are others trying to lead me in a direction that I know is wrong."

Caleb crossed his arms over his chest. "Which direction would that be?"

"That it was some kids on a thrill ride and it was all just an accident," Danny said. "That those kids ran off for fear of being caught."

Clayton snorted as he shook his head. "Driving a dump truck isn't like stealing a car."

"Exactly," Danny replied.

Naomi bit her lip in nervousness. She glanced at Brice before she said, "Sheriff Oldman, there might be some other facts that could be useful to this case."

"Like?" he asked.

Abby asked her, "You think the two are connected?"

"I asked Naomi that same question on our way here," Brice said. "I thought she was reaching, but now, I'm not so sure."

Caleb hooked his thumb at her and Brice. "I agree with them. It's connected."

"What the hell are y'all talking about?" Danny asked in frustration.

Clayton said, "Remember I told you that Brice sent Naomi to the house?"

"Right," Danny replied. "And that Whitney would be coming later."

Naomi's gut clenched in fear at what she was about to say. "What Clayton hasn't had a chance to fill you in about yet, is that last night, Whitney told me there's a group of men who have been assaulting a handful of girls. Including her."

Danny's brows snapped together. "Assaulting?"

"Yes," Naomi answered. "It's been going on for years. Whitney said it began slowly, and they put her in a position where she felt dominated, a position where she had no other choice."

"That's not true. She could have come to the police," Danny stated.

Abby patiently said, "One girl already did that. Jamie Adcock."

Danny rubbed his chin as he thought back. "I remember that name. I wasn't the sheriff at the time, and I didn't get the case."

"Well, she was run off," Naomi said. "It took some doing, but Whitney confessed to me that she had repeatedly been sexually assaulted over the years."

The sheriff squeezed his eyes closed for a heartbeat. "Who are the men responsible?"

"She wouldn't tell me. All she said was that they were men in positions of power. And she told me this morning that she planned to finish out her rodeo queen reign and out the entire group in just a few weeks. She said she had proof," Naomi replied.

Brice jerked his head to her. "Where is the proof?"

"She didn't tell me," Naomi said.

Danny's lips twisted. "Damn. Just when I thought things couldn't get any messier. There are a lot of coincidences here. But nothing that ties things together."

"But certainly a lot that doesn't rule the theory out," Brice stated.

"True."

"What about the pictures?" Abby asked Naomi. "Can you develop more?"

Naomi was nodding when the men started to speak at once, each of them stating why they thought it was a bad idea.

"I can do it," Naomi told them.

Danny rapidly shook his head. "It's a bad idea. Look at what they've done already. No doubt they'll be watching you."

"I agree with him," Caleb said. "I have two friends in the hospital, and both you and Brice already had run-ins with these people. I'd rather not push it."

Clayton said, "There has to be another way."

It was Brice who turned to face her. "I know you want to help, and I think you should print more pictures. We just need to keep this group from knowing what we're doing."

Naomi gave a short bark of laughter. "How do you expect to do that?"

"I'd be curious about that, too," Danny said.

Brice looked at each of them before his gaze landed on Naomi. "We talked about making everyone think that you left town."

"Yeah," Naomi said. "I remember. How am I going to

do that now with Whitney in the hospital? She's my friend."

"Even more reason to leave," Abby stated.

Naomi frowned, not sure she understood. She pursed her lips, but before she could pose a question, Brice continued.

"I have some friends at the community college," he said. "We get one of them to get the film. The rest of us will gather everything you need for the pictures. Then you develop them."

Caleb's look was hopeful as he asked her, "Can you do that?"

"I mean, yeah, I can put together a makeshift darkroom," she replied.

"Are y'all sure about this?" Danny asked.

Brice shrugged a shoulder. "Someone might recognize something. I want to put the photos everywhere."

"Make them feel cornered," Clayton said.

Naomi pulled her hand from Brice's and shook her head as she took a step back. "No. I don't want to do this. If they can't come after me, they'll go to the next best thing—all of you. What about Wynter and Brody? I won't put anyone else in danger."

"Clayton and I have already decided to keep the kids home for a few days," Abby said.

Clayton gave a nod. "Shane went to get them when we came here. Everyone is home and safe."

Naomi turned and looked at the hospital doors. "I was the one who kept pushing Whitney to give me information. If only I'd left well enough alone, neither Whitney nor Cooper would be in the hospital, and Ms. Biermann would still be alive."

"This isn't your fault," Brice said.

She faced the group. "But it is. I should've let them have my camera. I shouldn't have developed the film. I shouldn't have kept pushing Whitney."

"And that asshole shouldn't have been stalking Whitney," Brice stated.

Caleb snorted loudly. "Exactly. Those bastards are the ones I lay the blame on. They began all of this."

"I want to know who these guys are so we can stop them," Danny said.

Abby shifted uncomfortably in the wheelchair. "We need to talk to Jamie Adcock."

"I could find her, but if these men are as powerful as we think, then they'll more than likely have someone in my department," Danny said.

Everyone looked at Naomi then. She sighed and said, "Fine, but I have a few conditions."

"Name them," Brice said.

Her gaze landed on Abby before moving to Clayton. "You two have been amazing, but I won't continue putting either of you or your children in danger."

Caleb grinned and elbowed Brice. "Notice she left us out."

"Which means," Naomi continued after flashing a smile at Caleb, "I won't return to the East Ranch."

Brice's smile widened. "Of course, not. They'd look there. No, I have somewhere else for you to go. Somewhere no one will think to look."

Chapter 21

"Are you sure about this?" Caleb asked.

Brice pulled his eyes away from Naomi, who was on the phone with her mother and pacing the sidewalk in front of the hospital, to look at his brother. "Without a doubt."

"So much could go wrong."

"It already has," Brice reminded him.

Caleb ran a hand down his face. "Yeah, but someone should be there to watch your back."

"The more people at the house, the more it will draw attention."

"I don't trust these jackasses to keep their distance. Cooper is lying in a hospital bed with a concussion," Caleb said and pointed to the building. "I won't have you in there next."

Brice drew in a breath. "And I won't have it be you. Or Abby or Clayton or the kids or anyone else. This stops now, and the only way to do that is for these guys to think we've given up."

Caleb shook his head and walked a few steps away before he pivoted and returned. "What about the rodeo?"

"We pull out." Brice lifted his hand to look at it. He'd chosen not to put the bandage back on that morning, and the injury was throbbing. "We can blame my hand or the fact that our friend was in a serious wreck. I don't give a shit what excuse we give, but I can't be there now. I'd likely slam my fist into anyone I even thought might be responsible for this."

"Holy shit," Caleb muttered. "You're right. Returning would be a bad idea. I'll tell Darnell." He hesitated and looked at Brice. "What about the proof Whitney has?"

Brice shrugged helplessly. "She didn't tell Naomi where or what it was, and we can't intrude on her parents about it."

"I guess we can't break into their house and look for it?"

"No thanks. I've been arrested once. I don't need a repeat."

When his brother took out his cell phone to make the call, Brice turned and looked at where Abby, Clayton, and Danny stood, talking. Brice couldn't help but think of the first time he'd met Danny twelve years earlier.

"Everything all right?" Naomi asked as she walked up.

Brice nodded, shooting her a half-grin. "Just thinking."

"Don't worry about Abby. Clayton will make sure she's taken care of."

"Oh, I'm not at all worried about my sister," Brice said with a small laugh. "Clayton would willingly tear anyone limb from limb if they even thought about harming his family. Trust me, I know."

Naomi grinned as she raised a brow. "There's a story there."

"Oh, yeah. Clayton was a Navy SEAL. The man can kick some serious ass."

"And you?" she asked.

Brice lifted one shoulder in a shrug. "You can't spend years with a SEAL and not join the military. After college, of course."

"Of course," she replied with a grin.

"I went into the Marines, and Caleb the Army."

Naomi shoved her hair out of her face. "Is there anything you can't do?"

He grinned. "Not if I set my mind to something."

They stared at each other in silence for a heartbeat.

"Are you sure you're good with my plan?" he asked, needing to be certain she was a hundred percent on board.

She gave him a single nod. "Without a doubt. I like how we're taking me out of the equation so I don't have to worry about my mom or your family getting hurt."

"We have to go to extremes to make this work."

Naomi's lips curved into a grin. "I'll do whatever is needed to take these men down. In this day and age, I can't believe this type of stuff continues to happen."

"Some men like control. Others like to make women feel inferior and dominate. It makes sense that Whitney said each of them is in a position of power. Did she mean the rodeo or elsewhere?"

"I didn't think to clarify," Naomi said, grimacing. "I should have."

He waved away her words. "There was a lot going on last night, and what she told us was a lot to take in."

She rubbed her hands together. "When does your plan go into action?"

"As soon as you're ready."

"I was afraid you were going to say that." Her eyes slid

to the hospital. "I don't want to leave without seeing Whitney, but that could be hours or even days. That's time we could spend getting rid of the men who did this to her. But I keep thinking that a friend wouldn't leave another in such a situation."

Brice caught her gaze. "Who cares what anyone else thinks? We know the truth. And you can tell Whitney all about it when she wakes, and you're able to see her."

"You're right. I wonder if I should talk to her parents."

"We can have Jace do that."

Naomi bit her lower lip as she thought for a minute. "My mom thinks we should leave now and get going on this. I need to warn Abby and Clayton that she might take it upon herself to call them."

"She's welcome to visit the ranch, as well."

"And no one can know where we are?" she asked, a small frown puckering her brow.

He shook his head. "My family knows so they'll be able to find us if there's an emergency, but I don't want Danny or your mom to know."

"Fewer people who know, the less likely those men will figure out our plan. I understand."

Brice bit back a grin as she rocked back on her heels. That and biting her lip were quirks she probably didn't even realize she did, but he found them endearing.

She blew out a breath. "And you don't think we need to make it look like I'm going to the airport?"

"I doubt the group is that sophisticated. Besides, the airport is two hours away," he added.

"I just want to make sure all the bases are covered. Obviously, I watch too many movies," she said with a laugh.

Caleb joined them and gave Brice a nod. "Someone

from the rodeo will be here shortly to check on both Cooper and Whitney."

"We should be gone by then," Brice said.

Naomi nodded. "That's probably wise."

Brice thought about his house and winced. The papers had just been signed last week, and while he had moved a few things in, there was nothing stocked in the kitchen. "I'm going to need to make a few stops."

"Not a good idea," Caleb said. "Besides, you must not have seen the look Abby and Clayton shared when you mentioned taking Naomi to your place. They know there's not much there. Abby is already making a mental note of things to send over."

Naomi swung her head to Brice. "I agree with him. If I'm disappearing, then I can't be seen anywhere."

"Then we go whenever you're ready." Brice looked at Caleb. "Keep me posted on Cooper."

Caleb nodded once. "None of us will be staying long. I'll try to get Jace out so I can fill him in. He'll let us know about Cooper."

"And Whitney," Naomi added.

"And Whitney," Caleb said with a smile.

Brice pulled out his keys. "See if Jace can let Whitney's parents know that Naomi is . . ." He looked at her, trying to find the right words.

Naomi turned to Caleb and said, "Let them know I'm doing what I need to for Whitney. They'll understand that I didn't abandon her."

"I will pass that along," Caleb said. "Y'all get moving."

Brice held up a finger to tell them to wait. He turned his head toward his sister and found Clayton looking his way. A moment later, Danny's eyes landed on Brice for a long moment before he tipped his head forward and walked away.

Clayton wheeled Abby over. "You leaving?" Clayton asked.

"It's time," Naomi said.

Abby linked her hands over her stomach. "Both of you be careful. And stay in touch. We're here if you need us."

"Thanks." Brice leaned down and kissed his sister on the cheek. He pulled back and met her blue gaze. "If you go into labor, someone better call me."

"Don't worry," Caleb said. "We will."

Brice straightened, and Clayton pulled him into an embrace. Brice pounded his brother-in-law's back before they separated. "I've got this."

"I've no doubt," Clayton said. He then touched the brim of his hat, acknowledging Naomi, and wheeled Abby to his truck.

Caleb sighed loudly. "I really think I should be with you, but I'll be able to relay things to both of you. Just don't be stupid," he said and slapped Brice on the back as he walked into the hospital.

Brice then swung his head to Naomi. She offered a soft smile, and together, they made their way to his truck.

Larry strode into Raymond's office and took one of the chairs before the desk while his friend talked on the phone. It was a short while later that Raymond finally finished the call and hung up.

He laid his hands on his desk and looked at Larry. "Whitney survived."

"Maybe. Maybe not."

Raymond sat back in his chair and ran a hand over his

slicked-back, dark hair. "You aren't seriously considering what I think you mean, are you?"

"She's banged up pretty bad," Larry said with a shrug. "It won't raise eyebrows if she succumbs to her injuries."

Raymond looked out the window for a long time. "At least Sharon is out of the way. If I don't agree with your plan, it'll still be some time before Whitney is cognizant enough to talk to anyone."

"Do you want to take that chance?" Larry asked. "Our best course is to make sure Whitney can't say anything to anyone. Ever."

Raymond slid his faded blue eyes to him. "Do you really think Whitney would be brave enough to name us? Hell, she probably won't even realize we were responsible for this."

"Chances," Larry stated. "You said we had to take chances in life. By not ridding ourselves of Whitney, we'll be setting ourselves up to be taken down."

Raymond leaned back so his chair tilted backward. "Using my words against me now, huh?"

"One of the nurses in the ER owes us a favor. It'll be simple. And the smart thing to do."

"You're that worried about one little bitch?"

"She knows each one of us, Raymond. You said yourself last night that you wouldn't let anyone tear down what we created. As long as she lives, she'll be able to do just that."

He snorted, grinning. "Jamie Adcock or any of the other girls we're connected with could do the same. They haven't."

"Whitney is different now. You saw how she acted once Naomi returned. It's Naomi who could get Whitney to spill everything."

Raymond sat up and leaned his arms on his desk once more. "Then Naomi needs to be removed."

"So soon after the wreck? That might look suspicious."

Raymond raised a thick brow. "Call in one of the favors you collect for us."

"And Whitney?"

"Get rid of her, as well."

Larry grinned as he pushed to his feet. "I'll set everything up today."

"One more thing."

He sat back down and waited.

Raymond drummed his fingers on the desk. "Ethan has been calling the sheriff all morning, and when he couldn't get the answers he wanted, Ethan called the sheriff's station."

"You're concerned about the mayor?"

Raymond scratched his chin. "I think he's someone we need to keep an eye on. He'll probably settle once Naomi and Whitney are taken care of, but if he doesn't calm the fuck down, he'll make people start to take notice."

"Especially if the sheriff talks to the Easts. Everyone knows they're friends," Larry added. "I'll keep an eye on Ethan. I also know who to turn Curtis on now that Whitney is in the hospital. He'll be so obsessed with the new girl that he won't even realize it when Whitney dies."

Raymond smiled as he slowly leaned back. "Perfect planning as always."

"It's what I do."

Chapter 22

They were going to triumph. Naomi kept repeating that to herself as Brice drove them. She didn't know where they were going, but she trusted him.

He had shown what extremes he would go to for her. She glanced at him, and he met her gaze, a small smile pulling at his lips. Damn, he was gorgeous. She shouldn't be thinking about that, her mind should be on the men who tried to kill Whitney, but she couldn't help herself.

Brice Harper was as steady as a rock and utterly unruffled by the storm swirling around them. His calm, determined demeanor kept her from doing something irrational like returning to the rodeo and learning who those in power were.

At least by doing things Brice's way, they might actually succeed.

It wasn't that Naomi was a hothead. Normally, she was easygoing and let things slide off her back. But not when it came to Whitney or her family. Now, Brice and his friends and family had widened her circle of those she'd lose her shit over.

"You never said where your place was."

Brice put on his blinker and moved over into a turning lane, slowing to let a car pass before he turned onto a narrow road. "You didn't ask."

"I guess I didn't. I thought you lived at the ranch."

"I bought a place."

Her eyes widened. "That's great."

He looked at her, grinning. "You're wondering why I still live at the ranch."

"Well . . . yeah," she admitted.

"I just signed the papers last week. I've not had much time to do anything. And there are some things that I wanted to fix before I officially moved in."

She could understand that. "I have to say, with as close as you are to your family, I'm surprised you're moving."

"It wasn't an easy decision. Clayton saved my ass twelve years ago."

"What?" she asked, completely intrigued. "Are you serious or using a metaphor?"

His chest expanded as he drew in a breath. "Being serious. You see, my mother ran off when I was only ten. Abby had just graduated, and our mom left paperwork on the table signing over all rights to me and Caleb to Abby."

"Oh, God," Naomi murmured.

Brice lifted one shoulder in a half-shrug. "Abby could have turned us over to the state, but she didn't. She got a job and did what she could to keep us afloat each month. She saved up whatever she could and attended a night class at the university every semester, but I knew it would take her years before she got a degree. She was working well over forty hours a week, and still, we barely had enough money. I'm not sure how we survived. Caleb wore my hand-me-downs, and most of my clothes came from the Salvation Army. Same with Abby's. We saved the heater for those nights that dropped below freezing. Other times, we burrowed under blankets."

"But y'all were close, weren't you?"

"Yes."

His smile and that one simple word said so much about his formative years. "It sounds like a hard life."

"It was, but Abby made things fun. Caleb and I helped out around the house. We each learned to cook, and we'd try to have dinner finished by the time she got home. Not that we always made things easy. I let my grades fall, so I was getting in trouble at school. And, damn, Abby ripped me a new one for that. It didn't take long to straighten my ass up."

Naomi barely noticed the houses they passed. "So how did you meet Clayton?"

"When I was sixteen, I went to one of the feed stores to find a job after school. I met a man that said he'd hire me at his ranch. I'd always loved the idea of being a cowboy, so I jumped at the chance. It wasn't until later that I learned he was involved in cattle rustling. But when he told me how much my cut would be if I helped, I couldn't pass it up." He glanced at her. "The amount would have allowed us to buy the groceries we wanted and turn on the heat in the winter and run the AC all day long in the summer."

She studied Brice's profile and wondered if she would have taken the man's offer in his place. No doubt, she would have.

"They went after the Easts' cattle, and I got caught," Brice said. "It was Danny who arrested me. He and Abby went to school together, so he was the one who called her. From what Abby told me, her first meeting with Clayton didn't go well."

Naomi frowned, trying to follow the story while it played out in her head as he spoke. "But you told the police who was really behind it, right?"

He shook his head. "They said they'd hurt Abby and Caleb, and I couldn't take that chance. Somehow, Clayton figured it out. He offered me the chance to work off what I owed on the ranch."

"Was it a lot?" she asked.

"Well over two hundred thousand."

Her eyes widened. "Wow."

"Abby about died when she heard the amount. Yet I recognized the chance Clayton offered, and I really didn't want to go to jail. So I started working at the East Ranch. Almost immediately, I realized that Clayton was attempting to gain my trust so that I'd tell him who was responsible."

She gawked at him. "Don't stop there. Tell me the rest."

He shrugged while grinning. "Caleb wanted to work at the ranch, too. And Ben and Justine, Clayton's parents, took all three of us under their wing. It was obvious to everyone that Clayton and Abby had something between them. He kept coming up with reasons for her to be there, and she didn't even try to fight him. In the end, they fell in love."

"And the stolen cattle?" she pressed.

"Oh, Clayton used his SEAL skills and tracked them down. He allowed me to go with him, Ben, Shane, some other ranch hands, and Danny and a few other policemen." He paused. "You see movies with gunfire and people dying, but it's completely different in real life."

She formed an *O* with her lips and blew out a breath. "That's some story."

"Yep. We've been at the ranch ever since. Everything I learned, Clayton taught me. He was the one who encouraged me to buy my own place."

"Will you still work at the East Ranch?"

"Always."

The truck slowed, and Brice turned onto a driveway. Naomi saw the wooden entrance, which was brand new, along with the black metal sign that read *Rockin' H Ranch*.

That barely registered before they were driving along the fence line with rolling pastures beyond. She spotted a couple of barns in need of repair, and an old farmhouse that looked quaint and full of charm.

As soon as he stopped, she unbuckled her seatbelt and hopped out of the truck to take it all in. She noted that some of the fences needed fixing, and a couple of the gates were broken. Naomi fought not to go into the barns and inspect them.

"What do you think?" Brice asked as he came to stand beside her.

"I think it's amazing. You can feel the history here."

He grinned as he looked at his land with pride. "I thought the same thing the first time I saw it. A woman inherited it from her grandparents, but she wasn't interested in living here. She did do some remodeling in the house to help it sell."

Naomi turned and really looked at the house. Her mouth fell open as she took in the rustic exterior with the stone and brick façade and the wooden shutters. "She must have spent a fortune."

"She wanted it to sell quickly. Actually, she didn't do much to the outside," he told her.

Her head swung to him in surprise. "This is original?"

"It is."

She walked up the front steps and ran her hands over the wooden post supporting the roof of the porch. At the bottom of each of the six columns was rock that rose two feet high. "People pay a lot of money for this look. It's stunning."

"Come inside," he said and unlocked the door.

She walked through the extra-wide, arched door and smiled at the acid-stained concrete floors. Off to her left was a family room with a fireplace. To her right was what looked like a formal living room.

Naomi wandered through the space to find a new leather sofa and loveseat, as well as a TV hanging on the wall. Her exploration took her into the kitchen, and she smiled. It was a dream room.

Everything was white, from the cabinets, the quartz countertop, to the walls and ceiling. Huge wooden beams were set in large wooden squares on the ceiling, and there were other wooden accents as well from the stools at the large rectangular island in the middle of the kitchen to a set of shelves. The appliances were stainless steel.

She walked to the farmhouse sink and stared out the four massive windows overlooking the back of the property. If this were her house, she'd spend half her time in the kitchen. It was large enough to be a gathering place, and it had everything she could ever want.

When she turned, Brice was watching her, leaning a shoulder against the arched doorway leading from the family room. They stared at each other for a long moment. The silence was easy, but the feelings rising up within her made her stomach flutter.

She walked through the other doorway into a dining

room. There was no table, but she imagined something rustic and modern to match the rest of the house.

There was a good-sized laundry room and a mudroom that led to the back door. The last room she came to was empty, and there was no indication of what it had been.

She felt Brice come up behind her. Without turning around, she asked, "What will this room be?"

"What do you think it should be?"

"Your office." She shifted to look at him. "It looks out over the pastures and barn, just as Clayton's does. This is where you should do your work."

He didn't look away from her once. "That was my thought, as well."

Once more, they stared at each other. He brushed past her, their fingers grazing. Her heart skipped a beat as he walked out of the room without a word.

Naomi followed him to the set of wooden stairs that went straight up. He motioned for her ascend, and she could feel his eyes on her as he climbed up behind her.

At the landing, she looked right and left before she decided to head to the left. There were three bedrooms, not large but decent-sized, and one shared bath.

When she walked back to the stairs, Brice was waiting for her. This time, he trailed behind her into the master bedroom. The wood floors continued into the room and looked amazing with the wall of stone that accented the king-size, black metal bed.

There was a fireplace on the opposite wall. She glanced out the floor-to-ceiling windows that looked out over the land. Then she walked into the bathroom, which had obviously been remodeled. The white theme from the kitchen continued in the upstairs space with accents of black. There was a clawfoot tub, probably an original, set beneath a window, and a new corner shower in matching white tile.

She took her time looking at the double sinks and the two doors that led to a massive closet that ran the entire length of the room.

When she returned to the bedroom, Brice was looking out one of the windows. It was her turn to stare at him. While she wouldn't have thought he would fit in a house like this, seeing him inside it changed her mind.

He'd grown up dirt-poor and then lived in luxury for years. Now, he'd settled for a place in between.

Suddenly, his head swiveled to her. She walked to him as he turned to face her. So many times she'd thought of them kissing. Now that they were alone, would she finally learn the feel of his lips?

His hand reached out and rested on her hip before slowly moving to her back. He pulled her forward as he stepped closer. She couldn't catch her breath. Everything ceased to exist as she sank into his pale blue eyes.

They were breaths apart. Her hands were on his chest, desire swirling through her in a dizzying state.

Then his gaze dropped to her mouth. His head lowered slowly. Naomi leaned into him as she lifted her face, her eyes closing.

Her heart skipped a beat at the feeling of his lips on hers. He let out a moan and wrapped both arms around her as his tongue slipped into her mouth.

Naomi wound her arms around his neck as she was swept away on a tide of passion so swift and unrelenting that it had to be destiny.

Chapter 23

This was what he'd needed.

She was what he'd been craving.

Brice deepened the kiss, letting the taste of Naomi fill every fiber of him. His body burned for her, and she fanned those flames by returning his kisses with such fervor that his knees went weak.

She shoved his hat from his head to slide her fingers through his hair. And it drove him wild.

The kiss turned hungry as desire surged between them. He wound his hand in her hair and tugged her head back so he could kiss along her jaw and down her neck.

Her fingers dug into his arms as she released a soft cry. The sound was filled with hedonism and contentment. And he needed to hear more of it.

He lifted his head to look at Naomi. Her lashes fluttered as her lids opened, and he stared down into her chestnut-colored eyes that sparkled with desire. Her lips were swollen and wet from their kisses.

Brice couldn't remember ever wanting something as

much as he yearned for Naomi. An ache had begun deep within him when he first saw her, and the more time they spent together, the more that feeling grew until he realized she was the only one who could relieve it.

"Don't stop," she whispered, her voice thick with need.

Then she took a step back from him. Reluctantly, he loosened his hold on her hair as she smiled wantonly and shed her olive jacket. She turned and started toward the bathroom as she tugged her white tee shirt over her head and tossed it aside.

Brice palmed his hard cock and shifted it in his jeans. His mouth went dry when she removed her nude-colored bra and looked over her shoulder at him with a sexy grin. Then she disappeared into the bathroom.

A moment later, he heard the water running. His fingers fumbled with the buttons of his shirt, and finally, he gave up and yanked it over his head.

His strides ate up the distance to the doorway of the bathroom where he saw her bare leg before she stepped beneath the spray of the shower. He stared at the glass wall of the enclosure at her silhouette distorted by the water droplets and steam.

He leaned a shoulder on the doorway and removed his boots before unbuckling his belt and unbuttoning his jeans. His gaze landed on what remained of Naomi's clothes. He pushed down his pants and let them drop beside hers.

Brice made his way to the shower. He opened the door, and steam rolled out to surround him. His heart pounded, his blood drummed in his ears, and all because of Naomi.

His gaze found her beneath the spray. She faced him, her back arched and her head tilted as she ran her hands over her wet hair. He drank in the sight of her small breasts and hard, pink nipples dripping with water.

He couldn't wait to get his hands on her body and skim them along the indent of her waist and the curve of her hips down to her shapely legs. But what he wanted more than anything was to sink into her and join their bodies.

Her head lifted as she met his gaze.

The entire day had been surreal, but never more than that moment with Brice. Naomi raised her hand and placed it on his chest. She felt the erratic rhythm of his heart beneath her palm, and it made her own skip a beat.

Brice's hard body had been honed from working on the ranch and his stint in the Marines. He had wide shoulders thickened with sinew and a chest that made her mouth water. His washboard stomach made him look as if he'd come straight off a magazine cover.

Her eyes lowered to his thick arousal that jutted between them. The sight of it made her stomach flutter in excitement and expectation. She wanted him inside her, needed it.

When she looked back into his stunning blue eyes, her breath left her in a rush at the blatant hunger she saw there. It was the only warning she got before he yanked her against him and shifted them so he had her pressed against the cool tile as he savagely kissed her.

She clung to him, her blood heating in her veins while desire pooled low in her belly. His hard cock pressed into her stomach, and she moaned into his mouth when he rocked against her.

His large hands grabbed her bottom and lifted her. Naomi immediately parted her legs and wrapped them around his waist. She locked her ankles together and sank her fingers into his thick, dark locks.

He ended the kiss. She opened her eyes to find him staring at her. Water sluiced down his back and over his shoulders to run down his front. She didn't think she'd ever seen anything as sexy as the man before her. Part of her wished she had her camera so she could capture this moment forever. She might not have her equipment, but the image would be imprinted in her mind for eternity.

His voice was hoarse with desire when he said, "I need you."

Her lips parted when his head lowered. When his mouth wrapped around her turgid nipple, her eyelids fell shut, a moan falling from her lips.

She was helpless against the tide of ecstasy that engulfed her, and desperately rocked her hips against him. It wasn't long before her moans turned to cries as he suckled and teased her nipples. Her eyes flew open when she felt the head of his arousal at her core.

He lifted his head and trapped her gaze as he slowly lowered her onto his hard rod. She used her legs to pull him closer as her body stretched to accommodate him.

Once he was fully inside her, he drew in a ragged breath, a muscle in his jaw jumping as if it were everything he could do not to move.

But she wanted him to move. She *needed* him to, longed to feel his length deep within her.

She tried to shift her hips, but his hands held her immobile. Then he turned her beneath the spray of the water so that it hit her already sensitive nipples. Once more, she attempted to move, to no avail.

"Please," she begged.

His lips curved seductively. "What do you need?"

"You," she whispered and grasped his face. "I need you."

His blue eyes blazed with satisfaction as she leaned forward and kissed him ravenously. In answer, he lifted her until only the tip of his cock remained before thrusting hard.

Naomi tore her mouth from his and cried out at the feel of him. He shifted and had her back against the tile once more as he started to rock his hips, slowly building his rhythm until he was driving hard inside her.

Her orgasm built quickly, and before she knew it, the climax ripped through her with such intensity that she went weak for a moment. When she came to, Brice had stopped thrusting. He stood breathing heavily as he held her.

She opened her eyes and felt his arousal deep within her. He wasn't finished with her, not by a long shot. A thrill went through her.

This magnificent, amazing man had a way of making her feel beautiful, invincible, and shamelessly, wickedly wanton.

She turned off the water, and he carried her out of the shower to his bed, both of them dripping wet. Neither of them caring. The pleasure was too intense, the desire too powerful for them to stop and dry themselves off.

Naomi's heart thumped once again when Brice put one knee on the bed and laid her down. He pulled her legs from around his waist and grabbed her ankles before he thrust hard and deep.

She gripped the comforter with her fingers as pleasure easily and quickly built once more. Her gaze fastened on his hard body with beads of water rolling down his chest and over his stomach. His blue eyes looked from her face to their joined bodies.

Her breath hitched as she thought about him sliding into her, of him filling her again and again. Everything about him turned her on.

Suddenly, he released her ankles and leaned over her. He searched her face before caressing his fingers down her cheek. She had seen so many sides of Brice—determination, honor, friendship, family love, and strength. Today, she'd gotten a glimpse of his hungry, ravenous desire.

And now she was witnessing his gentle side.

Her stomach fluttered at the mix of passion and affection. No one had ever looked at her like that before, and it did crazy, wonderful things to her.

There were no words spoken between them. He kissed her, slowly, but it was filled with such need and yearning that it curled her toes.

And all the while, he moved his hips, his thick length sliding in and out of her. She slid her hands from his waist, up and around his back as the kiss ended and he started to pound into her, hard and fast.

Naomi clung to him, overwhelmed by the utter bliss she felt at being in his arms, of their bodies coming together. Time lost all meaning. Nothing mattered but the two of them.

He rose up on his hands and drove inside her hard and deep once more before he hastily pulled out of her. She held him as his body jerked from his orgasm and his warm seed spread over her belly.

After a moment, he rose up on his elbow and kissed the tip of her nose before he said, "I'll be right back."

She looked at the ceiling, reliving the last hour in her mind. Brice returned with a warm, wet washcloth that he used to clean her stomach.

Naomi curled onto her side, her head propped on her

hand as she inwardly laughed at herself while he disappeared into the bathroom again.

When he returned, he raised a brow. "What's that odd look for?"

"I'm normally very cautious about the men I sleep with."

His lips twisted as he glanced away while sitting beside her. "Okay."

"You don't understand," she said and sat up. "I like to have a talk where we discuss birth control and everything. I wasn't thinking about any of that with you. I'm glad you had the wherewithal to pull out."

He gave her a sheepish look. "I nearly didn't."

She fell back laughing. "Wow."

He stood and pulled the covers back and crawled beneath them before lifting them and raising a brow. As if she were going to turn down his offer.

Naomi quickly got beneath them, a smile on her lips when he pulled her against his chest. She rested her head on him while he put one arm around her and the other behind his head.

She wasn't the type of person to randomly sleep with someone. When she decided to have sex with a guy, it was because they were in a steady relationship. She and Brice hadn't discussed anything like that.

And maybe that was all right.

Maybe that's how it was supposed to be.

"So," he said. "It might be after the fact, but would it make you feel better to have that talk with me?"

She grinned and shook her head. "I think I like this better."

"Me, too."

"I'm not used to taking such risks," she explained. "I

play everything really, really safe. I think it started the night Suellen was killed."

His hand rubbed slowly up and down her back. "There's nothing wrong with playing things safe."

"Yeah, but I think by doing it, I took all the fun out of life. Especially my relationships. I was engaged for a bit, but I called it off two years ago for no reason other than both of us were playing it too safe. He didn't love me, and I didn't love him."

He rolled her onto her back and loomed over her with his blue eyes alight with something she couldn't quite name. "You're not playing things safe now."

"I like it."

"Things could go sideways."

She smoothed back a damp lock of his hair. "I know. It excites me."

"Me, too."

Chapter 24

The words were out of Brice's mouth before he realized it. But they were the truth.

Naomi excited him, yes, but she also caused him to feel so very much more. The need to protect her had only grown over the days they'd known each other, and he knew without a doubt that he had feelings for her.

Feelings he'd never experienced with anyone else.

He couldn't believe that she had almost married someone else. The thought that he might never have met her made him angry and upset all at once despite the fact that she was in his arms now.

"How about you?" she asked.

He blinked. Then he frowned at her. "What?"

"Have you ever been engaged?"

He shook his head and wrapped a strand of her damp hair around his finger. "No, but I did have a girlfriend for three years. She kept pushing to get married."

"Why didn't you?" Naomi's nose wrinkled. "I'm sorry. It's probably none of my business."

"I couldn't see myself spending the rest of my life with her," he answered.

Naomi's eyes widened. "Oh."

"Jill liked the name recognition of the Easts. She wanted me to change my name to Brice East."

"But you're a Harper."

"That's what I kept telling her. It didn't take me long to realize it wasn't me she wanted. She wanted the name and money I was associated with."

"You stayed with her a long time, though. Why?"

He sighed as he rolled onto his back. "I don't know."

Naomi rolled onto her side and came up on her elbow. "You don't have to tell me anything else. It's private. I understand."

"You told me about your fiancé," he said, cutting his eyes to her.

She shrugged, her lips twisting. "I didn't tell you specifics, like how he was boring as hell, and I went to extremes so that we wouldn't have sex because I didn't like it. I didn't tell you how I'd start arguments just to see if I could get him to some kind of emotion other than indifference. We lacked passion."

"Remember when I told you my mother left?"

"Yeah."

He grabbed a pillow and shoved it under his head. "It did a serious number on all of us. Jill used to tell me that I couldn't commit. It wasn't that. I . . ." He swallowed and glanced at Naomi. "I have a fear."

"Of abandonment," she said. "Anyone would in your shoes."

"I didn't even realize I had that issue until Caleb said something in passing. I blew him off. Then Clayton and I were talking about what I needed to do with Jill, and he said the same thing."

Naomi settled on his chest again. "Is that why you called things off with her? Did you think she'd leave you?"

"It's why I never confronted her on things. It's why I stayed with her so long. I liked having someone, and I'm embarrassed to say that it took me quite some time before I came to understand that Jill wasn't for me."

Naomi placed a kiss on his chest. "Abby seems to have gotten over her abandonment issues."

"Clayton was patient with her. Ben and Justine took us all in like we'd always been family. I think it helped Abby, and I know Caleb and I enjoyed it. I don't remember my father, and I barely have any memories of my mom. All I ever really knew was Abby. Then we had Ben and Justine, who became our grandparents. It had nothing to do with their money, and everything to do with the love they gave us."

Naomi took in a deep breath and released it. "I think unless anyone has been in your shoes, they take their families for granted. I know I did. I figured my parents would always be around until I was much older. My uncle's death was the first time I attended a funeral."

"That must have been difficult."

"Very. Still, I went on thinking things would remain the same. Except they didn't. Dad's heart attack only a year later took us completely unawares. My mom was devastated. By that time, I'd been to my uncle's and Suellen's funerals. I thought I was prepared. But it's different when it's a parent."

He held her tighter. She didn't cry, but he heard the sadness in her voice. "You still moved away."

"That was because of Mom," Naomi said and gave a little laugh. "She said I needed to get out and see the world before I decided if this was where I wanted to live. She came to visit me instead of me coming here most times. It was the strangest thing. Most of my friends in DC were always going home during the holidays, but I was usually preparing for Mom's arrival."

Brice grinned. "Are you glad you left?"

"It allowed me to see and experience things I would've missed. Mom was right. It was something I needed. And when I remained in DC, she wasn't at all surprised."

"Surely she misses you."

Naomi shifted her head to look at him. "Just as much as I miss her. We're all we have now."

"So you'll never move back?" He wasn't sure why he'd asked that. Perhaps it was because he liked the way she looked standing in his kitchen.

And he really liked her in his bed.

Naomi gave him a half-hearted shrug. "A week ago, I would've been able to answer that easily. Now, I don't know."

He might have believed he'd gotten past his abandonment issues, but the idea of Naomi leaving Texas made him rethink that. Each time he thought of her going back to DC, it made him feel as if someone were tightening a rope around his chest, constricting his breath.

"What are you going to do with this place?" she asked with a smile. "I think it suits you wonderfully."

"I want to raise horses. I might have an eye for picking out good ones, but Caleb is the one who is gifted at training them."

Naomi's head jerked up, her interest evident. "Really? That sounds amazing."

"It might have been helpful had I talked to Caleb before I bought this place, though."

"Oh," she said.

He sighed loudly. "If everything hadn't happened with you and Whitney, he'd probably still be ignoring me. He thinks I'm leaving him."

"Abandonment issues," Naomi said softly.

Brice blinked. Holy shit balls. How had he not seen that? Of course Caleb had gotten upset.

Naomi shook her head at him. "You didn't realize that, did you?"

"Not at all." He ran a hand down his face and looked at the ceiling. "Damn."

"What was your plan then?"

He liked that her body was next to his. He'd never had such a lazy afternoon, but he wanted to experience more just like this. Only with her.

"I wanted to surprise Caleb with the land. It's three hundred acres. I thought we could split it and go into business together. We've talked about it before. There's a perfect spot on the back part of the property if he wants to build a house. Or hell, anywhere."

Naomi rolled over to lie on her stomach, her chin resting on her hands as she looked into his eyes. "Did you tell him any of that?"

"I was waiting for him to calm down."

"You need to tell Caleb," she said. "Has he even been here?"

Brice shook his head. "Nope."

He heard her stomach growl. A laugh fell from his lips when she ducked her head. He was still grinning when she finally raised her gaze again.

"Hungry?" he asked.

She nodded. "It has been a while since breakfast."

That made him frown. He lifted his head to look at the clock on the bedside table to see that it was nearly three in the afternoon.

"I knew I should've stopped and gotten some food," he mumbled.

Naomi jumped up and started gathering her clothes. "You don't have even a box of crackers or anything?"

"I've got beer."

She laughed as she walked into the bathroom and returned with their clothes. "That's better than nothing," she said as she tossed him his jeans.

Brice wasn't too keen on them leaving the bedroom. Then again, they could make love in the kitchen—or anywhere else in the house. He rose and put on his boxers and jeans but left off his shirt.

They walked barefoot down the stairs to the kitchen, where he got out two beers. Naomi sat on the island, and he leaned back against the stove, watching her.

She raked her hands through her hair. "I bet I look a fright."

"You look beautiful."

Her smile was wide as she lifted the longneck bottle for a quick drink. "You must have it bad for me," she teased.

But he wasn't joking when he said, "I do."

Her smile dropped as she lowered the beer. She held his gaze, simply staring at him.

He pushed away from the stove and walked to stand between her legs. "Does that scare you?"

"No."

"The look on your face says otherwise."

She swallowed and shook her head. "I just didn't expect you to answer like that."

"I like you, Naomi. A lot."

After briefly biting her lip, she smiled and rested her arms on his shoulders. "Well, then I suppose I should tell you that I like you. A lot."

The morning might have gone to hell with the accident, but the afternoon was turning out pretty damn good. If only the men responsible for everything were already behind bars, but that wasn't the case. He couldn't lose his focus.

If he took his eyes off their goal, Naomi could get hurt. Brice would never forgive himself if that happened.

She brushed her fingers through his hair. "What are you thinking?"

"That I wish the outside world wouldn't intrude."

She glanced down. "But it will. It has."

"Yeah. Sorry about that."

"It's why we're here, right?"

He slid his hand around her neck and leaned in for a kiss. "Right."

There was a knock on the window that had both of them jerking their heads toward it. Brice rolled his eyes when he saw Caleb standing there with a wide grin.

"At least he'll have some food," Brice said.

Naomi laughed as he walked away to let his brother in. At the door, Caleb lifted a large basket filled with all sorts of food and snacks.

Caleb shoved it at him as he walked past. "There is another just as large in my truck. Abby went a little overboard."

"Hi," Naomi said as they entered the kitchen.

Caleb didn't hesitate to grab the beer Brice had left on the island. He ignored Brice and set the basket next to Naomi. Together, they began taking out the contents.

When Naomi found a can of nuts, she started eating them while looking at the rest.

Brice took the steaks, pork chops, chicken, and ground meat to the fridge along with the bell peppers, fresh carrots, broccoli, eggs, butter, and milk.

"Oh, a feast," Naomi said in excitement. She jumped off the island. "Where is the pantry?"

Brice directed her, and she helped put the food away while Caleb leaned against the counter, watching. Since Caleb wouldn't get the second basket, Brice walked out to get it, noting that it was mostly filled with wine, cookies, cupcakes, and other little snacks.

Naomi cheerfully took it from him and sorted through everything like it was Christmas morning. And all the while, Caleb didn't say a word.

Finally, Brice looked at him and said, "I'm glad you're here. Want a tour?"

"Can't," Caleb said as he finished off the beer and set it on the counter. "Gotta go."

Brice watched his brother leave and drive off.

Naomi walked up behind him and wrapped her arms around him. "He'll come around."

Brice hoped so.

Chapter 25

With her stomach full and her body still relaxed from making love to Brice, Naomi just wanted to curl up on the sofa and turn on the TV. But there was work to be done.

She gathered their plates and took them to the sink to wash. It would be so easy to get caught up in this beautiful house and Brice, but she was only there to help catch her friend's would-be killers.

Although, she wanted to think that she and Brice would've ended up together no matter what.

He came to stand beside her with another beer in his hand. "You don't have to do that."

"You cooked. It's the least I can do."

"It was an omelet," he said with a laugh. "I would've cooked you something else, but I was afraid if I took too long, you'd start gnawing on my arm."

She laughed and flicked water at him. "I do get a bit hangry when I've gone too long without eating."

"I'm thinking the steaks for tonight."

Her mouth watered just thinking about them. "Yes, please."

He grinned and lifted the bottle to his lips. She didn't think he had any idea how sexy he was standing there shirtless and barefoot. And he knew his way around a kitchen, which was nice.

She glanced at him again to find his gaze directed out the window. "What is it?" she asked.

"I was trying to think where would be a good place to set up your darkroom."

Right. She'd forgotten about that. And she'd just told herself not to get caught up in what was happening around her. She had to stay focused on the big picture. Then what did she go and do?

She wanted to roll her eyes. Instead, she rinsed off the plate and set it to dry. "It needs to be somewhere we can easily block out all light."

"How much equipment are you going to need?" he asked and turned his head to her.

Naomi went to the stove to grab the pan and then returned to the sink. "There's no way you'll be able to get everything, especially since we need to work fairly fast. That means we stick to the basics. I won't be able to play with the lighting on the pictures as I did before, but it didn't help enough anyway."

"I'll get whatever you need."

She cut her eyes to him and grinned because she knew that he was as good as his word. "I'll make a list. If I need more than that, we'll go from there."

"Okay."

After she'd finished rinsing the pan, she dried her hands and went to get her phone before she remembered once again that she didn't have one. Brice must have deduced what she was doing and handed her his.

"I'll send this over to Clayton and Caleb, and they can gather whatever you need," he said.

Naomi took the cell phone and quickly began jotting down the basics for the darkroom. Once she gave Brice the phone back, she said, "You realize if either Clayton or Caleb goes to a photography shop, anyone watching them will know the supplies are for me."

"I'll remind Clayton of that. They'll be careful," Brice promised as he sent off the text before calling his brother-in-law.

Naomi used that time to walk through the house, looking at each room as a possible space for the darkroom. With each area of the house fitted with new, large windows that let in tons of light, they were going to have to go to extremes to make a room pitch black.

Brice found her upstairs in one of the smallest rooms. "Will this work?"

"I think so," she said. "It's close to the bathroom for the water I'll need, and these windows are the smallest."

"Clayton says we should have everything sometime tomorrow before noon. He's sending several people out at different times, and out of the city, to gather the supplies. Caleb is loading some tables from the ranch into his truck. Do you want them now?"

She shrugged. "It would be a good way to bring him back. Maybe then you can tell him everything."

Brice hesitated, a frown forming.

"It was just a thought," she said with a shrug.

"A good one," he hurried to say. "It's just . . . I know my brother. He'd forgotten about me buying this place until I mentioned this place. Then he had to come bring the food."

She rubbed a hand along her arm. "I was an only child, so I don't really understand the sibling thing. I'll have to take your word for it."

He grinned and held out his hand. "How about a look outside."

"Yes," she happily agreed as she linked her fingers with his.

They returned to the master bedroom where she put on her boots, and he finished dressing. In no time, they were walking to the barn. It was as old as the house, which she found charming. While it might need repairs, it was in decent working order. At least from the outside.

Brice threw open the doors on either side of the barn to let in light before he flicked a switch. "The wiring needs to be replaced, and new lights fitted," he said looking upward.

She nodded and pulled open a door. The room had been used as a feed room. Across from it was the tack room that needed a good overhaul. Next, she went to each of the six stalls, noting the rotting boards and missing feed and water bins.

"It's workable here," she said.

He grinned while nodding. "I plan on building a new stable, something similar to what's on the East Ranch."

"Nice," she said, recalling the numerous stalls.

Brice leaned a hand on a bent stall door. "My realtor suggested I tear this one down, but I won't. I'll keep it because it belongs here, just like the house."

"I like that idea."

His blue eyes swung to her. She liked that he wasn't wearing his hat. The breeze ruffled his dark locks that were still in disarray from their shower and rolling around in bed.

"When will you start buying the horses?" she asked.

"I already have five at home. I mean, the ranch." He shook his head, his lips thinning. "The East Ranch."

She laughed, taking pity on him. "I knew what you meant."

"I could fail at this, you know. I could fall flat on my face."

"But you won't."

His brows snapped together. "How can you be so sure?"

"Because it's not you. Besides, Caleb will come around eventually, and with each of you bringing in your strengths, there is no way this place can fail."

"I hope you're right," he said with a sigh.

She walked to him and linked her arms around his waist. "I am."

He pulled her close for a long, lingering kiss. "I'm sorry you didn't get your ride this morning."

"Oh, I did," she said thinking back to the few minutes she'd spent atop London. "It may not have been for long, but it was enough to remind me how much I enjoyed everything to do with horses. They're big, beautiful, expensive creatures who take a lot of care, but I never regretted a moment of it."

"You sound like you miss them."

She nodded and glanced around at the empty stalls. "One of the things I loved about my parents boarding other people's horses is that all of our stalls were filled. I loved that. It meant more work for me, but to me, an empty stall is just lonesome."

He wrapped an arm around her shoulders and turned them to walk out of the back of the barn to look at the pastures. "I agree with you. There's never an empty stall for long at the ranch. If it isn't Clayton or Abby buying one, it's me or Caleb."

"What are you going to do out here?" she asked, spotting the giant oaks that looked older than the house.

"I've been reworking the layout of the land to accommodate the new barn and the numerous paddocks we'll need for training. A couple of years ago, Caleb mentioned how he'd set up his place if he ever got one. I took what he said then and used it."

She shook her head at his words. "Both of you are being so stubborn. Caleb because he won't listen to you, and you because you won't just tell him."

"You might have a point," Brice conceded and glanced down at her with a grin curving his lips.

"You already planned to tell him the next time you saw him, didn't you?"

Brice's smile widened. "Yes, ma'am."

She leaned her head against him. "I'm sorry you had to pull out of the rodeo."

"There'll be another. Besides, my hand could use the rest."

"How does it feel?" she asked as she leaned forward to take a look at it. The bruising had faded some, and the swelling had gone down.

He shrugged indifferently. "It's healing."

"You shouldn't have used it earlier."

He chuckled at her. "I wouldn't have been able to hold you up with one hand."

"Then you shouldn't have done that at all. I didn't even think about your hand."

"Good," he said as he turned to her. "I wanted you focused on other things."

She glanced away. "Well, you succeeded."

"I wasn't thinking about my hand either," he admitted.

Naomi turned to him, eyeing him suspiciously. "Surely, you felt pain."

"Darlin', I was feeling many things, but pain wasn't one of them."

No one said *darlin'* quite the way a Texan did. Hell, no one in DC said *darling* at all. She hadn't realized how much she liked—and missed—that word.

Especially when a handsome cowboy who made her heart race directed it at her.

"You belong in Texas," Brice suddenly said.

She was surprised by his words. "You mean because I grew up here?"

"Because it's in your blood. This land, this lifestyle. You should see the way your eyes light up when you talk about horses. You say you miss them. I say you yearn to have them back in your life. No, that's not the right word. You *need* them."

Naomi swallowed, unsure how to respond or even if she should.

Brice continued, unaware of her turmoil. "Tell me I'm wrong. Tell me that when you were at the rodeo watching the barrel riders that you didn't recall how it felt to sit atop your horse and wait for the buzzer, to feel the horse leap into a run. That you don't remember the feeling of the animal beneath you as you used your knees to guide him around the barrels before leaning low over his neck and racing back across the line."

"I can't," she admitted. "As soon as I arrived at the rodeo, the scent of the animals, the dirt, the hay, the sweat, and the manure hit me. The smells brought me back to a time that I'd forgotten. Briefly."

His blue eyes studied her. "And now?"

"You're right. Texas is in my blood. People in DC laugh when I tell them Texas isn't just a place. It's a way of life. Unless you live here, whether on a ranch or not, you can't possibly understand."

"That's true enough."

She pulled out of his arms and walked to the nearest fence. "I don't love living in DC. It's a nice place. Though it's crowded and a bit noisy. I'd grown used to it until coming back here. I didn't really choose DC after I got my degree. It was just easy to stay in my apartment and start my business. But now . . . now, I'm actually considering where I want to live." She turned to face him. "And it isn't DC."

Chapter 26

The future became crystal clear, as if a fog had been shrouding it. But the path was open now, and Brice knew Naomi was meant to be a part of his life.

Whatever elation he'd felt at her admission of where she wanted to live was dimmed by the fact that there were still people out there ready and willing to kill to protect not just their identities but also their actions.

He didn't let any of that show on his face, though. Naomi had enough to worry about. He didn't want her to know that he was deeply concerned about her safety. Taking her to his property had been the right move, but it was only a matter of time before the group of men uncovered his ownership.

And when they did, they'd come straight for him and Naomi. All Brice could do was get their plan moving quickly. However, until everything Naomi needed to develop more of the pictures arrived, there wasn't much they could do.

The entire time they were outside looking over the land

while he pointed out what he envisioned for the future, his eyes were scanning the area, looking for anything or anyone out of the ordinary.

"This place is already great, but it's going to be gorgeous when you're finished," she said.

He pulled in a deep breath and glanced down at her. "I hope so."

Naomi faced him then, her gaze direct and unflinching. "You've put on a good act, but I know you're worried. We can return to the house anytime."

He should've known she'd see right through him. Naomi had that ability. "I'm just being cautious."

"I'm thankful for that. After what those men already did to both of us, and Cooper, Whitney, and Ms. Biermann, I don't doubt for one minute that they'd send someone to kill us."

"Why didn't you say something?" he asked with a frown. "We would never have taken this walk."

She lifted one shoulder and swiveled her head to the empty, overgrown pasture. "Because this may be the only chance I get to come out here until everything is over." Her eyes swung back to him. "I wanted as much normal time with you as I could get."

"You can have all you want when we catch these assholes."

Her lips curved into a smile. "You're confident we'll succeed."

"I'm a Harper," he stated. "We may get beaten down, but we pick ourselves up and carry on. And one way or another, we succeed. No matter how long it takes, no matter what we have to do."

"There's no one else I'd rather be with right now. You,

Brice Harper, give me the courage to continue on, despite all the roadblocks before us."

He pulled her close and kissed her forehead before she rested her cheek against him. He placed his chin atop her head and briefly closed his eyes, sending up a quick prayer that they would be victorious.

"Give me a sec," he said as he walked to his truck and got inside.

He drove it into the barn and shut the doors to the building before he returned to her. They turned together and walked hand-in-hand to the house.

He left Naomi in the kitchen while he went into a storage closet and gathered all the blankets and quilts he could find, as well as duct tape. Brice tossed them onto the sofa and returned to the kitchen to find Naomi moving from cabinet to cabinet, searching for something.

She glanced over her shoulder at him. "I need coffee. It's an addiction. I drink way too many cups a day, and I've not had nearly enough today."

He walked to the pantry and moved some boxes aside to pull out the single-serve coffee maker he hadn't taken out of the packaging yet. When he brought it to her, Naomi's face lit up. She immediately took it from him and began to unpack it.

Brice grinned at her enthusiasm, as well as her obvious love of coffee. He went back into the pantry and grabbed another unopened box and returned to the island.

"Where do you want it?" she asked holding the coffee maker in her hands.

He shrugged. "You decide."

She turned in a circle, looking over the counters before deciding on a spot. While she finished setting it up, Brice started to unpack the numerous coffee pods from the variety pack with just about every flavor and roast available.

As the water heated in the coffee maker and she got out a mug, Naomi turned to him. Her eyes lit up at the sight of all the different pods. Her excitement was enjoyable to watch as she attempted to decide which flavor she wanted to try first.

Brice hadn't been thrilled when he realized he'd accidentally purchased the largest case of coffee pods available. He'd just assumed it'd be years before he needed to buy coffee again. Now, he was delighted that he had such a selection for Naomi to choose from.

And if she liked coffee as much as she said, he'd be buying coffee regularly. And that thought pleased him immensely.

"Are you laughing at me?" she asked, eyeing him with a grin.

"I like coffee as much as the next person, but I've never seen someone who loves it like you."

She lifted one of the pods and rolled it in her hands. "Oh, you have no idea. The coffee shop next to my house knows me by name, and they know my order. By season. I'm there like clockwork. They make my coffee ahead of time. I don't even have to wait in line."

"That is . . . impressive."

"Coffee is my drink of choice," she said, tossing the pod into the air and catching it.

He leaned a hand on the counter. "I'll be sure to remember that."

"Trust me, you don't want me to ever run out of coffee. It's not a pretty thing," she stated. Then with a wink, she spun and plopped the pod into the coffee maker and hit the start button.

Within seconds, hot water spat out into the cup along with the coffee. Once it finished, she added some sugar and then grabbed the cup to face him.

"Ready?" she asked.

"Lead the way."

She walked ahead of him out of the kitchen. Brice paused long enough to grab the blankets and tape before following her up the stairs to the bedroom she'd chosen. He dumped everything in the middle of the room as he looked at the window, unease filling him.

"What is it?" she asked.

"That window is unlocked."

Naomi's head whipped around to look at it. "Was it locked before?"

"I can't remember."

"Then maybe it was."

He walked to the window. "Maybe. I want to check all of them though."

"I'll help," she offered.

Brice locked the window, then they moved from room to room upstairs before venturing back downstairs and examining each window there. Once he was assured that the windows were all secure, he set the locks on the doors.

"Can you look in the utility room for the ladder?" Brice asked Naomi.

She nodded and walked to the back of the house. Brice might have brought only a few things to the house, but on his first trip, he'd stashed a couple of rifles and a hand-gun. He went into the pantry and reached on the top shelf for the rifle.

He turned with the gun and a box of bullets to find Naomi at the door.

"Do you have another one?" she asked.

"I do. As well as a handgun."

She gave a single nod. "It's been a while since I shot one, but I can use it."

"Good." He'd been a little worried about how she felt about guns. He trailed behind her as he asked, "Who taught you to shoot?"

"My dad. I tell you, though, my mom can shoot a mole off a witch. The woman is a dead shot."

Brice chuckled when they reached the bedroom again, where he set the rifle in a corner. "I'll make sure to remember that."

Naomi grinned while leaning the ladder against a wall. "My dad collected guns from all eras. He was fascinated with them. Safety, however, was his big thing. No one came into the house and touched his guns."

"Was he just a collector?"

"He was a hunter, like so many around here. Except he didn't do it for the thrill of killing. He did it to supplement our food. We ate more venison and wild pork than we did beef."

Brice nodded. "I wish I could've met your dad."

"He would've liked you," she said.

"You think?"

She raised her brows as she grinned. "Definitely."

That pleased him greatly. Brice pivoted and walked into the hallway before he made his way to the master bedroom. He went into the closet and turned to face the door. Then he reached over it and grabbed the rifle that hung there. On one of the top shelves was another box of bullets.

When he left the bathroom, Naomi was waiting. She held out her hands, and he placed the gun and the bullets into her grip. Then he moved to his bed and reached on the side of the table nearest the mattress, where he had fastened the holster. He pulled out the Beretta and checked the magazine before replacing it.

He had no desire to shoot anyone, but if someone came onto his property with the intention of hurting him or Naomi, he'd do what had to be done until Danny and his men arrived.

"That's convenient," Naomi said when he faced her.

"I got the idea from Clayton." He nodded at the rifle she held. "Let's keep one in the hallway for me. While you're in the darkroom, I'll keep watch over everything."

Her brows drew together. "You can't do it all yourself."

"I do wish I had a security system like the East Ranch, but we'll make do for now. The house is far enough from the road that no one can see it unless they drive here. That gives us time to see and hear them."

She briefly bit her lower lip. "If they come in vehicles."

"I think we have another couple of days before any of that becomes a worry." At least he hoped that was the case.

"Right," Naomi said and shot him a smile.

She walked from the bedroom to place the rifle in the hallway. Brice was a few steps behind her, except he paused at the top of the stairs and looked down. The best place for him would be upstairs to get a better view of the area, but if he were downstairs, he'd be able to stop anyone before they got into the house.

If anyone came for them. And he really, really hoped they didn't. He'd shot men in his time with the Marines. War or not, it had stayed with him. And probably always would. He'd thought he left that behind him when he finished his tours and resigned his commission. Yet he was thankful that he'd learned how to handle himself in such situations.

The ringing of a cell phone halted his thoughts. His gaze slid to Naomi as he pulled his phone from his pocket and answered it.

"Hey," Abby said on the other end of the line. "How are things?"

Brice kept his gaze on Naomi as he said, "We're good. About to start setting up the darkroom."

"I wanted to let both you and Naomi know that Jace got to speak to Whitney's parents."

There was something in his sister's voice that told him the news wouldn't be good. "So they know why Naomi isn't there?"

"Yes. They said they'd do what they could to help us. Jace gave them a condensed version of what's going on," Abby said.

He mouthed to Naomi that it was Abby. Then he said to his sister, "What other news do you have?"

"Well," she said with a long sigh. "Whitney's spine injury is bad. They say she'll be able to walk after extensive rehabilitation, but she'll never get on a horse again."

Chapter 27

"This is horrible news," Naomi told Brice when he relayed the update about Whitney's injury. "Horses are her life. They always have been."

He took her hand and rubbed his thumb on the back. "Doctors have been wrong before."

"What type of spinal injury?"

Brice shrugged as he shook his head. "All Jace told Abby was that there was a fracture in Whitney's lower back. That, along with her other injuries, are complicating her recovery. She's still in the ICU in a coma."

Naomi couldn't believe what she was hearing. It wasn't enough that the men had tried to kill Whitney. Now, they had taken away the thing she loved most in the world. "If we don't bring down these men, then this has all been for nothing."

"We're going to expose them," Brice stated. He squeezed her hand. "Do you believe me?"

She gazed into his blue eyes and saw his steely determination. "I do."

"Good. Now, let's get the room set up so when Caleb arrives with everything tomorrow, you can get to work."

Having something to focus her mind on instead of thinking about Whitney was exactly what Naomi needed. In the bedroom, Brice set up the ladder in front of a window as she grabbed a quilt and spread it out.

She then looped the duct tape on her wrist to easily hand to Brice. He was quick and efficient putting up the first blanket. After he'd tapped the top and some of the sides, Naomi took over and finished the sides before folding the bottom under.

The room became dark enough that they had to turn on the light in order to do the second window. They repeated the process before turning to the door.

Brice moved the ladder into the hall while she reached for another thick blanket that they then tapped along the top of the door.

Naomi stood back and admired their handiwork. "This looks good."

"Just what I wanted to hear. We'll leave everything here in case we need to make adjustments tomorrow."

She glanced at her watch. It was now ten after six. When she looked up, Brice was grinning at her.

"What would you like first? Food, bath, or bed?" he asked.

She laughed and shoved at his shoulder. "Do I smell?"

"Just thought you might want a soak in the tub," he said as he looped an arm around her waist and dragged her against him. "But, we can take that off the list."

"No, no. I was a bit hasty. It sounds nice," she said as he kissed her neck.

He groaned and looked down at her. "How about you soak while I start cooking?"

"All the coffee I could ever want and an offer to cook? You're spoiling me."

His eyes crinkled as he smiled. "That's what I'm here for, darlin'."

Dear lord. The man really had to stop talking to her like that. It made her weak in the knees.

He spun her and put his hands on her shoulders and pushed her into the master bedroom. "I have some clothes you can wear if you want me to wash yours."

"Seriously," she said as she stepped aside and faced him, a smile in place. "You want to wash for me, too? I'm not sure I know how to handle this."

His brows snapped together. "Just what kinds of men are there in DC?"

"Not the kind who do such things for women. At least not any that I know."

He shot her a sexy-as-hell, lopsided grin.

Naomi watched him walk to the top of the stairs, where he turned and winked before descending the steps. She made her way to the bathroom and started the water for her bath. She had to admit, the idea of sinking into the clawfoot tub and relaxing sounded amazing.

Besides, there was no telling what the next few days would hold. She should get in as much leisure time as she could. Rest her mind and her body for the anxiety of what was sure to come.

She undressed and piled her clothes near the door. As she turned, she saw the light switch was a dimmer. Curious, she tested it and smiled when she was able to turn down the lamps to a soft glow. The only thing missing was candles.

Naomi stepped into the tub. She sighed as she flipped her hair over the side and leaned back to be enveloped by the water and heat. Her eyes closed as she found her mind drifting until she thought of Brice. She hadn't lied earlier. She really was reconsidering moving.

Actually, *that* was a lie. She was no longer thinking about it. She was actually planning to do it. Not only would she be closer to her mom and Whitney, but Brice had also been right. Texas was in her blood. This was where she belonged.

And if that also meant getting to spend more time with Brice, then that was an added bonus.

She smiled as she thought of her brief horse ride that morning. Goodness. Had it really been just that morning? So much had happened over the course of the day that it felt as if it happened last week.

Being around the horses forced her to realize that she'd tried to forget something she was passionate about. Walking through the Easts' barn, petting the animals, smelling the hay and leather caused her to reevaluate . . . well, everything.

She had a nice life in DC. But she could have a fulfilling one in Texas.

Her grin faded when her mind shifted to Whitney. She had so much regret when it came to her friend, but this was her chance to make up for everything she'd missed. And she was going to set everything right for Whitney.

Once the men were behind bars, Naomi would help Whitney with her recovery, because the road back would be arduous and grueling. Whitney was strong enough to endure it, but she wouldn't be on her own.

But would Naomi?

Her eyes opened to stare at the opposite wall as she contemplated Brice. They'd confessed to liking each other a lot, but what did that mean?

She knew how she felt. She couldn't get enough of him. And it had happened without her even knowing it. Brice was always there when she needed him, standing by. His quiet strength and directness were things she appreciated.

If she had the nerve, she'd come out and ask him to explain how much he liked her. But she wasn't sure she could do it. Being forward like that had never been her strong suit.

In the city, men liked when women asked them out on dates. Perhaps it was her country upbringing, but Naomi preferred for the man to do it. Just as she liked having the door opened for her and being called *ma'am*. Not to mention having hats tipped in her direction.

It was all a show of respect. The country life.

She laughed at herself. Everything she disliked about the city was everything she could find right here in Texas. Why had it taken so long for her to realize where she belonged?

Or had it been that she'd been fated to meet Brice?

Now that was certainly a thought. He was simply everything she hadn't known she wanted or needed. And the way he looked at her! It was swoon-worthy to the nth degree.

She shook her head and laughed. Oh, man. She had it bad for him. Like, really bad. Did it mean she was falling in love? She had no idea, but she was curious to find out.

Her eyes slid to the door, where she looked into the bedroom. They had the entire night ahead of them. Alone. Her stomach fluttered with excitement.

She sat up and hastily washed, no longer wanting to relax in the tub. She wanted in the bed with Brice's arms around her and their bodies slick with sweat from making love.

Her hands shook with the images that filled her mind. She wanted him that badly, the need surging through her until she was dizzy with it. Her heart pounded, blood rushed loudly in her ears, and all the while, she smiled.

Because she was with Brice.

When she finished, she stood and grabbed a towel. After she'd bent and released the water in the tub, she dried off and happened to look down. Her clothes were gone. When had Brice come up here? And why hadn't she heard him?

She wrapped the towel around her and padded into the bedroom. He'd told her there were clothes, and when she looked into the closet and saw a denim shirt hanging up, she grabbed it and shrugged it on.

Then she paused in front of the mirror and pinched her cheeks for some color before running her fingers through her hair.

At the bottom, she heard Brice singing to an old Waylon Jennings song as he moved about the kitchen. She stopped in the doorway and watched him. Brice had removed his boots and socks, which were by the door where his Stetson hung on a peg.

He turned the steaks before placing them on a plate to rest before checking the potatoes in the oven. She spied the plates, silverware, glasses, and napkins set on the kitchen table, along with two tapered candles waiting to be lit.

No man had ever gone to such trouble for her. And it wasn't as if Brice had asked her out on a date. In fact, Naomi wasn't sure what this was, but whatever it was, she was pleased.

Suddenly, he looked up, their gazes clashing. His eyes slowly ran down her before rising back to her face. He let out a low whistle of appreciation. "My God, woman, is there anything you wear that doesn't look sexy as hell on you?"

"You like?"

"Oh, hell yeah."

She grinned and walked to him, rose up on her tiptoes, and placed her mouth on his. She let her tongue run along the seam of his lips. One arm snaked around her, holding tightly as he tilted his head and kissed her deeply, thoroughly.

While she might have begun it, he had swiftly taken over and left her breathless. And needy. Her body pulsed with a hunger that only he could quench.

He ended the kiss and gazed down at her. "If I don't stop now, our dinner will be burned."

"Then I suppose I'd better let you finish cooking. We're going to need our strength for tonight."

His eyes blazed with passion. "I was already burning for you. Now I'm ablaze."

"Good," she teased. "Now you know how I feel."

He briefly shut his eyes as his chest rumbled with a groan. "I swear, Naomi, I'm going to toss you onto the island and take you right now."

That sounded like something she very much wanted. But she wasn't about to let the food he'd gone to so much trouble cooking go to waste.

She kissed her finger and pressed it against his lips. "Until later, then. Wine? Or beer?"

"You pick," he said, turning back to the steaks.

Naomi chose a bottle of red and opened it. She finished pouring some into their glasses when Brice dished the steaks and baked potatoes onto each of their plates.

To her surprise, he pulled out her chair. It was another

reminder of her old life. She sat and inhaled the delicious aroma before her. She cut into her steak for a bite before fixing her potato.

The moment the beef touched her tongue, she moaned at the taste. "This is incredible," she said around her bite.

"I'm not sure I've made you moan like that," he said, desire darkening his eyes.

She cut her gaze to him. "Oh, you have. And you will again. But first, steak," she said and took another bite.

Chapter 28

Was it wrong that Brice liked the fact that he and Naomi had to be alone? He hated the circumstances that had put them there, but he very much liked being with her.

Liked was the wrong word. He relished every second, reveling in learning all there was to know about Naomi.

Yet his enthusiasm was dimmed by the fact that one of his closest friends was lying in the hospital, and Naomi's best friend would have a long road to recovery just so she could walk again.

After putting away the last cleaned dish, he found Naomi leaning back against the island. There was a seductive tilt to her lips that made his balls tighten in response.

She drained the last bit of her wine and set the glass aside. He strode to her, his gaze taking in the length of bare leg visible below the hem of his shirt. He loved the look of her in it and the way the collar parted enough to show him just a hint of her breasts while teasing him with the perfect view of her amazing legs.

Her fingers slowly ran up and down one side of the collar, tugging it open farther right before he reached her.

"You love to tease me," he said.

She raised a blond brow and shook her head. "It's the fire that sparks in your gaze when you look at me that I enjoy. It makes me burn."

The woman had a way with words. He grasped her hips and slowly lifted her to set her on top of the island. Her hands slid up his chest to his shoulders as her legs parted so he could step between them.

"Dinner was delicious, but all I could think about was dessert," she murmured.

Naomi would be the death of him. The hunger he felt for her consumed him and was so powerful that it made him forget everything but her. As if she were his entire world, as if she were the only thing keeping his heart beating.

And he was beginning to think that she was.

Her hands cupped his face as she gazed at him with her soft brown eyes. "What have you done to me, Brice Harper?"

Her question had him raising a brow. "Actually, I was about to ask you the same thing."

She didn't smile as he thought she might. Instead, her gaze lowered to his mouth for a moment. "I don't think I can return to my life before. Not after being in your arms."

"I like hearing that." He put his hands on top of her thighs and caressed upward, pushing the material with his hands.

"That doesn't scare you?" she asked with a small frown.

"Darlin', I want you here. Right here," he said before he leaned forward and took her lips.

Her arms wrapped around him as the kiss deepened,

passion and hunger pushing them hard. His fingers fumbled with the buttons of the shirt while she unfastened his pants.

A groan tore through him when he saw that she was completely bare beneath the shirt. It was a good thing he hadn't known that beforehand, or they never would've gotten through the meal.

He ripped off his shirt and jerked his jeans down to his feet. He freed one leg from his pants when Naomi shimmied her shoulders and let the shirt drop.

Brice forgot to breathe as he stared at the gorgeous woman before him. Her ankles locked around him, and her legs pulled him forward. Whatever thoughts he had of taking his time making love to her vanished as she guided him within.

The driving need to be inside her took control once he felt the tight, wet walls of her sheath. He thrust deeply, seating himself fully. Her head dropped back when he began to slide in and out of her. His gaze fastened on her breasts that swayed in time with his body.

He yanked her closer, pressing her against him. With every thrust into her, their bond tightened, strengthened. It didn't frighten him. It thrilled him.

Because he had something to hold onto.

Something to love.

Jace rubbed his tired eyes with his thumb and forefinger as he waited in line at the hospital for the largest cup of coffee he could get.

His body was sore from sitting—and sleeping—in the chair next to Cooper's bed. At least Cooper had woken earlier long enough to give his mom and Jace a smile.

After sharing a hug with Betty, Jace quickly sent off a

text to Brice and Caleb to let them both know Cooper's status. He hadn't heard from Brice yet, but to be honest, he figured his friend was taking advantage of being alone with the pretty Naomi.

Not that Jace blamed him at all. He'd do the same in Brice's shoes.

Jace covered his mouth as he yawned and stepped up to the counter to place his order. He paid and turned, cup in hand, to find Whitney's father.

"Sir," Jace said with a nod of his head.

The man looked dead on his feet. He swayed slightly and ran a hand down his worry-lined face. "Son, I'm wondering if I can ask a favor of you."

"Anything," Jace stated.

Mr. Nolan blew out a breath. "I've got to get my wife out of here for an hour or two. I want to take her home to shower and change, and maybe get some food. She's not eaten anything since we got here."

"You need help convincing her to leave?"

"Actually, her problem is that she doesn't want Whitney alone. Not even for a moment."

Jace couldn't blame Mrs. Nolan for that. "I'll sit with Whitney."

The man's eyes filled with tears. He glanced away, hastily blinking. "We had no idea Whitney had been . . . she never told us anyone had. . . ."

"It's all right, Mr. Nolan," Jace said and put his arm around the man, leading him back to the ICU doors. "Whitney didn't tell anyone. Not even Naomi."

"That's what has us so confused," he said with a shake of his head. "Those two girls are as thick as thieves, even with the distance separating them. Why didn't Whitney tell Naomi?"

Jace gave a shake of his head. "I wish I had an answer for you."

"You sure you don't mind sitting with Whitney?"

"Not at all," Jace replied with a smile.

They walked through the ICU doors together. Mr. Nolan then said, "I don't think I ever thanked you and the others for what you've done—are still doing—for my daughter."

"There's no need, sir. We look after our own."

The older man halted and faced him. "Will Cooper be all right?"

"Yes, sir. And so will Whitney. We'll all be here to help her."

Mr. Nolan smiled sadly, his eyes watering once again. "I don't know yet how Naomi and Whitney came to know you, Cooper, and the Easts, but I'm glad the girls have someone to look after them."

"That we will, sir. You don't need to worry. Naomi is in good hands with Brice."

The man grunted. "Maybe he'll be able to convince her to stay instead of returning to DC since none of us have managed to do it."

Jace grinned as Mr. Nolan opened a door and they quietly walked into the room. Mrs. Nolan looked at them as they entered. As soon as Jace saw the woman's pinched features and weary eyes, he understood the man's need to get her out, if only for a moment.

"I'm not leaving," she stated in a whisper.

Mr. Nolan opened his mouth, but Jace held up a hand to him and made his way to Mrs. Nolan. He squatted beside her chair and smiled at her. "Whitney has a long recovery. She's going to need you to be strong. You don't want her waking up and seeing you like this, do you?"

Mrs. Nolan's eyes slid to the bed where her daughter lay with tubs hooked to her. "You're right. I'm a mess. But my husband can bring me clothes."

"I'm going to stay right here with Whitney," Jace continued. "I won't leave this room until you return. Go with Mr. Nolan and take a hot shower. Get into some fresh clothes and stop somewhere for food. Take your time. I'm not going anywhere."

She considered his words for a long minute before she turned her head back to him. "I admit, I'd like a shower and clean clothes."

"Then go," Jace urged.

Mrs. Nolan drew in a deep breath and pinned him with a stern look. "Do I have your promise that you won't leave my daughter alone with anyone?"

There was something about her words that made Jace frown. "I swear I'll remain in this room at all times. Why are you so worried? Did someone say something?"

"It's just a feeling," Mr. Nolan said.

Jace glanced at Whitney's father before returning his attention to Mrs. Nolan. He knew from his own mom that, sometimes, mothers had intuition. It was probably nothing, but after everything that had happened, it put Jace on alert.

He gave the couple a smile and helped Mrs. Nolan to her feet before Whitney's parents walked from the room. Jace sent off a text to Betty to let her know where he was. Then waited a few minutes before he dimmed the lights and moved the chair into the shadows. If anyone did decide to come in, they wouldn't be able to see him.

For the next hour and a half, all was quiet. He kept hearing Mrs. Nolan's words in his head. She had a feeling her daughter wasn't out of danger yet, and it had nothing to do with her present injuries.

The fact was, the woman had a right to be concerned. No doubt those responsible for the accident hoped that Whitney would be killed in the crash. And had she been sitting where Ms. Biermann was, Whitney would have been.

Jace saw the shadow at the bottom of the door. There was a soft knock before a nurse poked her head inside. The smile she wore dropped when she didn't see the Nolans. The nurse looked over her shoulder and slipped into the room.

She stood at the foot of the bed, staring at Whitney for a long time. The nurse pulled her phone out of her pocket and looked at it for a long time. Her hand was shaking when she put the cell away.

The nurse began to sweat, her gaze filled with remorse and fear. Then she drew something else out of her pocket. Jace spotted the syringe when her hand cleared the material. He stood, but the woman was too intent on Whitney to see him.

He remained still, waiting to see what the nurse would do. He hoped she'd put the needle away and leave because it was obvious by her behavior that whatever was in the syringe hadn't been ordered by a doctor.

It wasn't until the woman moved to the IV with the intention of putting the contents of the syringe into the tube that Jace took action. He clamped a hand around the woman's wrist. Her head jerked to him as she jumped in surprise.

He glared at her, letting her see his rage. "Who sent you?"

"I do-don't know what you're talking about," she stammered. "I work here. Now get your hands off me."

"Not until you tell me what you're about to administer to my friend."

The nurse glanced at the needle, her pulse beating rapidly at her throat. "It's pain medication."

"She already had that less than an hour ago," he lied.

The woman tried to free herself from his grasp. "Let me go or I'll scream."

"Please do," Jace stated. "That way, we can find out exactly what's in the syringe."

That threat stopped the woman from struggling. "Please," she begged. "Let me go."

"So you can come back another time? Or will they send someone else?"

A tear rolled down her face. "I owed a favor, and it was called in today. I never expected them to ask me to do this."

"Who are these people?" he pressed. "Give me names."

She squeezed her eyes closed. "If I do, I'm dead."

Jace expected such an answer. He sent a quick text to Danny, letting him known that he had someone of interest in his custody. Within minutes, two deputies arrived and took the nurse away.

He was grateful that Danny had posted some men near the hospital just in case. No doubt the group after Whitney would strike again. Jace could only hope that Naomi and Brice's plan worked quickly.

Chapter 29

There was something utterly enchanting about waking up in Brice's arms while watching the sunrise. Naomi's body was sated after a perfect night making love all over the house.

She grinned, thinking about their time on the stairs. On the couch. The bed. The bed again. And the bed a third time before rolling off and onto the floor.

He took a deep breath, his chest puffing out as he rubbed a hand down her back. Brice kissed her forehead. "What are you grinning about?"

"Last night," was all she said.

He chuckled. "Ah. I'm sorry I didn't let you get much sleep."

"Or I, you," she said and shifted to lay on her stomach with her chin propped on his chest.

"I regret nothing," he stated firmly, a grin still pulling at the corners of his mouth.

She couldn't stop staring at him dreamily. "Me, either. Though I really wish we could stay just like this."

"There's no reason we can't once we solve this fiasco we're currently embedded in."

The delight that shot through her at his words left her dizzy. "I'd like that."

"Naomi," he began, his face shifting into nervous lines. "It might not be the best time to say this, but I—"

The shrill ring of the phone interrupted him. She wanted to scream because she had a feeling whatever he'd been about to say was important. But his phone rang again.

She sat up so he could roll to the side and reach for the cell that rested on the side table.

"Hello," he said. His gaze swung to her as a frown formed while he listened to whoever it was. "Son of a bitch," he murmured.

Naomi was all too aware that their night of decadence was at an end. She scooted to the edge of the bed and stood before she rushed downstairs in the buff to the laundry room to get her clothes out of the dryer.

After hastily dressing, she fixed two mugs of coffee and made her way back upstairs. By the time she entered the bedroom, Brice had his jeans on and had just slipped his arms into a button-down. By the stern set of his jaw, he was none too pleased with whatever the call was about.

"Everything okay?" she asked and held out his mug.

He shook his head and finished buttoning his shirt before he took the coffee. "That was Jace. Apparently, Mrs. Nolan had a feeling that Whitney shouldn't be left alone. They asked Jace to stay with her so they could go home to shower and eat. While Jace was there, a nurse came in with a syringe filled with something meant to kill Whitney."

Naomi sank onto the bed as her knees went weak.

"They don't want her to wake. They know she'll tell the authorities everything."

"Exactly."

She gathered her courage and got to her feet. "I'm not going to let them get to her."

Brice put a hand on her arm and looked deep into her eyes. "None of us are. The nurse is in custody. Danny will get names from her."

The sound of an engine had both of them walking to the window. As soon as they saw Caleb's truck, they made their way downstairs.

Naomi's blood felt cold as it rushed through her. How many times could Whitney escape death? These men who had abused her wanted to silence Whitney, and they were getting others to do their dirty work for them.

She started to walk outside to help the guys unload the truck, but Caleb and Brice told her no in unison. She eyed them, confused. "What's wrong?"

"Stay inside," Brice said, pointing at her.

Caleb issued a single nod. "Anyone could be watching."

She rolled her eyes. "And if someone is watching, then they'll know I'm here by everything you're unloading."

"Naomi, please," Brice implored. "Stay inside."

As if she could refuse that. She threw up her hands and walked back into the kitchen. While she waited, she began cooking some sausage and made toast.

The brothers carried a table upstairs, and on their way back out, Caleb snatched a piece of sausage and shot her a wink. She smiled in return.

They made three more trips with the other table and bags of the things she'd requested. She put the last bit of butter on a slice of toast when the guys returned.

She pointed to the table and ordered, "Sit."

"Bossy," Caleb said with a grin.

Brice dumped out their coffee and made more for all three of them. Caleb hooked his hat on the back of the chair as they sat down. Naomi looked between the brothers as they each put food on their plates.

"Oh, I almost forgot." Caleb leaned to the side and pulled something out of his pocket. He handed her the roll of film that she eagerly took.

"How did you get it?" she asked.

He shrugged and speared a sausage link with his fork. "A friend of a friend."

"Thanks," Brice said.

Naomi gave Caleb a bright smile. "Yes, thank you. Are you sure no one saw this friend of a friend."

"I'm ninety eight percent positive."

She swallowed her bite of toast. "Thank goodness. How is Abby?"

"Irritated that she's not more involved," Caleb replied.

Brice grunted as he took a sip of coffee. "I bet Clayton is at his wits' end keeping her there."

"Actually, it's Abby's swollen feet that are keeping her at the ranch."

Naomi looked at the brothers, each eating and talking about anything but the house they were in. But that was fine with her. She would keep the conversation going until breakfast was over.

"There's nothing suspicious happening at the ranch?" she asked.

Caleb shook his head as he took a large bite of toast.

Brice pushed his clean plate away and leaned back in his chair. "Clayton would've contacted us if something had happened with either the ranch, Abby, or the kids. Silence is a good sign."

"Yeah, but I'm still worried," Naomi said. "Especially after Jace's call."

Caleb tossed his napkin on his empty plate and rested his forearms on the table. "Now that we have the nurse, who will hopefully give up the names we need, developing the picture might not be needed."

"How long until we know something?" Brice asked.

Caleb lifted his shoulders to his ears in a shrug. "The last Clayton heard from Danny, the nurse had refused to talk and asked for a lawyer. Danny put her in a cell to await her attorney's arrival."

Naomi couldn't stop the small niggle of worry that wouldn't go away. "What about the syringe? Do we know what was in it?"

"It's being tested now," Caleb said.

"All this waiting is killing me." She caught Caleb's eye. "I have something I need you to do."

He quickly said, "Anything."

"Follow me," she said and got to her feet.

"Naomi?" Brice asked with a frown.

She glanced his way, sending a reassuring smile when Caleb stood. "This way."

Behind her, a chair scraped against the floor as Brice moved to follow them. Naomi knew she might be overstepping, but she had to try something. And she hoped Brice wouldn't be angry at her for it.

"What is it?" Caleb asked as she stopped in the family room.

Her gaze met Brice's before she slid her eyes to Caleb. "The favor I have is that I get to show you the house."

Caleb's easy smile grew tight, his eyes hard. "You tricked me."

"Yes," she admitted. "Brice would've waited until you

were no longer angry before he said anything, and while your brother has said that you don't hold grudges, my guess is that this is something altogether different."

"This doesn't concern you," Caleb stated.

Brice took a step toward his brother, anger filling his face.

Naomi held up a hand to Brice and faced Caleb. "No, it doesn't. I apologize to both of you. But I don't have siblings. What I did have were two best friends, and occasionally, two of us would get pissy with each other. It always took the third member to make the other two remember why they were friends. That's all I'm trying to do."

She really wished she hadn't done anything now, but it was too late. She turned her head to Brice. "I see you hurting for what has happened, and I wanted to make it better."

Brice took her hand and gave it a squeeze.

Caleb watched them warily. "I should go."

"Wait," she said. "There is so much to see, and I wish you'd let Brice tell you his thoughts."

"Another time," Caleb said and strode away.

Naomi turned to Brice. "I'm sorry. I know I should ha—"

His lips silenced her words. The kiss was slow, sensual, and entirely seductive. When he ended the kiss, he lightly caressed his hands down the side of her face. "Thank you for trying."

Relief surged through her that he wasn't angry. "I wish it would have gone better."

"I plan on sitting Caleb down when this is over. I don't care if I have to tie him to the chair, but I'm going to make him listen. I'm going to tell him everything."

"Good," she said and pulled his head down for a quick kiss. "I know it might not be needed since they have the nurse, but I'd like to get to work."

"Agreed."

They returned to the kitchen, scraping plates and setting everything in the sink. Brice locked the door, and they made their way up the stairs.

The entire time, Naomi kept wondering what it was that he'd been about to say before Jace had called that morning. She desperately wanted to ask him, but she figured if it were important, he would've brought it up again. For all she knew, he wanted to tell her to put more sugar in his coffee.

They closed the door to the bedroom and stood in the darkness for several minutes while their gazes grew accustomed, as she looked for any light coming through the quilts. There were a few spots, and once they were taken care of, they put up the tables. Naomi guided him, telling him what she wanted where until everything was in its place.

She lifted her gaze as she watched him replace the normal bulb with a red one. Then Brice folded the ladder and took it out the door.

Naomi lifted the canister of film and drew in a deep breath. Regardless whether the police needed her photo, she wanted to reprint the ones she had done for Brice of him and Caleb at the rodeo. They had been good shots, and they would look nice in the house.

She started to pull out the film when Brice's phone rang from the hallway. She stilled, waiting to hear what was going on.

"Naomi?" Brice said through the door.

"You can come in," she told him. "I've not started yet."

The door opened, and he stepped through. Even in the red light, she could tell it hadn't been good news.

"The syringe was lost," he stated.

Surprise rippled through her. "What? How can that happen? I thought there were fail-safes to prevent such a thing."

"So did I," he said wearily.

She studied him a moment, noting the agitation and worry. "There's more. Tell me Whitney is alive."

"Whitney is fine," he said. "She's being guarded by Jace, her parents, and two sheriff's deputies."

"Then what is it?" she asked.

He blew out a long breath. "The nurse killed herself."

Shock went through her. "But . . . how?"

"Someone gave her a razor blade. She slit her wrists."

Naomi rested her hand on the table to keep on her feet. "It's the group of men, isn't it?"

"It sure looks that way."

"They've bullied people long enough. It's time someone took a stand." She tossed the roll of film in the air and caught it. "I'm getting to work."

Chapter 30

Though he was curious to see her work, Brice couldn't remain with Naomi. He had to keep a lookout around the house. The fact that it was daytime helped since it would hinder anyone looking into the house. Not to mention, he was better able to see if anyone approached.

As he walked the house, he thought about his brother. Brice had been wrong in assuming that Caleb would cool off quickly as he usually did. The fact that Caleb was still upset told Brice just how badly he'd hurt his brother.

It didn't matter that it had been unintentional. Or had it? Brice wanted to buy the property himself. He hadn't once thought about going to Caleb and getting him to go in on half. Not because he didn't want Caleb's name on it. Quite the opposite, really. Brice intended for him and Caleb to share everything equally. Hell, the ranch was in both of their names.

So why had Brice gone about it alone? He looked at the ceiling, his thoughts going to Naomi. She had asked him if he still had abandonment issues, and he'd replied that he didn't. But it was a lie.

He saw that now. She had allowed him to face that truth. If it hadn't been for her, he might have never recognized that he'd bought the ranch on his own in case Caleb changed his mind. That way, if his brother didn't want to join him, then it wouldn't be Caleb leaving. It would simply mean that Caleb wasn't joining him.

Brice braced his hand next to the window. Because of a long-held problem, he might have irreparably damaged his relationship with his brother.

His mother's disappearance had been the best thing she'd ever done for them, but a child shouldn't have to suffer through something like that.

The stable life Abby had given them—including the years he and Caleb had at the East Ranch—had soothed the hurt. He'd thought maybe even healed it. But what really happened was that he buried it instead of dealing with it as Abby had.

"Fuck me," he murmured, running a hand down his face.

Naomi's simple question had uncovered years of him ignoring a serious problem. He had a chance to fix everything now, and he intended to take it.

That wasn't the only opportunity he was going to grasp. The woman upstairs had casually strolled into his life, knocking him sideways and causing him to crave her with every breath in his body.

She meant everything to him. It hadn't been a bolt of lightning that let him know that he'd fallen in love. It had come quietly, softly. But once he realized where his heart was, it shone as brightly as the sun.

He'd tried to tell her that morning before Jace's phone

call interrupted them. And it wasn't something he wanted to just blurt out the first time he said it.

Actually, he worried that it might be too soon. He didn't want to push Naomi away, but he also couldn't hold back his feelings. If she knew how he felt, then that might be the very thing that brought her back to Texas.

The fact was, he would use anything he could to entice her to return. Horses, friends, and himself. They were good together. Great, even.

And he should know after the last couple of years with Jill, where everything had felt forced. With Naomi, everything fit easily, as if it were meant to be.

He pushed away from the window and made another round of the house before heading upstairs to get a better view. The sound of Naomi moving about in the bedroom eased him somehow. With her, he was able to see himself and the world clearly for the first time.

Brice stopped next to the quilt that he'd hung over the door into the darkroom. "How's it coming?" he asked.

"Slower than I'd like," her muffled voice said through the door. "Some of this equipment is state of the art. I was expecting used items."

He grinned and leaned a shoulder against the wall. "You do know your list went to Clayton, don't you? He is all about reusing items when possible, but he also recognizes that new things can sometimes get the work done quicker."

"Remind me to thank him for that. It's all going to cost me a fortune, but if I was building my own darkroom here, this is exactly what I would've bought."

Brice didn't bother to tell her that Clayton wouldn't accept any payment from her. She'd figure it out soon enough. "Do you need anything?"

"You." Her footsteps approached the door, and her voice was louder as she asked, "What if this doesn't work? We've put a big target on ourselves and everyone we know."

"It'll work."

"But what if it doesn't?" she insisted.

He drew in a deep breath. "When my mom left, I was the one who discovered the note she left Abby. The first thing I felt was anger that my mother would do such a thing to us. But I was still a kid who wanted her around, no matter how messed up she was. Abby came downstairs the next morning after Caleb got her up. Do you know what she told us?"

"What?" Naomi asked softly.

"That we were going to be fine. That it might be hard at first, and we'd definitely have rough patches, but we'd make it. Because we were together."

Naomi whispered his name. "I wish I could see your face right now."

That made him smile. "What I'm trying to say is that we didn't focus on everything that could have gone wrong. We remained together through it all, watching each other's backs."

"Because you were family," Naomi said.

"Exactly. You're one of us now. No matter what happens, you're not in this alone. Ever."

She kicked the door. "I want to kiss you. The wet, slobbery kind."

"Keep talking like that, and I'll yank this door open, the pictures be damned."

Her laugh filtered through the door. "I'm so glad you came to help me that night."

"So am I."

"And . . ." she began, her voice trailing off. "I'm glad we're here together."

He put his hand over the blanket on top of the door, wishing he could have her in his arms. "There's no one else I'd rather be with. You're special, you know that, right, Naomi?"

"You were going to tell me something this morning. What was it?"

His eyes closed as he dropped his hand. When he lifted his lids, he focused his gaze down the hallway past the door of his room to the bed.

"Brice?" she called.

"I'm here," he said.

"You remember what I'm talking about, don't you?"

He recalled every moment with her. "Yeah."

"Will you tell me?"

"Yes."

She issued a little laugh that held a note of sadness. "Just not now."

"Not through a door," he corrected.

"I don't know. There could be benefits to saying things through a door or on a phone call."

His gut clenched. Was she trying to tell him that he wasn't enough to keep her in Texas? "Do you have something to tell me?"

"There's a lot I'd like to share with you," she admitted.

"Do you want to do it now?"

There was a lengthy pause before she asked, "Do you?"

"I've got time."

Her laugh reached him again. God, he loved the sound of it. It was pure, her humor not just in the laugh itself but also in her eyes and the vibrations she gave off.

"Now that I think about it, I'd like to be looking at you when we talk. I love your eyes, by the way."

He smiled. "Do you?"

"Definitely. I could stare into them all day. The blue is so striking."

"I heard your laugh first," he said. "I was walking through the rodeo, and it stopped me in my tracks. I had to find the woman who could do that to me."

"You're coming perilously close to making me forget I'm in a darkroom, Brice Harper," she said.

He glanced at the bed again. "One night with you isn't enough. I want more. And I think you do, as well."

"Yes."

Brice smiled his relief. "Good. And I'll take you on a proper ride."

"On you or a horse?" she teased, her voice growing distant as she walked back to the tables.

He began to harden as he imagined her straddling his hips. "Which would you like?"

"Definitely you first."

"I beat out a horse?" he asked, laughing.

The laugh died when he spotting something moving in the distance. Brice moved closer to the window in the hall and narrowed his eyes, but he still couldn't make it out.

He strode to the corner where his rifle was perched and lifted it to his shoulder to look through the scope. Moving the gun left to right, he searched for whatever was out there.

"Brice?" Naomi's voice said close to the door.

He didn't take his attention from searching the grounds. "Keep working."

"What do you see? Your voice is farther away."

"I'm right here," he told her. "At the hall window. I saw something in the pasture. It's in a grove of trees right now."

She asked, "A person?"

"I don't know yet."

He said the lie to keep her calm, and while he hadn't seen anyone yet, the movements were those of a person, not an animal like a deer. With no livestock in the pastures, any movement caught his attention.

His phone vibrated with a call. Brice didn't move as he pulled out his phone and brought it to his ear. "Yeah?"

"If you shoot me, I get to shoot you," Caleb stated.

Brice frowned at the statement. "What?"

"I'm the one out here in the trees, idiot. I know you saw me, and I'm sure you have your gun trained on me."

Brice blew out a breath when Caleb leaned from behind a tree so he could see him. "I could've blown your head off."

"While I admit you're a better marksman than me, I doubt you could've taken off my head," Caleb retorted.

"Why didn't you tell me you were coming?"

He shrugged before disappearing behind the tree again. "I thought I might change my mind once I arrived."

"I'm glad you're here, little brother."

"I am the one always saving your ass, so it's only fitting I be here to do it again."

Brice lowered the gun and straightened, a smile on his face. "Any news from the others?"

"Nothing. And, frankly, that has me concerned."

"Why? The nurse can no longer identify them, and the syringe is gone."

Caleb grunted. "Do you really think they'll stop going after Whitney? And how long do you think you have before they realize Naomi never left?"

"They aren't going to touch her," Brice angrily stated.

"No, they aren't. We're going to make sure of that. But I know you, Brice. You've thought ahead for just that scenario. You always do."

He rubbed his eyes with his thumb and forefinger. Brice then looked over his shoulder at the door to the darkroom. He knew Naomi was listening.

"The way I see it," he told Caleb. "There are only two options. The pictures work so someone recognizes the man."

"Or?" Naomi asked through the door.

Brice turned and faced it, wishing it were her face he stared at instead of the blanket. "Or . . . you take Naomi to the ranch, and I take care of things here."

"You're out of your damn mind if you think I'm leaving you alone," Naomi said through the door.

At the same time, Caleb let a wry laugh. "No fucking way. You won't face them alone. I'll be standing right there with you."

Brice didn't argue with either of them. He knew what he had to do to protect those that he loved, and he would do it without hesitation.

Chapter 31

"I can't stand this."

Clayton pulled his gaze from looking outside to his wife. Abby's anxiety wasn't doing her or the baby any good. Her discomfort had grown worse, and he was more than a little nervous.

"Do you need another pillow beneath your feet?"

She shot him a withering look. "I'm talking about you and Brice and everyone else leaving me out of things," she snapped.

It was her worry that caused her to lash out, that and the discomfort from the pregnancy. Clayton walked to the sofa and sat beside Abby, facing her. He took her hand and brought it to his lips where he kissed it.

She turned her head away, tears forming to fall down her cheeks.

"Come here," he said, trying to draw her to him.

Abby shook her head. "No. Stop," she said as she cried harder.

If she wouldn't go to him, he would go to her. Clayton

scooted closer and held her. It was only a heartbeat later that her arms wrapped around him, and she buried her face in his neck.

"If anyone can come out of this, it'll be your brothers. I've known a lot of men in my life, my love, and those two are the toughest I've ever encountered."

She sniffed loudly. "You're just saying that to make me feel better."

"I'm stating the truth." He leaned back to look at her. "Both of them begged me to teach them things I learned as a SEAL, and despite knowing how much you hated it, I did it anyway. They took that knowledge, and each entered the military, where they did their tours and returned home safely. These men, whoever they are, don't stand a chance against your brothers."

Abby wiped at the tears on her cheeks. "When the two are united. They haven't been since Brice bought the ranch."

"Caleb left about forty minutes ago to take up watch outside Brice's house."

"Really?" she asked, her eyes brightening.

He grinned. "Really. I know it's a habit, but you don't have to mother them anymore."

"I spent too many years as their mother, father, and sister. I worry about my brothers just as much as I do our children," she said with a lift of her chin.

"Just one of the many reasons I love you."

She sniffed again and looked into his eyes calmly. "My search for Jamie Adcock has proved futile."

"If we had time, I'd hire a private investigator, but I have a feeling Jamie and her mother got as far away from the men's reach as they could. We're likely never to find them."

"Everything hinges on Naomi's picture. Will it be enough?"

Clayton lifted one shoulder. "It's going to have to be. Our only other option is to wait for Whitney to come out of the coma to tell us where her evidence on them is. And that could take weeks."

"How did this happen to our town?" Abby asked in outrage.

He'd been wondering the same thing. "I wish I knew."

"The fact Whitney and who knows how many other girls felt they had to keep quiet breaks my heart. I fear that these men are so powerful that none of the women will step forward to admit what happened—or what is currently happening to them."

"It only takes one," Clayton said.

Abby's brow eyes widened. "Who is that reporter friend of Shane's? The one who flirts with him but he hasn't asked out yet?"

Clayton frowned, trying to think who she might be talking about. Then it hit him. "You mean Beverly Barnes? Honey, she runs the local paper."

"Whatever," Abby said with a dismissive shake of her head. "See if she'd be interested in running a story about this. With a copy of the picture Naomi is printing. But it has to be front page."

"You're a genius."

Abby smiled and linked her hands behind her head. "Yes, I know. I married you, didn't I?"

Clayton gave her a quick kiss before he jumped up and rushed to find Shane. He found the ranch manager in the east pasture, looking over the cattle.

Clayton moved his horse alongside Shane's. "I have a favor."

"I'll do anything for this family. You know that," Shane said.

Clayton looked into his friend's dark eyes. "I need you to ask Beverly Barnes on a date."

Shane's dark brows snapped together, unease filling his face. "I gather this has something to do with our visitors the other night and the wreck?"

"It does."

Shane returned his gaze to the cattle grazing and leaned his forearm on the saddle horn for a long, silent minute. "You want me to convince her to run the story."

"That's right."

Shane turned his horse around and nudged it into a walk. "I can't promise anything, but I'll do my best."

Clayton watched him ride away. He still couldn't believe there had been a time when he hadn't wanted to return home. Now, he wasn't sure how he could do anything without the support of Abby, his family, and friends.

The ranch wasn't just how they made a living. It was a small community, and they looked after their own. And right now, it was Brice who needed their help protecting both Naomi and Whitney.

Clayton let out a click as he leaned low. The horse bolted into a hard run back to the house.

Shane couldn't remember ever being so nervous. He lowered the visor in his truck and checked the cut on his neck from shaving. It had finally stopped bleeding, allowing him to remove the spot of toilet paper he'd used.

He looked into his own eyes through the mirror and frowned. "This isn't a real date. It's for Clayton and the others. That's all. So, take a deep breath and get out of the truck."

But not even that pep talk got him moving.

He shoved the visor up and jumped when he spotted someone standing beside his truck. Shane rolled down the window and came face-to-face with Beverly. She was a stunning woman with a head of vibrant red waves that fell to her chin. Her hair was as fiery as her personality. Her amber eyes crinkled slightly at the corners, amusement lighting them.

Though in her late fifties, she looked much younger—and had a killer body to go along with it. It took everything Shane had to pull his eyes away from her big breasts.

Beverly preferred to wear all black, and was rarely seen in anything but stilettos. Divorced for over fifteen years, she had no kids, but she was sought after by many.

"Hello, sexy cowboy," she drawled.

Shane's heart thumped so loudly, he was sure she could hear it. "Good afternoon, ma'am."

"You know, most women who've grown up here aren't swayed by a Texas drawl, but I've always been a sucker for a true cowboy. Well, one in particular," she said, smiling at him, her meaning clear.

He shifted uncomfortably under her gaze. "Would you like to get in?"

"Would I ever," she replied.

Once she was in his truck, Shane took a deep breath and turned his head to her. "Beverly, I need to say something. I wanted to tell you from the start, but I was afraid you'd refuse me."

"Well, I'm intrigued," she said. "What is it?"

He put his hands on the wheel and looked out the windshield. "First, let me say that I've wanted to ask you to dinner for some time."

"Why didn't you?"

"That's a long story, which I will share with you. But not tonight." He looked at her and was immediately caught by her gaze.

Amber eyes studied him. "If you haven't noticed, Shane, I've tried to make my interest in you known for some time. Whatever you need, all you have to do was ask."

"I have a story for you."

Her brow furrowed. "For the paper, you mean?"

"Yes. It's a doozy. Know that if you print it, you'll likely be threatened."

She crossed one slim leg over the other. "I keep my finger on the pulse of the area, and it takes very little to figure out that whatever you do, you do for the Easts and Harpers. So I'm assuming this has something to do with the rumor I heard about Brice Harper getting hit on the head at the rodeo?"

"It's so much more than that." Shane blew out a breath. "There are many people connected, and we're not sure who all is involved. You probably heard about the nurse who was arrested this morning."

"I did hear something about that."

Shane scratched his chin. "She's dead. Suicide. And the syringe they were going to test that was used in the attempted murder is now missing."

Beverly's gaze intensified. "I think you better start from the beginning, but I'm going to need a drink for this."

"We have to go somewhere no one will overhear us."

She smiled and buckled her seatbelt. "I have just the place, cowboy."

Shane's nervousness eased as he drove. Until he pulled to a stop in front of Beverly's house. She laughed at his obvious unease and opened the door. He put the truck in park and slowly turned off the ignition.

He swallowed hard, his gaze following the sensual sway of her hips as she walked to the front door. She gave him a long look before she walked inside—leaving the door ajar.

The last woman Shane had dared to care about had been killed. He hadn't held a woman since, and he wasn't sure he knew how anymore. But this wasn't about him. It was about the family he had in the Easts and Harpers.

At least that's what he told himself. Otherwise, he probably wouldn't be sitting in front of Beverly's home.

With no other choice, he climbed out of the truck and adjusted his hat before he made his way to the house. At the entrance, he paused and looked inside at the wide foyer as he ran a hand down his shirt. His gaze lowered to the floor as he stepped over the threshold.

"I was beginning to wonder if you'd come inside," Beverly said as she appeared in a doorway, a beer in each hand. "Close the door and get your cute ass in here so you can begin your story."

Shane wasn't sure if anyone had ever called his butt cute, but it made him smile. He shut the door and removed his hat, carrying it in his hand as he walked to the doorway where Beverly had been.

He found a tidy room done in all cream with accents of gold. Or was it rose? He didn't know the correct name of the color, and soon forgot when his gaze landed on Beverly. She sat on the sofa watching him. She smiled and motioned to the overstuffed chair opposite her. Shane made his way to it and set his Stetson on the glass table between them before grasping the cold bottle of beer.

"I have something stronger if you need it," she said.

He took a long drink, letting the cold liquid slide down his throat. "This will be fine."

"I can't cook to save my life," she suddenly stated. "But I have a young man who will deliver anything I want. Let me know when you get hungry, and I'll make a call to one of the restaurants."

Shane gave her a nod. "That sounds fine."

She pulled out a narrow device and set it on the table between them. "I thought I'd spend the evening flirting with you, and maybe even get a kiss if I was lucky. Seems that will have to wait. Unless you want to start off with the kiss," she offered with a wickedly sexy smile.

In the course of his life, Shane had never done anything without thinking it over repeatedly, and yet he had the desire to yank Beverly to her feet and kiss her.

"Keep smiling at me like that, cowboy. I like it," she told him with a wink.

"Why me?" he asked. "I've seen the men pursuing you. Why do you want me? I'm nobody, and I have very little to my name."

She crossed one leg over the other and held his gaze. "I don't care what you do or don't have. It's always been you, Shane. You just never noticed me."

"Yes, ma'am, I certainly did."

"I'm not getting any younger, and I figured I'd never know if you were interested if I didn't tell you what I wanted."

His thoughts briefly drifted to the past. "You may regret that."

"There are a great many things I regret, but being attracted to you isn't one of them. Now, as much as I want to keep discussing this, I get the feeling timing is an issue. Why don't you start your story?"

He ran a hand over his jaw. "It really should be Brice and Naomi sitting here, but since they can't be, I'm here. I'm going to tell you this to print it, but all names have to be omitted."

"I'll see it done," she promised.

"It started when Naomi Pierce returned to town to visit her best friend, Whitney Nolan."

Chapter 32

Naomi couldn't remember a time when a picture had ever been so important. Most of her work was done digitally, but she had always been obsessed with the development of pictures. And she was glad that she had learned the process and kept up with it all these years.

She hung the last photo on the string and blew out a breath. Her back ached, her eyes hurt, and she was thirsty, but the work was now done.

The thump of Brice walking up the stairs in his boots was now a familiar sound. It brought a smile to her face because he came straight to the door to check on her.

"Hey," he called. "How's it coming?"

She walked to the door and opened it a crack before moving aside the quilt and slipping into the hall. Without a word, Brice pulled her into his arms and held her. That simple gesture did so much to bolster her. In the comfort of his embrace, the world couldn't touch her.

If only she could stay there.

"Hungry?" he asked.

"Starving." She straightened and glanced out the window to see that it was late afternoon.

She was the one who'd decided to work through lunch, but she had assumed she'd finish quicker. She was paying the price now with a dull headache that signaled she had gone too long without anything to eat or drink.

Brice took her hand. "Come on."

They walked down the stairs to the kitchen, where he pushed her onto one of the island stools as he began getting things from the fridge and pantry.

Naomi turned her head to the windows, but after a moment, she closed her eyes and yawned. Something cold was placed in her hand. She looked to find a bottle of water that she quickly opened and drank.

She licked her lips and set the empty bottle aside. "Thanks. Any word about Whitney or Cooper?"

"There's no change in Whitney, and there are two deputies outside her room along with her parents inside with her."

Naomi shoved back her hair from her face. "I want to see her."

"You will soon," he said as he began cutting some cheese, which he then handed to her. "To tide you over," he explained with a grin.

She gobbled the slices as quickly as he handed them to her.

"As for Cooper," Brice continued. "He's awake, though groggy. Based on what Jace told us, Cooper is pretty pissed about everything. Unfortunately, he didn't see anything that can help in the investigation."

Naomi swallowed her bite and slipped from the stool to grab another bottle of water. "How long will he be in the hospital?"

"Another day for observation," Brice said with a shrug. He put down the knife and pulled out a slip of paper from his back pocket. "Do you think you can forward one of the pictures to this email?"

She took the paper and read the email address. "Sure. Who is it?"

"Our county paper. It seems my sister had the brilliant idea of having them run the story."

Naomi couldn't believe her ears. "That's a great idea." But then she frowned. "Except I'm not sure I want my name listed."

"None of our names will be printed," he assured her.

"How can you be so sure?"

Brice popped a piece of cheese into his mouth. "The editor of the paper has been flirting with Shane for months. He finally asked her out and offered her the story."

"And she wants to run it?"

"She sure does. Beverly is determined to find out who the men are, and she's willing to put her life and career on the line to help us."

"I haven't met her, and I like her already," Naomi said.

Brice brought the knife to the sink and wiped off his hands before grabbing a box of crackers and returning to her. "Beverly is outspoken and unstoppable. I wish I'd have thought about talking to her earlier. With this story going out in the paper tomorrow, along with the picture, we just might bring all this to an end quickly."

Naomi jumped up. "I need your computer. And please tell me you have a scanner."

"I do," he said and walked her to a stack of boxes in the family room.

After moving some of them, Brice found the printer and hooked it up while she ran upstairs to grab one of the prints. By the time she returned, the laptop was open, and the printer was on and waiting.

She sat on the sofa and quickly scanned the picture before signing in to her email account and sending it off to Beverly. Naomi lifted her gaze to Brice and smiled.

"Is Caleb still outside?" she asked.

"Yep."

"Want to invite him in for dinner?"

Brice gave a shake of his head as he moved the computer and sat beside her. "He won't come in."

"He can't stay out there all night."

"Sure he can," Brice said with a chuckle. "We both did it often enough when we were on missions. He has food and water to get him through the night. Then I'll go see him in the morning."

She leaned her head against Brice's shoulder. "No one has bothered us here."

"They'd be fools to try."

Raymond softly set down the receiver of the phone on his desk and lifted his eyes to Larry, who was leaning against a filing cabinet. "Call the others. Our . . . poker game . . . tonight is cancelled."

"Why? Who was that on the phone?" his friend pressed.

"My contact at the paper. It seems Beverly Barnes is revamping the entire front page for tomorrow's edition."

Larry frowned, shrugging. "So."

"So, her new story features a copy of the photo Naomi Pierce took."

"Oh, hell," Larry murmured and pushed away from the cabinet.

Raymond controlled the rage that bubbled within him. "I thought you said you looked for the film?"

"I did," Larry stated. "There was nothing in her rental car. It must have been on her."

"You think?" Raymond snapped. He slammed his hand on the desk and drew in a deep breath to dam the tide of anger that took him. "We had a chance to halt all of this. What the fuck went wrong?"

Larry ran a hand down his face. "Naomi should've died when I pushed her. The fall alone should have kept her down long enough for the horses to trample her. I still don't know how she survived."

"Luck, I suppose."

"Can we stop the story from printing?"

Raymond cut his eyes to Larry. "Everything is digital now. I could burn the building down, but the information would still be in the cloud. And you forget, the story won't just be on paper delivered to every home. It's online, as well. There's nothing that can stop this from getting out."

"What do we do then?"

Raymond stood and smiled. "There is an easy way to get ahead of this."

Larry stared at him a few minutes before he grinned. "We frame Ethan, Curtis, and Billy."

"That's the easy part, but there's another step I want to take."

"What's that?"

"Curtis is the one in the picture. It won't take long for someone to figure that out. We need our three comrades to meet in the mayor's office where Curtis, in a fit of despair, will pull out a gun and shoot the others before taking his own life."

Larry issued a half-shrug. "The only part that will be a problem is getting Ethan to agree to have the meeting there."

"I'll tell him I'm coming, but we'll make sure he doesn't know about the other two. There's no way he can refuse them once they're there."

A glance at his watch had Larry frowning. "You'd better make the call."

"You notify the other two."

Raymond opened a drawer and pulled out one of the burner phones and dialed the direct line to the mayor's office. Just as he expected, Ethan was more than happy to stay late and take a meeting before their poker night.

After disconnecting the call, Raymond considered the other players in this game. It would be nearly impossible to get to the Easts. Everyone knew the ranch had state of the art security that was updated yearly.

Then there was Naomi Pierce. No one had seen her since she left the hospital the day before, but he doubted she'd left the area. Though that's what Naomi's mother wanted everyone to think based on the reports coming in.

Raymond had no reason to believe that Naomi hadn't gone back to DC, but he had a nagging feeling that warned him the meddling bitch was still around.

He'd had the world in the palm of his hand until Naomi arrived. Somehow, she'd been able to get through the layers of fear and threats they had piled on Whitney and got her to talk. Raymond dearly wanted Naomi dead. He wanted to take his knife and cut her for every minute she had disturbed his carefully laid out life.

If she was still in the area, he'd find her. And as long as Whitney remained in her coma, there was no one to point the finger at him. At least there wouldn't be once Ethan, Curtis, and Billy were dead.

Larry's tall frame filled the doorway. A suspicious man would take Larry out of the picture, as well. While

Raymond was cautious and distrustful, he didn't doubt Larry for a minute. They had been through too much together.

He was Raymond's enforcer, the one who either got another to kill or killed himself. He had more on Larry than his friend had on him.

"It's all set," Larry stated. "Your four o'clock is here."

Raymond walked to his friend and handed him the burner. "Get rid of that before you leave."

"I'll be back once I'm finished."

Raymond paused on his way out the door. "Do a little more digging into Naomi Pierce. I want to see if she really did leave."

"I'll go have a talk with her mother. If Diana knows anything, I'll get it out of her."

"Carefully," Raymond cautioned. "We don't know how much the Easts know."

Larry's brows snapped together. "Since when have you feared Clayton East?"

"I don't fear him, but I'm not going to underestimate him either. Someone with his kind of money has connections, just like I do. So be careful," he repeated. "And while you're at it, do some digging on the Harpers, especially Brice. We might get lucky."

Larry looked away, offended. "I've never let you down before."

"Heed my words now and you won't."

"In a few hours, our three comrades will be gone and unable to point to you, and you'll know where Naomi is."

Raymond reached for his hat from the hook and set it on his head. "If Naomi is still in the area—"

"I'll take care of her," Larry said over him.

"My friend, you're big and strong. Most times, that's

enough to scare the shit out of people. But Clayton East was a SEAL."

Larry snorted. "That doesn't scare me."

"He taught Brice and Caleb all he knows. And those boys were in the military themselves."

"They're nothing. You act like I should fear them," he said with a sneer.

Raymond put his hand on Larry's shoulder. "We've always done everything together. I want to make sure no one dares to end that."

"They won't," Larry stated and walked out.

Chapter 33

Brice's eyes flew open. He lay silently on the bed with Naomi snuggled against him. The house was quiet, just as it should be, but something was wrong.

He put his hand over Naomi's mouth as he turned toward her. She woke instantly, her body tensing.

"Get your shoes on," he whispered.

She turned her head, their eyes meeting in the moonlight. She nodded slowly as trepidation tightened her features. As much as he'd wanted to spend the night making wild love to her again, something had cautioned him against it.

Naomi's exhaustion sent them to bed not long after dinner, but he suggested they sleep with their clothes on. Now he was glad he'd made that call.

With slow movements, she lifted the sheets and got to her feet. Brice's gaze was on the doorway. He kept it there as he rose and reached for the pistol on the side of his nightstand. He didn't bother with his boots. It would make too much noise. On silent feet, he moved to the side of the window and peeked outside. He saw nothing, but his gut was telling him that something was out there.

If Caleb had seen anything, his brother would've let him know. The fact that there had been nothing from Caleb was worrying. Brice refused to even consider that something might have happened to his brother.

His gut clenched painfully as he recalled the last time he'd thought he lost someone in his family. Abby had been shot. Thankfully, it hadn't been serious, but it could have been. Back then, none of them had been trained for an attack.

Brice and Caleb had sworn never to be unprepared again. Clayton had helped with that, as had their military training. Whoever was in the house was about to get a rude awakening.

He glanced at Naomi to find her staring at him. Backing away from the window, he gave it a wide berth and made his way to her. He took her hand to find it ice cold.

"Keep your hand on me at all times," he whispered. "I'll get us through this."

She swallowed hard and nodded. As soon as he turned to face the doorway, she put her hand on his back. He raised his gun and aimed it before he started slowly walking toward the entrance.

Once he reached it, he paused and looked over his shoulder at Naomi. Her fear was evident, but she was holding it together. Brice wasn't sure where to take her. The best scenario was his truck, but that was exactly the place he would target if he were after someone. He would have to leave her in the house while he sorted things with whoever had come for them.

The loud ringing of a cell phone broke through the silence of the night. The light from the phone lit up on the bedside table. Naomi started to turn away to answer it, but Brice grabbed her arm and shook his head for her to leave it.

It felt like an eternity before the ringing finally stopped. A few moments later, there was a ding of a voicemail.

As much as he wanted to find out who called, he wouldn't. Because he knew someone was on the stairs. He pushed Naomi back and down so she would make the smallest target possible.

Then he drew in a deep breath. As he released it, he spun around the door and aimed his pistol down the stairs.

Only to find Caleb on his stomach with his gun aimed at him.

Both pulled up their weapons simultaneously.

Caleb jumped to his feet and put his back against a wall. He shot Brice a crooked grin. "I feel like I'm back in the Army," he whispered.

Brice shook his head and leaned into the bedroom to get Naomi. "What the hell are you doing?" he asked Caleb.

"I saw a man headed this way."

That wasn't good news. Brice watched Naomi rush to get the phone. His head swung back to Caleb. "How the fuck did you get in?"

"It wasn't easy, if that makes you feel better."

"Brice," Naomi whispered as she hurried to him. "The call was from Danny."

Without another word, Brice went to his voicemail and put it on speaker as he hit play.

"Brice? Pick up. I'm leaving Diana Pierce's house. She had a visitor who beat her pretty badly trying to get information about Naomi. Tell Naomi that Diana is safe. She didn't tell the man anything. Not even when he threatened her life. Unfortunately, Diana didn't get to see his face since he was wearing a ski mask."

Brice wrapped an arm around Naomi and briefly met Caleb's gaze as the message ended.

"I thought keeping her ignorant of where I was would help her," Naomi murmured as she lifted her eyes to him.

"Danny will look out for her now."

"We need to get ready," Caleb said.

Naomi drew in a shuddering breath. "Someone is coming for me, aren't they?"

"Our trucks are hidden," Caleb stated. "This place looks abandoned. They might pass us by."

But Brice knew better. Whether Diana Pierce had told the man or not, they had figured out where Naomi was. And they were already here.

Naomi's gaze landed on him as she patiently waited for him to tell her the truth.

He turned to face her. "Caleb and I are going to take care of anyone who tries to come in the house. Stay up here away from the windows."

"I can use a gun, remember?" she said.

"And it may come to that, but shooting a person is entirely different than a target."

Caleb made a sound at the back of his throat and handed Naomi the rifle that was in the hallway. "Just don't shoot us," he teased.

There was a ghost of a smile on her lips that quickly vanished as she checked the bullets in the chamber. "I thought this was over."

"The group of men must have found out about the article running in the morning," Brice said.

"That can't be stopped," she stated angrily. "Killing me certainly won't do that."

Caleb gave a wry shake of his head. "No, but they're worried that Whitney might have told you something that could out who they are."

"If that was the case, why wait to come after her?" Brice asked. "They could have gone looking for Naomi at her mother's yesterday but they didn't."

Naomi rested the butt of the rifle on the floor. "That's true, but it still doesn't tell us why they're coming now."

Brice's phone buzzed. He took it out and saw a text from Clayton that rocked him. "There was a murder-suicide in town a few hours ago. It appears our mayor and another man were shot before a prominent businessman then took his own life. Right there in the mayor's office."

"Damn," Caleb murmured. "Do you think they're the ones Whitney was talking about? She did say they were powerful."

Naomi held out her hand for Brice's cell. Once in her hand, she did a search. "No one seems to know why Curtis Moore killed the mayor or Billy Gonzales before he turned the gun on himself." She lowered the phone and met Brice's gaze. "It's suspicious that it would happen right before the story went out in the morning."

"Very," Brice agreed. "If those three men were involved, I don't think they were the only ones."

Caleb ran a hand through his hair. "That much is obvious. Whoever is running the show is tying up loose ends so no one can point the finger at him."

"Whitney can," Naomi pointed out.

Brice frowned as he tried to sort through all the details. "There's no telling how long it'll be before Whitney wakes up. No, those remaining wanted to make sure the weaker ones, the men who might break under interrogation and spill everything, were out of the way."

"And since Naomi took the picture, and they never found the original, if she isn't around to distribute it or tell her side of the story, then that only leaves Whitney," Caleb said.

Naomi raised a brow. "Are y'all forgetting the other women this has happened to?"

"They've kept silent for years out of fear or who knows why," Brice said. "I doubt they'll come forward now after the deaths and Whitney's accident."

Caleb's lips twisted. "Not to mention what happened to the two of you at the rodeo."

Naomi blew out a breath. "Then these men have won again."

"You're still standing," Brice reminded her.

Caleb gave Naomi a nod. "I'm going to take my position. It won't be long before the guy reaches the barn and house."

After Caleb left, Naomi handed Brice back the phone and asked, "Why didn't Caleb wake you instead of scaring us?"

"He knew I'd hear him. You going to be okay up here?"

She smiled and lifted the rifle. "I'll be fine. Go do what you need to do."

Brice yanked her to him for a long, lingering kiss before he headed down the stairs. He stood against the wall facing the windows in the kitchen and called his brother-in-law as he put on his boots.

"Clayton, I know Danny has his hands full, but Caleb spotted a man on my land."

"Have you seen the man yet?" Clayton asked.

Brice was about to answer when he saw movement near the barn. "I do now."

"I'm on my way," Clayton said and hung up.

Brice tucked the phone into his pocket and walked to the back door. He didn't want his house shot up, but he also didn't want any guns fired in case a stray bullet found its way to Naomi.

He quietly unlocked the door and slipped outside before closing it behind him. Brice looked to his left when he saw something out of the corner of his eye and spied Caleb behind a tree.

Their gazes met. Brice pointed to himself and motioned to the intruder. Caleb gave a single nod before using hand gestures to tell Brice he was going behind the man to make sure there were no others.

The fact that this was so similar to the missions they acted out as kids would have made this humorous if lives weren't on the line.

Brice watched the man come around the barn, never looking inside. He didn't wear a mask, but there was a black beanie covering his hair. The attacker glanced around, his gaze skimming over the shadows where Brice hid. When the man reached the house, he came right up to the kitchen window to look inside.

That's when Brice raised the barrel of his gun and moved out of the shadows. Only four feet separated them, so the man noticed Brice immediately.

"You've come to the wrong house," Brice said.

The man smiled and turned, bringing up a weapon. Brice immediately knocked the attacker's hand away before the gun could be fired, causing the pistol to hit the house and fall to the ground. At that same time, a gun cocked behind the would-be intruder.

"You're finished here, man," Caleb said and kicked the pistol away.

Brice raised a brow as the intruder stood defiant against

two guns trained on him. "Did you hear my brother? Perhaps I should beat you like you did Diana Pierce?"

"Or rape him," Caleb suggested.

Brice laughed. "Castration."

"You wouldn't dare," the man said, eyes narrowed.

Brice lowered his gun and got in the man's face. "Wouldn't I? After what you've done to Naomi, her mother, Whitney, Ms. Biermann, and countless other women?"

The man snorted loudly. "Sharon Biermann was in on it with us."

Anger surged through Brice. "I think you should be beaten, raped repeatedly, and castrated."

"We've cut enough balls off horses," Caleb said. "We could ensure that you don't feel much. Or . . . well, we could make you suffer horribly."

The man shifted uneasily as he glanced over his shoulder at Caleb. "You're bluffing."

"I'm not," Naomi said from behind Brice.

He turned as she walked out of the house, her face pale in the moonlight. Brice watched her carefully. She'd left the rifle inside, but there was no mistaking the cold fury within her.

"I'd happily cut off all your manly bits. And I'd do it right now," she said.

Caleb pulled a knife from the scabbard at his waist and handed it to Brice. Brice watched the man's face go slack when he then placed the knife in Naomi's hand.

"You came to kill her," Brice said to the intruder.

Caleb slammed the end of his rifle into the back of the man's knees to bring him to the ground. "Hold him with me, Brice, so Naomi can cut."

"No!" the man bellowed and held up his hands in surrender. "Stop her, and I'll tell you everything."

Chapter 34

It was now up to her. Naomi stared at the man on his knees before her. Brice and Caleb were waiting for her decision. They were leaving it up to her whether she castrated him or not.

And she was sorely tempted.

Finally, they had a face to put to the group of men who had assaulted Whitney and countless others.

"Please," the man begged, his troubled eyes on her.

Brice and Caleb had a firm hold on him. It was the only reason Naomi felt safe enough to move a step closer. "Who are you?" she asked.

"Larry," he said, swallowing loudly. "Larry Anderson."

"Well, Larry, how many of the women that were groped and raped and bullied begged to be left alone?"

He frowned, glancing at Brice.

"How many?" Naomi demanded again, her voice rising.

Brice twisted Larry's arm hard. "Answer her."

"A-all of them," Larry said with a wince.

Naomi looked away as emotions rose quickly inside her. She wanted to cry for Whitney and the others, but her anger was too great. Her eyes swung back to Larry. "Why should I listen to you then?"

Larry's head jerked from Caleb to Brice, trying to find an ally. He looked imploringly at Naomi. "I've agreed to tell you everything I know. Just don't hurt me."

Caleb glared at Larry. "I have a particular hatred for men who think they can bully women. The only reason you feel that way is because of the dick between your legs. We take that away, and you have nothing."

"I have a family," Larry protested.

Naomi was appalled by his words. "What about all those women? Did you think of their families? Did you stop for even a second and wonder what your assault would do to them mentally?"

"You might not have left a physical mark on them, but the scars are still there," Brice said.

"Look," Larry hurried to say. "Look! I was just one of five. Names. You want names? I'll give you names."

Naomi met Brice's gaze. He was waiting for her verdict. Never in her life had she wanted to do physical harm to someone before. Not even the man who had been driving drunk and struck the car that killed Suellen.

But this was different. Someone had laid hands on Whitney, forced her to do things against her will and made her feel as if there was no one she could turn to. These men had intimidated, frightened, and terrorized. They used their strength, their standing in society, and their power not just for assault but for murder, as well.

She wanted justice for herself and everyone involved. And she feared that this asshole might get away with all of it if he got the right lawyer.

But she wasn't a vigilante. Not now. Not ever. However, she wasn't going to pass up the opportunity to get all the answers.

"Start talking," she demanded.

Larry nodded, relief filling his face. "Raymond Bell is who you want."

"The construction guy?" Caleb asked in surprise.

Larry's gaze moved to the side. "We've been friends since elementary school. Where he goes, I follow."

"And when he decided to force women, you eagerly joined in?" Naomi asked.

His hazel eyes met hers. "Yes."

While she digested that, Brice asked, "I'm guessing our mayor and the other two men killed were part of your group?"

"Yeah," Larry answered. "Raymond wanted to make everyone think those three were the ringleaders."

"That would leave just Whitney and me to deal with," Naomi said. She gave a sad shake of her head. "Where you the one driving the dump trunk that plowed into Cooper's truck?"

There was a slight hesitation as Larry glanced at the knife she held before he said, "Yes."

"You were trying to kill Whitney."

He closed his eyes for a moment. "Along with Sharon, yes."

Naomi looked past Brice and Caleb as Clayton and Danny came around the house with a flashlight that he pinned on Larry. She didn't move as Danny walked to stand beside her. Larry drew in a deep breath, blinking against the harsh light. This was the part where he could claim that they'd forced him to confess under duress.

"What have we here?" Danny asked after looking at Brice and Caleb.

Brice shrugged. "A trespasser who intended to kill Naomi."

Danny eyed Larry's pistol on the ground. "Trespassing with the intent to harm. And caught in the act."

"Not to mention you have his weapon with his fingerprints on it," Clayton said from the corner of the house.

Danny's lips twisted as he nodded. "That's very true." The sheriff rested his hand on the gun at his hip. "When I walked up, I heard you telling the others a fine story. How about you repeat everything for me?"

"Sure thing, sheriff," Larry said. "Can you put the cuffs on me and get me away from these people?" he asked.

Naomi backed up as Danny cuffed Larry and got him to his feet. Another deputy took Larry away while Caleb relayed the conversation to Danny and Clayton. Brice moved to her side, linking his hand with hers as Danny hurried to his car to go and arrest Raymond Bell. She should be rejoicing, but she was numb.

A few minutes later, Clayton and Caleb joined them. Clayton smiled at her. "Y'all did good."

"I didn't do anything," she said. "It was these two."

Caleb grinned at her. "Larry really thought you were going to geld him. Hell, I even thought you were."

"I nearly did." She met Caleb's brown eyes. "He and the others hurt women in ways you can never understand. And I wanted to hurt him in kind."

"I did, too," Brice admitted. "Hell, I still do."

Caleb ran a hand down his face as he sighed. "Yeah."

Clayton's lips turned up into a soft smile. "Danny will have Raymond in custody shortly. I'm sure you'd like to see your mom and Whitney."

"Yes," Naomi said. She'd forgotten everything but Larry over the last few moments.

Clayton nodded to Brice. "Take her and go. I'll lock up here."

"I'm coming, too," Caleb said.

The three of them walked to the barn, where the trucks had been hidden. On the drive there, she looked out the window, thinking about the fierce rage that had consumed her when she faced Larry.

Had she been alone, she may well have shot him. He had come to kill her, after all. Yet those feelings were something new and entirely disturbing.

Brice took her hand that had been lying on the seat. She turned her head to him as the lights of a passing car illuminated them and smiled when she met his gaze. They pulled into the hospital parking lot and hurried into the building with dawn fast approaching.

Caleb jumped into the elevators to see Cooper, while she and Brice stopped at the reception desk to find out where her mother was. When she learned that Diana had already been treated and left, she could only shake her head.

"I can take you home," Brice offered.

Naomi looked at the elevators. "I'd like to see Whitney and Cooper."

"Come on," he said and took her hand.

On the ride up in the elevator to the ICU, she couldn't stop looking at him.

"What?" he asked with a grin.

She scraped the pads of her fingers along the dark shadow of his beard. "You're amazing."

"Woman," he said as he faced her, pulling her against him. "I've never felt such need as I do when I'm with you."

The desire that flared in his eyes made her heart skip a beat. "Show me."

His head lowered, their lips brushing just as there was a ding and the elevator doors opened, signaling their arrival. They both laughed and walked out together.

After a word with a nurse, Whitney's father came out the ICU doors and got both of them. The sight of her best friend lying motionless on the bed with all the tubes hooked to her brought a rush of tears.

Naomi walked to the bed and took Whitney's hand in her own. "Hey," she said to her friend. "I'm sorry I haven't been here. I was trying to catch the men who did this to you. And, we did. So you can wake up anytime now."

"Look," Brice said as he pointed to the TV that was on but muted.

Naomi glanced at the screen to spot Danny putting a man in handcuffs into a squad car. The banner at the bottom of the television said, "*Local businessman, Raymond Bell, arrested for sexual assault, conspiracy to murder, and several other charges not yet released by police.*"

"See?" Naomi said to Whitney as she blinked through her tears. "This part is over. Those men will never bother you again."

The hardest part was yet to come. Not only would Whitney have months of physical therapy, but she would need to address the assault with help, as well. But she was strong. Naomi knew Whitney would come out stronger in the end.

Naomi lifted her head to find Mrs. Nolan crying in her husband's arms. She walked to the couple, and they pulled her into their embrace.

"Thank you," Mrs. Nolan said through her tears.

Mr. Nolan sniffed loudly. "Whitney is lucky to have you as a friend."

Naomi remained with them for a little longer before she and Brice went to see Cooper. They found him sitting up in bed, joking with Caleb and Jace.

It was good to see him smiling again. Brice pulled her into the room after him. Cooper wanted to know everything that had happened, and Caleb was happy to retell everything.

Naomi listened, but her attention was on Brice. His head turned to her before he gave her a sexy smile. That's when it hit her. The thing that had brought them together was over. She had no reason to remain in Texas anymore.

But she didn't want to leave. She'd known that for some time.

Once the story was finished, Brice said, "Hey, guys, it's been a long couple of days. I'm going to take Naomi home."

She smiled and waved goodbye as the three of them laughed and winked. Neither she nor Brice said anything until they were inside the truck. Both sat there silently staring at the sky streaked with pinks and yellows from the sunrise.

"You need to see your mom."

Naomi nodded. "I know."

"Yeah," he said with a small frown.

When he'd said that he was taking her home, she had immediately thought his house. Not her mother's. And she did want to see her mom, but she really wanted to be with Brice.

"Danny is going to want statements from us," he said.

She glanced at Brice. "Right."

"I can drive you when the time comes."

"That would be nice."

He started the engine and pulled out of the parking spot. She kept trying to find something to say that would keep them together, but he had responsibilities and a family he needed to return to just as she did.

They had been inseparable for days now, and she'd gotten used to that. She'd gotten used to *him*. His smile, his touch, his scent.

She decided to let him know that she wanted to see more of him when he pulled into her mother's driveway. Then all her courage fled.

It had been so easy to say things to him at his house, but now, she couldn't find the words. What was wrong with her? Why couldn't she tell him that she had fallen in love with him?

She turned to him, ready to tell him everything when, suddenly, her door was yanked open, and her mother's arms were around her.

Chapter 35

There had been few occasions in his life where Brice hadn't known what action to take. Yet, now was one of those rare times. He softly ran the brush over his horse while his mind drifted, thinking about Naomi. It had only been five hours since he'd dropped her off, but it felt like five years.

They were good together. Great, actually.

While she might have said she was considering moving back to the area, she hadn't yet. She had been forced into a situation that brought them together, but he hadn't talked to her about what he wanted.

Now that the danger had passed, he wanted to give her some time with her mom and Whitney. But he ached to have her near. The sheer weight of the longing was crushing.

"Damn, man. You've got it bad."

He turned his head at his brother's voice and found Jace and Caleb leaning against a stall. Brice patted Jigsaw before giving him a good scratch behind the ears. "I'm surprised you aren't at the hospital."

Jace snorted loudly. "Cooper is driving everyone nuts trying to get out. I was either going to tie him to the bed or leave. I opted to come see the two of you."

"There's not much going on," Caleb stated. "Clayton is doting on Abby, who grows more uncomfortable by the minute. Then there's Brice, who has spent the last several hours out here pining for Naomi."

"Thinking," Brice corrected.

Jace lifted a shoulder in a shrug. "What is there to think about? You want her. She wants you."

"It's not that simple." Brice walked from the stall and shut it behind him. "Naomi doesn't live here."

Caleb shook his head as his lips flattened. "Sometimes you can be so dense."

Brice made his way past them to the tack room where he put away the brush. "I'm not just going to let her go. I plan to . . . do something."

"Then what are you waiting for?" Jace asked from the doorway.

Brice faced his brother and friend. "I don't know."

"Don't wait," Clayton said from behind Caleb. "That was my mistake."

Brice walked out of the tack room and faced the three of them. "I don't know what to say to her."

"Sure you do," Caleb said. "So get to it."

Jace let out a sigh and looked at Clayton. "Now that that's settled, I was wondering what there might be to eat?"

Clayton laughed as the two pivoted and strode to the back door.

Brice swung his gaze to his brother. "I've been trying to talk to you for a few days now."

"I know," Caleb said and kicked the toe of his boot into the earth. "I wasn't ready to hear any of it."

"Are you now?"

Caleb's brown eyes met his. "I'd rather you go see Naomi, but I'm going to listen anyway."

"Good." Brice ran a hand over his jaw. "First, I want to apologize. I should've talked to you before I did anything with the ranch. I didn't realize until Naomi made a comment that my actions stemmed from Mom leaving."

Caleb's gaze moved out the barn doors. "Being abandoned by a parent leaves a deep scar."

"Yeah, well, I thought I was over it. Turns out, I'd only buried my emotions. For years, we've talked about owning our own place. It was something I began seriously considering a year ago. I talked to a realtor, and when the ranch came available, I jumped on it. I didn't even tell Abby until it was all done."

His brother's gaze met his briefly. "I know."

"I put the ranch in both of our names. I even used the business name you came up with."

There was a smile on Caleb's lips when he turned his head to Brice. "The Rockin' H."

"The paperwork is in and waiting to be signed by both of us. I was going to surprise you with all of this. I thought I was doing both of us a favor. It wasn't until Naomi that I realized I'd done it by myself in case you no longer wanted to go into business together."

Caleb's frowned as he stared aghast at him. "You thought I'd back out? For the past twelve years, this has been our dream. Why do you think I got so pissed? We should have been looking at places together, with both of our money buying it. I thought you were going out on your own."

"Never," Brice said. "I was protecting myself, is all. I messed up, and I'm sorry."

"Ah, hell. How can I stay pissed now?" Caleb asked with a grin.

Brice pulled his younger brother in for a hug. When he glanced at the house, he saw Clayton and Abby at the window watching them.

Caleb clapped him on the back and stepped away. "Mom leaving really fucked us all up. I thought Abby was past it, but every once in a while, I hear Clayton reassuring her that he's not going anywhere."

"What about you? I buried my issues, or at least I'm in the process. Have you?"

"Naw," Caleb said with a shake of his head. "They're with me all the time."

That made Brice frown. "You never say anything."

"Why? What's done is done. We can't change Mom leaving. We three dealt with the carnage she left behind. Hell, Brice, we're still dealing with it."

"We shouldn't have to. It's time we put that behind us."

Caleb shot him a wide smile. "You're right. Now, enough about this shit. Go to Naomi and tell her you love her."

"I think I will," he replied with a grin.

Brice waved to his sister and brother-in-law as he hurried to his truck and drove away. His excitement in seeing Naomi again pushed out all thoughts, so he was no closer to knowing what he wanted to say to her by the time he pulled up to her house.

He climbed out of the truck, his mind racing with thoughts of how to tell her. Then he spotted her walking from around the back of the house, and his mind went blank. The minute she saw him, her face split into a welcoming smile.

Without hesitation, he strode to her, his heart thumping wildly.

"Hey," she said. "What's—"

He silenced her with a fiery kiss. Having her in his arms again calmed the storm that had begun to rage inside him. She sank against him, moaning softly as she responded to his kiss.

Tearing his lips from hers before his desire pushed him to take her right then, he pressed his forehead against hers and looked into her eyes. "I love you. You're . . . everything to me, Naomi. With you, I'm able to face my past and see my future. I want you to be a part of that future. I *need* you to be a part of it. This is what I was going to tell you yesterday morning. It's what I should have already told you."

Her chestnut gaze held his. "I love you."

"I know you don't live here. I don't know how a long-distance relationship works, but I'll do it. As long as I have you." When she smiled up at him, he blinked. "Wait. What did you say?"

Naomi chuckled and pressed her lips to his in a soft kiss. "I said, I love you."

He closed his eyes as joy spread through him, making his knees weak.

"As for the long-distance relationship. It won't work."

His eyes snapped open as he lifted his head to look at her. "What? Why? I'll do whatever it takes."

She put a finger to his lips to silence him. "It's not going to be an issue because I'm moving back."

"You're going to be the death of me, darlin'," he said

with a grin as he lifted her so that she wrapped her legs around his waist.

"I suppose you're Brice Harper?" a woman said.

Naomi rolled her eyes. "Mom!"

Brice looked to the front door, where a woman with dark blond hair cut in a bob stood smiling at them with two black eyes and a face discolored by her beating. He set Naomi down and tipped his hat to her. "Mrs. Pierce."

"We can chat later," Diana said as she smiled at Naomi. "Y'all go have fun."

Brice watched as Naomi ran to his truck and got into the driver's seat. When she started up the vehicle, he hurried to the passenger side and climbed in. "Where are we going?"

"To have some fun," Naomi replied with a wicked grin.

Within minutes, he figured out that she was heading to his ranch. "I told Caleb everything."

"And he's good with it?"

"Yep." Brice put his arm along the back of the seat and stared at her.

She glanced at him. "Do we have enough food? I don't want to leave the bed once we're in it."

"I could have Caleb bring some over if we run out."

"No interruptions."

He nodded. "Good point. I want you all to myself."

When she finally pulled into the drive, Brice unbuckled their seatbelts. She threw the vehicle into park and turned off the ignition before hurrying out of the truck. He quickly followed, chasing her into the house. Brice caught her at the base of the stairs and pulled her against him for a hungry kiss. Their laughter died as they stumbled up the stairs and straight to the bed.

He'd found a home, a new business, and the love of a

woman who would stand beside him in the years to come. The gnawing within him to keep searching for something was finally quiet.

Because he had the ultimate prize—Naomi.

Epilogue

Three days later . . .

Naomi walked from the sheriff's station with Brice's arm around her. They had given their statements, but it was discovering that bail had been denied for both Raymond and Larry that had them smiling.

"Hospital?" Brice asked.

She nodded as they got into his truck and headed to see Whitney. Naomi wanted to update the Nolans as well as check on her friend.

The two days she and Brice had taken for themselves had been the best of her life. Between bouts of making love, they talked about everything, watched a few movies, read, and ate. It had been relaxing and just what they needed after the stress of before.

They sat naked in his office, eating ice cream and deciding where furniture would go. They looked at horses he considered buying, and searched for a mount for her. Though, in truth, she really wanted London. She and the horse had a connection.

Naomi glanced at Brice and smiled. They were closer

now in mind and spirit, as well as body. She knew there would be struggles that came their way, but there was no one she would rather have beside her than her very own cowboy.

As soon as they entered the hospital, Caleb, Jace, and Cooper were waiting for them.

"She's awake," Caleb said.

Naomi didn't need to ask who he was talking about. She rushed to the elevator and impatiently waited for it to take them to the floor and then waited impatiently some more to get through the ICU staff.

Finally, she walked through the doorway of Whitney's room. Her friend's gaze swung to her. Immediately, they both started crying. Naomi hurried to her and carefully took her hand.

"They told me everything that happened," Whitney said, motioning to her parents.

Naomi wiped at her tears. "I told you I wouldn't let you down."

"I'm so glad you came back for a visit. Without you, I might still be stuck in that nightmare."

"Well," Naomi said and looked over her shoulder at Brice, who remained at the door. "You'll get to see a lot more of me. I'm moving home."

Whitney's smile was huge as she glanced at Brice. "I told you he was a good one."

Naomi licked her lips. "I'm going to be here beside you through it all."

"I know. I'm not scared, though. After all of this, I know I will walk again. And one day, I'll be back on a horse. I have the strength to face anything now."

"You've always been strong. You just forgot."

Tears fell down Whitney's face as she beamed up at her. "And you helped me remember."

"Naomi," Brice said anxiously from the doorway. "Clayton just brought Abby in. She's having the baby."

"Go," Whitney urged with a laugh.

Naomi waved to the Nolans. "I'll be back with news of the newest East addition," she promised.

Then she took Brice's hand as they hurried to the maternity ward where Caleb, Jace, and Cooper were already waiting. The next few hours crawled by before Clayton finally came out to see them.

He wore scrubs and looked as if ten years had been taken off his life. "The baby got stuck. They had to do an emergency C-section."

"Is Abby all right?" Brice asked.

Clayton slowly nodded. "She's resting now, but there was a point where the doctor said she might not make it. But Abby pulled through."

"Abby wouldn't leave you or the kids," Caleb said.

Naomi held Brice's hand tighter. "And the baby?"

"A girl," Clayton said proudly. "We're naming her Hope."

Jace slapped Clayton on the back. "Congratulations."

Naomi hugged Clayton and asked, "What do you need us to do?"

"Get ready to babysit," he said with a smile.

They all laughed before Clayton took them to see little Hope. As Naomi stood between Brice and Caleb and they looked at the newest edition to the East family, she couldn't help but think about having kids running around the ranch and teaching them to ride.

"How many do you want?" Brice asked in her ear.

She looked at him. "I don't know. You?"

He shrugged. "I never really thought about it."

"Well," Caleb said. "I think you two better."

Clayton chuckled, though he didn't take his eyes away from his little girl. Finally, he turned to Naomi. "Abby will be pleased to hear that Brice got his head out of his ass and talked to you. The two of you are prefect for each other."

She glanced at Brice. "Thank you."

"I'm going to buy Abby a ton of flowers for when she wakes," Clayton said and walked away.

Caleb winked through the glass at the young nurse tending the babies. "I gotta get back to the ranch and get Wynter and Brody fed before I bring them up here to meet their new sister. You two be good," he said before he left, as well.

"Wait for me," Jace said as he hurried after Caleb.

Naomi leaned against Brice when he put his arm around her and then they slowly walked down the corridor. "What do you want to do now?"

"Take you back to the house." He kissed the side of her head.

"I need to head to DC in a couple of days to get everything packed up."

"Yeah, about that. Why don't we go together? I can help you, and we can drive the U-Haul back."

She faced him when they reached the elevators. "I was hoping you'd offer."

"I don't think I've officially asked, but will you move in with me?"

She wound her arms around his neck. "Hm. I don't know. I mean, I'd see you every day. We'd have meals together and sleep beside each other."

"That's very true," he said with a nod. "But think about the darkroom. It's already set up for you."

"Oh, good point."

"Does that sway you?"

She shrugged, her lips twisting ruefully. "Not really."

"How about if I tell you that I can't live without you?"

Her brows rose as she grinned. "That's helping."

"What if I say that I love you more than anything?"

She bit her lip, her eyes going briefly to the ceiling. "Yep. That pretty much does it."

Brice's face split into a wide grin as he bent and kissed her. The elevator dinged, and the doors opened. She and Brice stepped aside as Shane walked out, holding hands with Beverly Barnes.

Beverly smiled at them while Shane tipped his hat to Naomi. Then he shot Brice a bright smile.

"I'll be damned," Brice murmured as the couple sauntered away.

"I'm happy for them," Naomi said as they hurried into the elevator before the doors closed.

Brice punched the button for the ground floor and took her hand. "Ready for whatever is to come?"

"Very. Thanks for coming to my rescue."

"I'll always be here for you."

She faced him and gazed into his blue eyes. "I love you, Brice Harper."

"Ah, darlin', you stole my heart when I saw you in the stands. I've been yours ever since."

The doors opened, and they stepped away, hand-in-hand as they walked from the hospital into a future as bright and exciting as the sun.

Look for the first novel in
the Heart of Texas series from

DONNA GRANT

THE CHRISTMAS
COWBOY HERO

And don't miss Grant's Sons of Texas series

THE HERO
THE PROTECTOR
THE LEGEND

From St. Martin's Paperbacks

Stay updated at
www.donnagrant.com